INTENT TO COMMIT

By

Michael J. Reidy

To Julianna
Hope you
enjoy !
Mike Reidy
Jan 201~

Published in the United States by HW Publishing, a subsidiary of House of Walker Publishing, LLC, New Jersey

Permission for lyrics comes from Westside Steve Simmons "Someone Who Loves You" copyright 2009 and " Island Time" copyright 2009. Limestone Cowboy CD created by Steve Simmons

Library of Congress Control Number: 2011940249
Copyright © 2011 by Michael J Reidy
Intent to Commit/Michael J Reidy
Cover design by: Andrew Saffron
ISBN: 978-0-9834762-2-1

Dedication

This book is dedicated to the men I admire most: Joseph, Dennis S. Reidy Jr., Harvey Ritchie, Anthony M. Reidy, Fr. Jerry Lajack, John Slater, Jim McElhaney, and Paul Nemec. It is also dedicated to a special little boy, Benjamin Reidy.

Special thanks go to my wife of forty years, without whose help and support I would have accomplished nothing, and also to my daughter Jane Burgett. Thanks also to Tommy Coletti, author of Special Delivery and Dishonorably Interred, for his guidance and advice. I also thank Westside Steve Simmons and Harry Plotkin who are real people who gave permission to include them in this work.

There are two unwritten rules governing criminal trials; they all involve an element of luck and they never go as planned. Ted Chase expected nothing different in People-v-Grundy, a vehicular manslaughter prosecution. Ted's client, Jerry Grundy D.C., had turned down a plea deal from the prosecution, angering the judge who promised Ted his client will get the max if found guilty. The judge was well aware of Grundy's two other arrests, both inadmissible in the present case. One charge ended in a reckless operation plea and $400 fine and the other, in a not guilty jury verdict. Though totally improper, the judge viewed People-v-Grundy as an opportunity to even the score.

Grundy had retained Ted for the two prior DWI's and, based upon those experiences, was willing to roll the dice once again. However, this time, the stakes were much higher. The office receptionist who died in the crash, Terri, was young, pretty and recently engaged. She should never have trusted Grundy to get her home that evening.

Ted believed Grundy had surely hit the trifecta this time. The personal injury case would be huge and Grundy's license to practice chiropractic was now in jeopardy, let alone Judge Granders' promise regarding sentencing. The civil matters - the PI case and the license issue - both depended upon the outcome of Grundy's criminal trial. Grundy's insurance policy, like all others, denied coverage for accidents "while under the influence of alcohol or drugs of abuse," and the State Board of Chiropractic Examiners would not step in in the absence of a criminal conviction. In reality, Grundy could not cop the plea. It would ruin him financially.

Ted Chase disliked Jerry Grundy, or, as he demanded to be called, DOCTOR Grundy. *Doctor, my butt,* thought Ted to himself- *he is nothing more than a glorified masseur. Frankly,* Ted thought, *he should "hang"* but it was his job, within the bounds of the law, to seek Grundy's acquittal. Grundy was the wealthy client of a senior partner and Ted had no choice in the matter. His thoughts drifted to the dead girl's family and fiancé and then to his own daughters.

Ted Chase was forty-six years old, happily married to Dorie for almost twenty years, and the father of three children, two girls with a boy sandwiched in the middle. He was a graduate of John Marshall Law School and a partner in the medium-sized law firm of Kurt Carrothers Co LPA of Crawford. His practice was mostly criminal but he did some civil as well and was really the only lawyer in the firm who tried cases.

He was six feet tall with sharp features, deep blue eyes, and a full head of black-gray pepper hair. He was still in pretty good shape, only ten pounds or so over his college weight.

Law was his second choice for a career. His real ambition was to play center field for the Cleveland Indians, but, needless to say, that didn't happen. He played some ball in college and soon realized he couldn't hit a curve ball or even see a ninety-two mile per hour fastball. After two years, his batting average never got off the interstate and Ted began to consider other career paths.

He was a good "earner" for the firm, however, his compensation lagged behind most of his partners. He refused to engage in the office politics and he refused to "churn" files.

"Mr. Chase......Mr. Chase, are you still with us?"

"Oh...sorry Your Honor," he said as he stood up.

"Is the defense ready?"

"Yes, Your Honor. The defense is ready."

Judge Granders was the "bad luck." The "good luck" was the prosecutor and the very young arresting officer, an inexperienced deputy sheriff.

District Attorney Carl Picker fancied himself as Clarence Darrow, Louis Brandeis and Perry Mason all in one

2

fantastic package. In truth, he was none of these. In truth, he was best described as "adequate." He only had his job because no other member of the county bar wanted it. No successful Anders County lawyer considered public office because he couldn't afford the job. Consequently, it was the underperforming lawyers who viewed it as career advancement. How ironic - if you were a marginal lawyer, you stood a better chance of becoming a prosecutor or even the judge. And don't fool yourself, the Anders County Bar Association "arranged" everything behind closed doors before the first vote was ever cast; hence District Attorney Carl Picker and His Honor, Curtis Granders - both starving lawyers who "rose to the pinnacles of their profession."

Picker had already led the tenderfoot law enforcement officer through his direct testimony. He got the call from the dispatcher at 1:15 AM and arrived at the scene within ten minutes. There he saw that the chiropractor's automobile had plowed right through the "T" intersection of County Road B and State Route 2 and came to rest some eighty feet or so into the cornfield north of the state route. The path of the automobile was easily discerned by the mowed-down corn. He made note of the absence of skid marks before or after the sign which directed northbound traffic on the county road to stop before entering the east-west state route. He also noted that the car had apparently skipped like a stone over the ditch and was airborne for some thirty feet. This was also evident from the corn. (The speed was later estimated at over fifty miles per hour.) Doctor Grundy was found under the lone street lamp, which gave light to the intersection leaning up against the telephone pole upon which it was mounted. He was bleeding from the nose, mouth, and from a laceration above his right eye.

Not unlike every other DWI Ted had tried, the little-experienced deputy sheriff testified the chiropractor's eyes were glassy, his speech was slurred and he had the odor of alcohol about him. *How quickly they learn*, Ted thought to himself. The greenhorn inquired whether the Doctor had

3

consumed any alcohol, but even in his present state, the good chiropractor knew not to answer. He also knew to avoid the breathalyzer. In truth, Grundy had more experience with this than Deputy Sheriff Klein. What followed was Klein's testimony how he administered the field sobriety tests to Dr. Grundy and how Grundy had failed them miserably. By the time the tests had been administered, Klein had been there about twenty minutes and was so excited about his first DWI arrest and "bagging" the prominent doctor, he failed to look into the car eighty feet away where the young girl was dying.

Klein also testified that he asked the chiropractor a series of questions including what time it was, what day of the week, what road he had been on, what was his direction of travel and so forth and that his answers, all wrong, were recorded on the arrest form along with the results of the field sobriety testing. He then informed Grundy he was under arrest for DWI, handcuffed him, and guided him to the backseat of the patrol car. It was only then that young Officer Klein went to the car buried in the cornfield and discovered the horror of the partially decapitated body of the receptionist. He testified that he vomited before he got back to his cruiser and its radio. Ted began slowly.

"Officer, let's begin by discussing the field sobriety tests you administered to Dr. Grundy on the night of the accident.

"Okay."

"Did I understand your testimony that they were conducted along State Route 2 under the very light the Doctor was standing when you arrived?"

"Yes sir."

"Did you conduct them on the roadway or on the berm?"

"The berm."

"Where was your patrol car parked at the time?"

"On County Road B."

"Were the headlights of your car pointed anywhere near where the tests were conducted?"

"Yes, right at the spot."

"So do I understand you correctly, there was some light shining down from above on the Doctor and some light shining directly at the Doctor from your car?

"Yes sir."

"High beams?"

"Yes."

"As vehicles went by on State Route 2, did they momentarily block your high beams pointed at the doctor?"

"Yes."

"So the light would appear to be flashing somewhat?"

"I guess you could say that."

"Were the red and blue lights mounted on the roof of your car flashing at the time?"

"Yes."

"Did the reflections from those red and blue lights hit the Doctor?"

"Yes, I suppose so."

"Kind of like the strobe light in a fun house?"

"Objection."

"Sustained."

Never mind, the jury was beginning to form the picture.

"Tell me Officer, State Route 2 is a very busy route isn't it?"

"Yes."

"Even early in the morning." More of a statement rather than a question.

"Yes."

"What is the speed limit along that stretch?"

"55."

"A lot of truck traffic?"

"Yes sir."

"How many trucks went by during your field testing of Dr. Grundy?"

"I dunno, I didn't count."

"Several?"

"Maybe four or five."

"Did you brace yourself as they approached?"

"What do you mean?"

"Officer, let me ask it this way. When the trucks went by, did you feel any type of "wash" from them?"

"I guess you could say that."

"They moved you around a little bit?"

"A little, maybe."

"Now as I understand it, you asked the Doctor to walk a straight line is that correct?"

"Yes."

"On the berm of the road?"

"Yes sir."

"Officer, isn't it true that State Route 2 like all other state routes within our state, crowns at the middle and tapers off to the berm?"

"Yes."

"So that the rainwater runs off to the ditch?"

"Yes sir."

"And the berm is likewise tapered off toward the ditch?"

"Yes sir."

"So you admit, do you not, the test was conducted on an uneven surface?"

"It was on the berm."

"Yes, I know, but the berm slopes doesn't it?"

"Yes," tersely.

"And this sloping berm was made of cinders was it not?"

"Yes."

"Loose cinders?"

"I suppose."

"Officer Klein, what color was the line?"

"What do you mean?"

"What color was the line the Doctor was told to walk?"

"I asked him to imagine a straight line and then walk it-heel-to-toe. There was no color."

6

"So the Doctor was not walking a real line, a painted line, but only an imaginary one, is that right?"

"Yes."

"Did you also imagine a line?"

"I don't know what you mean."

"Let me ask it this way-was the Doctor's imaginary line the same line you imagined?"

"I don't know."

"However, you did report he failed the walking-the-line test and I just wanted the jury to know which imaginary line he failed to walk - his or yours."

A snicker from the jury. No answer, however none needed. The jury appeared to be getting it.

Now it was time for the "experiment" - something Ted picked up at a seminar downstate. This question is to be asked only after the arresting officer has been sitting for a good long time. Ted was hopeful because young Officer Klein was nervous from the get-go and it showed.

"Officer, I would like you to demonstrate one of the field sobriety tests, the touch-your-nose test. I understand the instruction to the defendant is to stand, close both eyes, tilt the head back and then touch the tip of the nose, first with the right index finger and then with the left. Are you familiar with this test, Officer?"

"I am."

"Did you administer this test to the good Doctor?"

"Yes, and he failed it."

"Would you please demonstrate this test for the jury?"

The poor young guy stood up ramrod straight, closed his eyes, tilted his head back and then promptly lost his balance. He had to grab the railing on the front of the witness stand to prevent himself from falling. More than just a snicker this time; score one big one for Chase.

Picker had his head in his hands.

"Officer, you had better sit down before you fall."

"Objection."

"Counselor, just ask the questions."

7

"Yes, Your Honor."

"Officer, did you have anything to drink before you came to court this morning?"

"Objection!"

Ted didn't hear the ruling, and frankly, at that point, could not have cared less.

"So officer, to put this thing in perspective...the tests were conducted on loose cinders on a sloping surface with light coming down from above, light from high beams pointed right at him, light from flashing red and blue beacons on top of your car, with semis going by at 55 miles per hour leaving you and the Doctor in their wake, with invisible imaginary lines, not one, but perhaps two...and all this done by an individual who had just been in a car wreck and sustained serious head injuries? Is that about it?"

No answer. No need for an answer.

"Officer Klein, handing you what has been marked State's Exhibit One, that is the arrest form you completed, isn't it?"

"Yes sir."

"And part of the reason you suspected Dr. Grundy was under the influence was the way in which he answered the questions you put to him and recorded on the back of the form, isn't that true?"

"Yes sir."

"Some of the answers appeared to you to be incorrect, is that right?"

"Yes sir."

"Officer Klein, did you work last Friday evening?"

"Objection. Relevance."

From the eminent jurist: "Mr. Chase?"

"Your Honor, in just a few questions, the relevancy will become apparent even to Mr. Picker." (Ted couldn't resist the jab.)

"You may proceed."

"No, I was out with my girl."

"How late did you stay out?"

"I dunno, pretty late."

"Did you stay out past midnight?"

"Probably."

"What did you do Saturday?"

"Slept in and then did some work in the yard."

"Officer, isn't the true answer to my question that you *began* Saturday still out with your girlfriend, returned home, slept in and then did the yard work?"

"I suppose, if you want to get all technical about it."

"When you answered my question just now, you gave no consideration to the fact your Friday night date carried over into Saturday morning, did you?"

"I suppose not."

"And when you questioned Dr. Grundy regarding what day it was, he said Friday when, really, it was early Saturday morning, is that not true?"

"Yes sir."

"And you recorded that answer as a mistake didn't you?"

"Yes."

"But, in truth, he only made the same mistake you just made now didn't he?"

"Yes sir. I guess so."

"And you are cold sober."

"Yes sir." (Score another one for our side.)

"The question you asked him regarding the direction of travel...how did you phrase it?"

"I read it right off the form."

"Please read it now."

"What direction were you traveling?"

"It does not say: What direction were you *driving*, does it?"

"No sir."

"As a matter of fact, NONE of the questions you read him off of that form inquire as to who the driver of the car was, do they?"

"No sir."

"In fact Officer, you went through the whole battery of questions and never once asked him if he was the driver of the car up in the cornfield did you?"

"I did not ask him, no sir."

"Officer, is it fair to say that you *assumed* the Doctor was the driver because there was no one else there at the time, at least no one else you saw?"

"I guess so."

"And isn't it also true that it was only *after* you arrested Dr. Grundy for DWI and had him handcuffed in the backseat, that you discovered that there was another person at the scene of the accident?"

He swallowed hard. Ted couldn't tell if it was from nerves, the pounding he was taking, or his recollection of the receptionist. "Yes."

"The other person could have been the driver of the car, isn't that true?"

"I dunno, maybe, but it was the Doc's car."

"Officer, isn't it true that neither you nor anyone else from your department has ever determined who was driving the car at the time of the accident?"

"Yes, I guess that is true."

At that point, Ted had just earned a directed verdict of acquittal which he knew Granders would never give him. However, closing argument was a "breeze" with this latest admission and the jury was out all of an hour. Ted surmised they took that long because lunch had been ordered for them. Grundy had dodged the big one this time. Ted Chase had helped him do it.

When Ted returned to Crawford, there was a pink note on his desk from Phil Carrothers: "See me as soon as you get in." Ted crumpled the note and threw it in the trash can. "See me....forget you," he mumbled to himself.

Phil Carrothers was the heir apparent to his brother's law firm, Kurt Carrothers Co LPA, though he lacked the know - how and people skills to fill the post. He would never be described as handsome, was two years junior to Ted Chase, and had the personality of a door knob. He headed up the civil litigation branch of the firm and, no doubt, his Martindale Hubbell biography was impressive, if not totally overblown. He held himself out as a civil litigator but, in his early forties, had yet to sit first chair in a jury trial. He suffered from a terminal case of "fearus courtroomus," as did the other four members of his department. The last civil matter to be tried by the department was some twelve years ago - and that, by two lawyers no longer with the firm.

Ted always wondered how Phil and the other "litigators" slept at night. How could anyone deceive themselves for so long into believing they were something they truly were not? Even "The Pirates Who Don't Do Anything" admitted as much in their song during the last Veggie Tales movie. The bigger question was: when were the firm's insurance defense clients going to wise-up to it?

When a new civil matter came into the firm, the department's MO was to bill the hell out of it, research this and re-research that, file for a summary decision, and, if that were denied, talk the client into settling the case for much more than it was worth. They had to, to avoid the courtroom. They even used the estimate of their future (excessive) fees to force the issue. "Fearus courtroomus" was a dreaded, deadly disease.

Because he billed his clients to death while avoiding the "heavy lifting" in court, Phil's numbers were much better than Ted's and so was his compensation. It was clear to Ted that the firm rewarded mediocrity and the "churning" of files. Ted's practice, mostly criminal defense, was snubbed by these younger, talentless lawyers - all civil "litigators."

Ted was aware the civil defense of Dr. Jerry Grundy had already been assigned to the firm and he pitied the poor adjuster who had made the referral. No doubt the Grundy matter was what Phil wanted to discuss. Ted made it a point to avoid Phil upon his return other than to send him a reply: Back in the office. Come see me after lunch.

Ted ate lunch at his favorite diner and took the rest of the day off. Regardless of how often he had been through the drill, he was always amazed at how exhausting a trial could be. The heaviest object you lift is your own briefcase, but when the verdict comes in, you just feel mentally and physically "drained." Other trial lawyers had expressed the same to him. The prevailing thought was that trials command your every sense, your entire focus, every minute for days or even weeks. Your body reacts at the end as though you had just come in last in an iron man competition.

When he finished his sandwich, he remembered that Dorie and the kids were with her parents up at the lake so he drove to Progressive Field to watch his beloved Indians. It was a "get away" day for the club, an early afternoon game followed by a long plane ride to the west coast. Once again, due to the team's lackluster performance up to this point in the season, down front boxes were still available to the walk-ups. When it came to the Indians, Ted always treated himself to the best seats. Being a major league center fielder had long been Ted's Walter Mitty existence; he simply loved professional baseball, Cleveland's yearly swoon notwithstanding.

It was the third week of August, that melancholy time of year for Ted when the sun took a different angle as the earth tilted toward fall. Most people never notice the subtle change but Ted always paid close attention. He always tried to pinpoint the exact day the sunlight "changed." For Ted, that day marked the end of summer and it always came too soon. *Perhaps*, he thought to himself, *if the Tribe ever made the playoffs again, the sun would be forced to cooperate and extend summer all the way to October.* Anyway, not this year. Their opponent this day was the Royals who, remarkably, were only four games out.

As was his practice, Ted arrived at the office the next morning at 6:15. He made a pot of coffee and grabbed a banana from the pile on the counter. He knew what was in store for him that day and he wasn't looking forward to it. Just like post-trial exhaustion, the first day back in the office always led to some degree of let-down, a kind of postpartum depression for trial lawyers. *"The baby"*-the verdict, was *"born"* after months of preparation and days of intense stress. Returning to the daily grind of the office was a huge let-down. Thank God it was Friday.

He expected the message light on his phone to be lit up and he was not disappointed. While in trial, Ted did not answer his phone nor check his messages. His belief was that his client paid for, and expected, his undivided attention to the matter at hand and he delivered; even if it were for the likes of Jerry Grundy. The day before trial, Ted religiously changed his recorded phone greeting to indicate he could not be reached and left the names and extensions of both his secretary and paralegal. Ted finished his banana breakfast, took a slug of his coffee, and hit the button.

"Ted, this is Kurt (Kurt Carrothers, patriarch of the firm and Phil's older brother.) We are coming up on our fiscal year-end and I wanted to speak with you regarding year-end distributions. Call me or stop down when you get back."

Ahh..., the other harbinger of fall, the yearly determination of bonuses. This year was a bit leaner than most for the firm and, to make an understatement, it was going to be interesting.

Psychologically, Kurt Carrothers was hard to work for because he was a twice-divorced, fifty-seven year old, childless spendthrift. The other members of the firm created wealth for Kurt, ultimately to be squandered on women, gambling, over-the-top trips, and bad investments - while they strived to pay the tuition bills of their children. Ted wondered how such a gifted lawyer could be so reckless in his personal affairs.

The rest of the messages triggered the expected depression. Most people come to "know" the law by watching television shows which only misrepresent it. Truth be told, many of Ted's contemporaries became lawyers only because they watched Raymond Burr or Andy Griffith. Little did they know or appreciate the "invisible" daily grind of a law practice. Ted survived because he was blessed with a great secretary and the best paralegal, probably in the entire city.

Ted was not looking forward to meeting with Kurt Carrothers. The general practice firm started out as a benevolent dictatorship; Kurt set the direction of the firm and decided compensation. When Ted joined the firm, he did not fully comprehend how it worked; he was just happy to have an income and so were the bankers who held his student loans. Early on, Kurt was very fair, having the firm's best interests as his guide. However, as his life style began to catch up with him, he clearly lost his way. Then younger brother Phil rejoined the firm after a hiatus and the writing was on the wall. Even partners senior to Ted had discussed the change and some had left for better, fairer opportunities with other firms.

Kurt and Phil lived and died with the financial "Prospectus". How Ted came to despise the word. They hid behind it as a rationale for every unfair, cockeyed decision they made. None of the partners believed the numbers as reported bore any semblance to reality and the whole thing degenerated into a modern day version of *"The Emperor's New Clothes."* The partners knew their numbers were a joke but the brothers Carrothers naively believed they had everyone fooled.

The goal each year was to generate a bonus pool to be distributed to the partners based upon their overall contribution to the firm. The two factors taken into account included business origination and billable time. The inequity in the process was twofold. If you charged your time honestly, as Ted did, you suffered at the hands of the "churners" who billed the shit out of every file they touched - creating little value for the client and significant "write-downs." Secondly, it was only Phil and Kurt who determined origination credit so they could, and did, skewer the numbers.

Due to a general economic downturn, the bonus pool was less than half of the preceding years. Everyone, including Ted, knew it and expected the distributions to reflect it. He trudged down to Kurt's corner office trying to steel himself to the fairy tale he was about to hear.

Ted tapped on the door as he entered Kurt's 'Temple of Self Accomplishment.' Surrounding the 'altar' of the huge mahogany desk, the walls were covered with pictures of Carrothers with this politician or that judge at a black tie dinner or posing on the first tee at some charity outing. One line of tributes circled the entire office like the Stations of the Cross. They were framed proclamations extolling the great things Carrothers had done for the community and its civic organizations. The Lions, Kiwanis, and Rotary clubs were all represented, sometimes two and three times. Carrothers certainly believed the parable about not hiding your light under a bushel basket; he did nothing anonymously. He also did nothing unless there was something in it for Kurt and Phil.

"Ted, as you know, this was a down year. Weakest year the firm has had in the last four. We really struggled and agonized over these decisions. I wanted to have a talk with you face-to-face rather than have you open an empty envelope. We determined that this year there were two partners who did not earn a bonus and, unfortunately, you are one of them. There just wasn't enough to go around. I really am sick about this. We really struggled trying to make a decision fair to everyone." Classic Kurt: *Please feel sorry for me as we stick it to you and your family.*

As soon as Ted saw the distribution report which included the salary figures for the next year, he made the decision to leave the firm. A lateral hire and friend of Phil's who had been with the firm less than three years and whose numbers were not quite as good as Ted's, was going to make a thousand dollars a week more. The message was clear; Ted and his practice were not valued. It was clearly time to move on, even if it meant some lean years ahead.

4

After dinner that evening, he had a long talk with Dorie who expressed support for whatever decision had to be made. They had some savings which would keep the wolves from the door until Ted could land on his feet with another firm or, perhaps, open his own shop. Unlike the Kurt Carrothers of the world, the Chase family had always lived within their means. Their life was simple. The kids adored Dorie's parents and spent much of their time with them up at the lake.

"I'll talk with your Dad tomorrow and I think I'll call Mac too."

"Oh, that's a good idea. Tell Mac I'm still in love with him."

Ted's Dad passed during Ted's third year of law school and there were two men who filled the void. Ted came to love Dorie's father, Jack almost as much as he loved his own. He placed great value on his advice and sought it often. Jack too, valued their relationship which created in him a sense of pride; after all he was giving advice to a sharp lawyer. Mac was James McIlvaine, Ted's trial practice teacher from law school. Mac had seen a special talent in young Ted and helped him cultivate it. They remained close even this many years out. Mac continually professed his "undying love" for Dorie and warned Ted he would, someday, steal her away, notwithstanding he was old enough to be her father. Mac and Dorie always "flirted" with each other and took swipes at Ted in the process. The three of them truly had a special relationship.

"Mac, this is Ted."

18

"No, she's not here," followed by a belly laugh.

"Like you would tell me if she were."

"You are smarter than I thought." Another laugh.

"How's everyone?"

"Fine, Mac. Dorie sends her love."

"In-laws?"

"Yes, very well, thanks. How have you been?"

"Good, Ted. Hey, by the way nice job on that Grundy thing. Is he as big a jerk as I've been told?"

"Bigger."

"Didn't deserve it."

"Tell me about it."

"I was a little surprised that you took his case."

"Didn't have a say in the matter."

"Oh...one of those."

"Yep............. Mac, I think it's time for me to leave Carrothers."

"Well, I wondered how long it would be before you got the hell out of there."

"Really? Mac, you never..."

"I know. That may be one of the few things you and I never discussed, but I always believed you were too good for that bunch. Let me guess, things getting a little tight over there?"

"That's part of it..."

"So, have you got a plan?"

"Not yet, Mac, kind of flirting with the idea of flying solo."

"How's the book of business?"

"Nowhere like it should be, less than four hundred thousand if everything comes."

"So you would have to start hustling right away, expenses being what they are nowadays."

"That's the way I see it."

"Anyone you can share space with?"

"Don't know, haven't got that far yet."

19

"How's Dorie with it? You'll be having a lot of late nights you know."

"Heck, Mac, you know how she is."

"Yes, I do. You're very lucky. Any chance Carrothers will be an asshole about you leaving and taking some business with you?"

"I really hadn't given it much thought. He really couldn't gripe about my core clients - the ones I do all the work for."

"Well, be careful. You know him much better than I do. Ted, I'll tell you what, would you be interested in doing some plaintiff PI work?"

"Well, I guess at this point I need to consider whatever work I can get my hands on."

"We need to get together then. I have an interesting case coming in and I need someone to carry the water. I am much too old to go it alone."

"What do you mean you have a case? Since when did you starting taking cases?"

"I really haven't. This is just a favor for a friend of a friend. Do you recall that horrendous semi versus car crash out on the Birney Road about six months ago? Father and little ones trapped in the car and burned beyond recognition. Truck driver also died."

"Yes, I do. I remember talking with Dorie about it."

"Well, what you probably didn't know is the truck driver's autopsy revealed a .18 blood alcohol level."

"Wow, that I didn't know. What company was it?"

"Priem Transport Logistics."

"Nice defendant - they're huge. Who's the client?"

"Name's Laurie Giffen - she's barely alive."

"What do you mean she's barely alive? I don't remember her being in the car."

"No, that's just it. Probably would have been better for her had she been. Some coroner's assistant left some photos out and she saw them. She's a real mess. Company maintains

20

it had no knowledge of this guy drinking, says it was a one-time deal."

"You mean a last time deal."

"Look, she has an appointment this coming Tuesday 10:00 AM. She's coming to my office at the law school. Can you make it?"

"Sure. I will see you then."

"By the way, did you want to talk with Dorie?"

"Go screw yourself, you dirty old man."

Ted hung up the phone and thought to himself: *not bad, haven't even announced yet and already I have a client, or, at least, part of a client.* He thought just a little about what he knew so far and jotted down some notes: negligence, employer liability for its employees, independent contractor, Giffen's comparative negligence. The legal issues started cascading from his mind. Each defense, and surely more he had not yet considered, were potential land mines, or more appropriately, hand grenades insurance defense counsel would lob at the plaintiff. Each one had to be overcome in the quest for Widow Giffen's monetary recovery. Any one of them could be fatal to the case. Given the stakes, Ted knew it would be a war and a *lot* of legal work. A case like this could occupy sixty or seventy percent of his time, without a guarantee of seeing even a dime. On top of that, the case had to be funded: depositions had to be purchased, experts had to be retained, court costs paid etc. It's an extremely rare case where the damaged plaintiff could bear these costs; nine times out of ten, they were advanced by the lawyer. Ted knew that for every big jury verdict reported in the papers, there were probably five or six where the plaintiff was "zeroed out" and the lawyer took a huge hit. Many firms had crumbled under the weight of a "sure winner," that, for one reason or another, had ended up in the toilet. He also knew there would be a team of insurance defense lawyers who would have the toilet as their goal for Laurie Giffen's case. He took some bit of comfort knowing that Mac had completed at least a cursory evaluation of the case and had recommended Ted's participation.

Returning to the office early on Monday was different; Ted having made the decision it was now his goal to leave it behind. For some reason, over the years he had saved a memento from each one of his cases and they were displayed on some wall shelves to the right of his desk. In truth, it all looked like a pile of junk, but Ted recognized it as a career in the law. He wondered if his first case as *"Ted Chase, Solo Practitioner,"* would lead to another trophy or a bankruptcy petition.

He did not have a lot of time to ponder his new situation; he was due in Crawford County Court at 9:00 to defend young Danny Longer who had been charged with felony theft.

If you wanted to make good money in a law practice, you had to hustle and that meant having a lot of different irons in the fire all at the same time. Finish one case, move on to the next. Most people were unaware of that part of the practice. If Ted realized in school he would have homework every night for the remainder of his life, he would have learned how to hit a fastball.

The 18 year old was the son of one of Carrothers' fellow country-clubbers and, like all other juvenile defendants he had represented over the years, young Danny *"had fallen in with the wrong crowd."* If Ted heard this lame parental excuse once, he had heard it a thousand times. *"My kid's not a bad kid; he has just fallen in with the wrong crowd."* No parent had ever admitted to Ted that, indeed, their kid was a willing member of that crowd. Ted was not enthused about the case because he was certain Carrothers had offered Ted's services as a freebie to his country club buddy and that meant all the billable time Ted put in on the case would not show in the ledger at the end of the year. *How ironic,* he thought, *the client who can more than afford to pay for the defense gets a pass and Ted's family takes the hit.* This was the type of inequity completely lost on Carrothers.

Ted found Danny leaning up against one of the marble pillars outside courtroom three with his foot against it.
"Hello Danny."
Silence.
"Danny, I thought we had discussed that you were going to lose the hardware in your nose and ears, get a haircut, and wear a tie today."
Silence.
"Danny?"
"Yea, whatever."
"Danny, where are your parents?"

Danny was the product of a broken marriage. His father was a very successful entrepreneur who, over the years, had sacrificed his family in the pursuit of wealth. When he had finally "arrived," at age forty-eight, he realized a successful guy like he was, should have a young, attractive wife, hence, the divorce a year ago and Danny cast adrift on his own at age seventeen. The "evil stepmother" was an incredibly attractive thirty year old who now enjoyed the lifestyle Danny's mother had helped to create but would not share. *"The Step",* as Danny lovingly referred to her, couldn't care less about the outcome of Danny's trial. She saw it as an opportunity to get him out of the house, the longer the better.

"Danny, get on your cell and call your father."
"Why? He doesn't give a shit."
"Look, Danny, he might not, but I do, so give me a break."
The look he gave Ted could only be described as "curious."

24

"Okay, look at it this way, I don't like to lose cases no matter who my client is. Does that work for you?" At that point, Danny had his back turned and he was on the phone to his father.

The case was called just as they entered the courtroom. The Honorable Richard McCarthy was presiding, a stroke of luck for Ted. (Every criminal trial had some element of luck.) Judge McCarthy, one of the newest judges to ascend to the bench, in Ted's estimation, went right to the head of the class. He had no leanings, no hidden agendas and he was fair. Unlike judges in the small surrounding counties, he'd had a very successful law practice and saw the bench as his opportunity to give something back. He could have worked for free. Ted knew he would get a fair shake.

Ted stood rather than sat when he got to counsel table, "Your Honor, this case was scheduled to commence at 9:00 AM but the Defense requests a very short postponement until 1PM."

"And the reason is..."

"Your Honor, there is a defense witness who has yet to check in with the bailiff....."

"Mr. Green?"

"Yes, Your Honor."

Ted had been right about this jurist. "Mr. Green" was universal lawyer code. If a lawyer told the judge Mr. Green had not yet appeared, it meant he had not yet received his retainer, no greenbacks. Ted did not feel he was deceiving the Court because his representation was technically true, even though he knew Mr. Green would never show. He needed time to get Danny groomed.

"Well, we can move the arraignments up....any objection from the State?"

"No, Your Honor."

Everyone played along. Even the prosecutor realized that retainers had to be paid upfront in criminal cases. Danny had no idea what was happening. Back in the marbled hallway

25

Danny asked, "Who the hell is Mr. Green? The clerk at the convenience store was a lady."

"Danny, don't worry about that. Look, here's the deal. Go across the street there and get a haircut, go home, take *all* the earrings out, and come back here at one-o'clock in your best suit. Don't do it, and you'll have to find another lawyer. Also, I want at least one of your parents here with you. I would prefer both, but I will settle for one. Same deal, they don't show and you'll need new counsel."

Ted met Danny and *"The Step"* at one o'clock in the corridor outside the courtroom. To say she was a "stunner" would have been an understatement, but Ted was more concerned with Danny's appearance. Appropriately shorn and dressed, Master Danny could pass for a responsible young adult.

"The Step" began the conversation, "Look, Mr. Chase, you need to understand something, I...."

Ted cut her off, "Sorry, no time. Court starts at one o'clock and this judge does not appreciate tardiness. You just have to sit there and not say anything. Please follow me." On top of not getting paid, Ted was not about to take any crap from the trophy wife. In that same instant, he realized his decision to leave the firm afforded him a greater measure of independence in dealing with its clients.

Ted had waived a jury, being perfectly happy with McCarthy as his draw. Bench trials streamline the whole process. Objections are held to a minimum - there is nothing to try to hide from a jury, and opening statements are rather perfunctory - the judge being totally familiar with the file. The State's star witness was on the stand by one-thirty. The prosecutor led her through her testimony.

No one was in the store when she left the register to go to the back room. She admitted that she had inadvertently left the cash drawer open, a mistake which ultimately cost her her job. It was about eight PM and it had been a very busy Saturday. As she walked toward the back, out of the corner of her eye, she caught some movement in the security mirror mounted in the corner of the store near the ceiling. She saw a young man go straight to the counter, reach over, and grab the money out of the drawer. He immediately left to join a group of similar young men loitering outside the front door.

She was scared to death but she kept her wits about her. She quickly went to the door and locked it and then to the counter to push the alarm. She tried to keep her eye on the group milling around outside but she stayed clear of the door. She was unaware how many boys were outside.

The patrol car was there within two minutes. Danny had a wad of bills on him and he was arrested immediately. The prosecutor saved the identification until the end.

"Mrs. Lampley, do you see the individual in the courtroom who entered the store that evening and emptied the drawer?"

"Objection, there is no evidence the drawer was 'emptied.' Ted made this objection to confuse the witness but it was a good objection - there was still some money left in the drawer - some change.

"Mr. Bonner, would you like to rephrase the question?" The Judge asked.

Mrs. Lampley said quietly to herself, "*What is going on?*"

"Yes, Your Honor. Mrs. Lampley, do you see the individual in the courtroom who entered the store that evening (staring at Ted) and took the cash from the drawer?"

She thought to herself, *wasn't that the same question?*

Ted perceived just a hint of hesitation.

"I think so. I think it may have been that young man sitting over there," pointing at Danny Longer. "But he looks a little bit different today."

"How so?"

"The boy who took the money had longer hair and his clothes were a lot different, baggy." No mention of the head hardware. "But I am pretty sure that is him. Yes, that's him."

"Thank you Mrs. Lampley. Your Witness."

As Mac had instructed him years ago, Ted had been to the convenience store after the heist and had made copious notes. He was ready to go.

"Mrs. Lampley, you did not see anyone outside the store before you elected to go to the back room?"

"No."

"And after the money was taken, you kept your eye on the group outside the door but did not go close to the door once you locked it?"

"That's right."

"How many boys were outside the store?"

"I do not know."

"Did any of the boys have long hair?"

"Yes, they all did."

"Did any of the boys outside have baggy clothes?"

"Yes, they all did."

"Did anyone leave the group after the money was taken and before the police arrived?"

"I don't know."

"Did anyone join the group?"

"I don't know."

"Did you see any one particular boy holding money outside the store?"

"No."

"Now, as you were walking *away* from the register, toward the back, you said that you, "...caught movement in the security mirror out of the corner of one of your eyes," is that correct?"

"Yes."

"Just movement, not a particular person?"

"That's correct."

"Which eye?"

"My right eye."

"Mrs. Lampley, how far were you from the front counter when you looked into the mirror?"

"I dunno. I am not good with distances. Maybe from here to about where Mr. Bonner is sitting."

"Mr. Bonner, would you stipulate for the record a distance of approximately twenty feet?"

"I have no problem with that."

"Thank you. Mrs. Lampley, how far were you from the mirror mounted up in the corner?"

"Probably another ten feet farther than the counter."

"You mean you were twenty feet from the counter with your back to it, walking toward a mirror which was thirty feet away?"

"Yes, that's about right."

"That puts the object at the counter fifty feet from the mirror, doesn't it?"

"Yes, that would be about right."

Ted knew that was "about right" because he had measured it. It was forty-eight feet.

"Mrs. Lampley, the lighting in the store is bright fluorescents, isn't it?"

"Yes."

"And those lights are reflected in that mirror, are they not?"

"Yes."

"And isn't it also true the products on the shelves are also reflected in that mirror, are they not?"

"Of course."

"Would you agree with me that most of the products in the store have very bright, colorful packaging?"

"Yes."

"And, to some extent, the lighting of the parking lot was also reflected in that mirror, wasn't it?"

"Yes, I guess so."

"Mrs. Lampley, have you ever been to Six Flags?"

"Objection!"

McCarthy: "Relevance, Mr. Chase?"

"Your Honor, the next couple of questions examines the witness' familiarity with a certain type of mirror."

"Overruled. Ms. Shaw, please read the question to the witness."

The court reporter read the question.

"Yes, with my children when they were young."

"Did you take the kids into the funhouse there?"

"Yes."

"And you stood in front of the mirrors in that funhouse?"

"Yes, the ones that make you look goofy." (Gold!)

"I'm sorry, I didn't hear you, could you repeat that?" (A trick Mac taught him - get the witness to say it twice.)

"Those mirrors make you look goofy." (Bonner was beginning to lose interest.)

"That's right. They make you look goofy by distorting your figure, isn't that true?"

"Yes."

"Isn't it also true that the security mirror way up in the corner is round and that objects reflected in the middle of the mirror appear larger than those along the rim?"

"Yes, later on, after I got fired, I went back to look at it."

"Really? Did someone ask you to do that?"

"Yes."

"Who?"

"Mr. Bonner." Ted wondered now about his jury waiver, but only for a split second.

"So you would agree with me that whatever you saw in that mirror on that day was somewhat distorted?"

"Yes."

Audible groan from Bonner.

"Mrs. Lampley, while you were walking away from the counter, your head was bobbing a little up and down wasn't it?"

"How do you mean?"

"Well, when you walk, your head does not stay 100% on the same level - it moves a little bit up and down, doesn't it?"

Reflecting, "I guess so, just a little bit."

"Let me ask you this, how big was the distorted figure you saw in the mirror?"

"Objection."

"Overruled."

31

She held up her right arm and spread her thumb and index finger about an inch and a half apart.

"Mr. Bonner, will you stipulate to an inch and a half?"

Bonner, by now, had seen the writing on the wall. "Yes."

"Mrs. Lampley, I won't bother to ask you how big the figure's head was. By the way, was the figure facing you when you looked in the mirror or did it have its back to you as it was reaching over the counter?"

"It had its back to me."

"And you had your back to it, right?" By using the word "it," Ted moved the focus further away from young Dannyboy.

"Right."

"And what you want this Court to believe is that someone committed felony theft, and then elected to wait outside the store for the local gendarmes to arrive, and you have no idea how many boys were in the group or if any of them left. That about right?"

Weakly, she said, "I guess so."

Bonner put the arresting officer on the stand, but the case was already over. Just because Danny had some money on him proved nothing and Danny had the good sense to keep his mouth shut.

Bonner rested.

Ted was sure the Judge did not have enough to convict. He could have asked for a directed verdict, but took a gamble and rested his case without putting on any evidence. He guessed right. McCarthy ruled the eyewitness testimony was so faulty that the standard of proof beyond a reasonable doubt was not met by the State.

Ted felt sorry for Danny, a casualty of his father's ambition rather than the subject of it. He was a "Cat-in-the-Cradle" boy. After the judge announced his decision, Ted turned to him, "Listen, try to keep your nose clean. Here is my card. I'm writing my cell and home numbers on it. Use those

first. Call me if you need to talk or whatever." He ignored
Mother Theresa.

7

Here it was Tuesday already and Ted had not given much thought on how to engineer his exit from the firm. There were clients to contact and that gave rise to ethical considerations. The ethics rules govern what can and cannot be done. The one thing he was sure of was he would talk with Mike, his paralegal, before anyone else, even Carrothers. The goal would be to bring Mike over at the earliest possible time and that, of course, would depend on the new numbers. Mike had a wife and two kids; a steady income and health insurance was a must.

At ten minutes to ten, he was standing outside Mac's office at the law school. Mac had not changed in all these years; the office was a pigsty. Books were strewn all over and the bookshelves were empty. You could not walk on the floor because there were papers wall to wall and magazines. The wastebasket was empty and looked as though it had never been used. The computer was covered in dust. In the middle of this mess, reading a law journal, as content as could be, sat James J. McIlvaine, the eminent Richard R. Hoeflinger Professor of Trial Practice.

"Well, I see things haven't changed much."

"Ted! Don't sneak up on an old man like that!"

"Mac, I think I may have left a sandwich in here in '88. Could you look under that stack behind you on the credenza?"

"You know, you should be happy you are a lawyer, you would starve as a comedian."

"I am about to start starving as a lawyer, so what's the difference?"

At that point, Mac's secretary announced that a Mrs. Giffen was here to see him and was waiting in the faculty law library.

"Have you given your notice yet?"

"No, I had to take care of something yesterday and I burned up the weekend to prep."

"Oh yea? Anything exciting?"

"Not really. Bench trial with McCarthy. Mac, how deep have you gotten into this thing so far? I think we are going to be in for a war. I was concerned about how much we would have to invest."

"Ted, we have a legally drunk trucker who incinerated a 31 year old father and two children. He was going too fast and couldn't stop. The widow is a basket case, barely clinging to sanity."

"Well, we have filing fees, discovery costs, expert witnesses...."

"Oh, on the expert, I took the liberty of making an appointment. He will be here at 11:30. Thought it best to get him in the case sooner rather than later."

"Who is he?"

"Name's Charlie Howe. He's local. I sent him the accident report and BCI investigation documents last week."

"I have never heard of a local PhD by that name."

"Neither have I."

"Mac?"

"Come on, let's meet Laurie."

Laurie Giffen could best be described as a broken little rag doll. She was barely 5'2" and she had the figure of a little boy. She looked like she had been through a war. Ted thought: *take away the ragged hair, incredibly pale skin, red eyes and visible tremor, and there was an attractive young woman underneath it all.* His heart began to melt as soon as he laid eyes on her. He could not begin to fathom her loss.

"Hello, Laurie. This is the fellow I was telling you about. His name is Ted Chase and he and I are going to work your case together."

"Hello Mr. Chase."

"Ted, please."

"Thank you for taking on my case."

"Laurie, what we wanted to accomplish today is to talk with you about what we are all in for over the next year or so - so that you would know what to expect. A lawsuit, such as the one we are about to file on your behalf, is not to be entered into lightly. All of us are going to have to invest an incredible amount of time and resources to see this thing through. Undoubtedly, there will be both successes and failures along the way. It is not just a single battle, it will become an all-out war."

Laurie was nodding her head as Mac spoke but interrupted him to say, "Mr. McIlvaine, I have no money to pay you."

"Laurie, start by calling me Mac and don't worry about the money. A case like yours is normally taken on by the lawyers with a contingency fee. You only pay us if we are successful. Now I am going to let Ted talk with you about how a suit like this normally goes."

At that point, Ted spoke of the filing of the complaint and the answer in response; the initial paper discovery to be exchanged and then the depositions. Ted told her of the need for multiple experts including a physician, an expert in trucking, and perhaps an economist. He gave her a general idea of a timeline to expect. He spoke of the possibility of settlement and what a trial may be like. Ted briefly touched on the defenses which will be hurled at them and the fact they will be up against insurance defense lawyers whose ultimate goal will be to "zero them out." It was a delicate discussion because Ted needed to be honest with her about what to expect, but he did not want to discourage her. She kept her eyes on his the whole way through.

"Do you have any questions?"

"I am sure I will later when all this sinks in."

"Then you call me, here is my card. I will give you my cell and home numbers as well. One thing I must warn you about. Once you leave this room, Mac and I are the only people you can talk with about this. You cannot say a word to another human being. I should also warn you that in a case such as this, it is not uncommon for an insurance company to enlist the services of a private detective to watch every move you make. They could place you under intense scrutiny. Are you up for this?"

"I think so."

Mac had a retainer agreement already prepared. At the very bottom of the form were several lines where the client was asked to write in her own hand that she had thoroughly read the agreement, accepted its terms and desired to retain the lawyers' services on the conditions set forth in the agreement. Having the client write it out was prudent. In the event a dispute arose later on, having the acceptance in the client's own hand made it harder for the client to refute. She wrote it out, signed it, and handed it back to Mac. Mac had the secretary make a copy for Ted which he placed in the rear pocket of his briefcase. Laurie said she was very thankful for the help and she left the library.

Mac and Ted just looked at each other. At that point, Mac's secretary announced that a Mr. Charlie Howe had arrived and was waiting to see him. Mac told her to send him back.

8

Charlie Howe walked through the door of the library. He was about six feet tall. He was wearing worn Mucks caked with dry mud, Carhart bib overalls tattered at the cuffs and a green duck hunter's cap. His beard had to be at least two days. He needed a haircut. He had a crinkled manila envelope tucked under his right elbow.

After Mac made the introductions, Ted asked him to step out into the hall, closing the library door behind them.

"Mac, who the hell is this guy?"

"My brother-in-law's best friend."

"Where's our expert?"

"He's our expert."

"Mac, what the hell...."

"Ted, did you forget *everything* I taught you?"

"What are you talking about?"

"Where does this lawsuit have to be filed?"

"Depends."

"Well, the accident occurred on the Birney Road just over the line in Anders County. Priem's headquarters is in Anders County and that is where the Giffen family had lived and where Laurie still resides. So we will have an Anders County jury pool, won't we? And you know for a fact, defense counsel is going to fly some fellow in from some east coast university who speaks with an accent, has an alphabet soup after his name for credentials, will most likely be arrogant and will talk about stopping coefficients, ratios of braking power and some such bullshit no one will understand. Most likely, their expert will have never set his butt inside the cab of a semi. We, on the other hand will have good-ole Charlie Howe, local farmer and over-the-road truck driver who has driven over four hundred thousand miles without so much as a fender bender."

"Well, let's not make any commitments to Charlie just yet,"

"Suit yourself," he said as they re-entered the room.

"So, Charlie, did you look over the materials I sent to you?"

"Yep," he said lifting the crinkled envelope.

Mac stole a look at Ted.

"What do you think about the accident?"

"Well, the guy was deadheading turnpike doubles/covered wagons that had no anti-locks back to the terminal, had too much to drink, was going too fast coming over a rise, got the brakes chattering and plowed into the back of those poor people in the old Volvo wagon. They didn't stand a chance."

"Excuse me for asking Charlie, but could you do it again, this time in English?" Ted asked.

Mac just smiled. "Charlie, forgive him. He is just an ignorant lawyer. Ted, I will translate. Covered wagons are trailers with wood staked sides about four feet tall with canvas tarps over the top. Turnpike doubles means there were two of them, forty-eight feet long and deadheading means they were empty. No anti locks mean they were old, before anti-lock brakes were mandated. Chattering means the brakes were not slowing them down."

Charlie offered some additional information. "Shouldn't a had the doubles on that road and he was going the wrong way."

"What do you mean by that?"

"I mean turnpike doubles are only allowed on certain interstates and the road he was on ain't one of 'em - musta been lost."

"Lost?"

"Yeah, he was empty and was supposed to be headin' back to the terminal."

"So?"

39

"He was drivin' away from the terminal, not toward it. Musta been lost."

Ted began to understand Charlie's value and thought he would offer a thought or two on the subject. "God, it's a good thing the trailers were empty. He could have taken out all the cars at the light, not just Giffen."

Charlie hung his head and stole a peek at Mac.

"Go ahead and tell him Charlie."

"Ted. That's your name? Ted?"

"Yes."

"If the trailers were loaded, there wouldn'ta been an accident."

Ted could see Mac was enjoying his consternation.

"I'm sorry?"

"He got a bad case of the wheel hops because the trailers were empty. Look here at this picture with the skid marks. Do you see how the skid marks start and stop over and over again? When the skid marks stop, that means the tires are up in the air and are not in contact with the road. Now how much braking do ya thinks goin' on when the tires are up in the air?"

"None."

"Now you're catchin' on. If the trailers had a load, the weight of the load woulda kept them tires on the pavement and the damn truck woulda stopped. Ted, it takes longer to stop an empty trailer than a full one."

"Well I'll be a son of ......"

Mac chuckled.

"Charlie, tell me about CDL's. I know that in order to keep your commercial driver's license, you need to be examined every two years, but what happens if the trucker develops a drug or alcohol problem? Is he let go right on the spot?"

"No, he's put on a waiver. It's like a probation where he has to prove he's clean. Gets tested once a month by a doc. The bigger outfits have EAP's too, employer assistance programs, which usually kick in and give the guy some help.

40

If he continues to screw up, they'll put him on what they call a "last chance" agreement - come up "dirty" one more time and you're done."

"Thanks Charlie." Mac stepped out of the library with Charlie, leaving Ted to ponder all he had just heard. After a rather lengthy discussion, Mac returned alone.

"So what do you think of our expert?"

"Yes, he'll work. He'll definitely be talking to his own kind."

"Here's more good news - he won't cost us a dime. He said he just wants to help that poor young lady. Gave him an idea what he may be in for but he said to me (trying his best to mimic Charlie's voice), "It just ain't right to charge a person for tellin' the truth about somethin' like this."

"You know Mac, Anders is a one judge county."

"Yeah.....I know, I know."

"And I just pissed him off."

Ted and Mac agreed to meet at the law school Friday morning. Mac was going to take a stab at the first draft of the complaint and Ted was going to make a list of all the documents they would be requesting from Priem Transport in their initial discovery requests.

9

When he returned to the office, the message light was lit.

"Ted, Kurt. Come see me when you get in. Jim Longer called and I need to talk with you."

Well, Ted thought to himself, *maybe he had underestimated Mr. Longer after all.* Sure, Kurt gave him a pass on the fee, but at least Longer appreciated Ted's efforts and the fact he lost a weekend with his family in order to pull his son's ass out of the fire. After all, had Danny been convicted, some reformatory time was not out of the question. Kurt should be happy too. Ted delivered for him. Ted thought it was about time he got some recognition for his efforts. First time he looked forward to seeing Kurt in a long while.

"Hey, Kurt."

"Oh, Ted, come in. Look, Jim Longer called and complained; said you gave his wife a hard time. Said you didn't make any arrangements and pulled her out of the spa or some such thing at the last minute. Said you ignored her or were rude to her even though she bent over backward to get to court to help you out. How are we going to fix this? You know he's a member at Brentwood. We need to handle this today."

Ted immediately rose to his feet. "I'll tell you what Kurt. You want to know how to fix this? The way we fix this is to tell Mr. Longer and his lovely wife to go screw themselves." He walked out of Kurt's office knowing he would never set foot in there again; he had crossed the Rubicon.

He got back to his office and told his secretary to cancel his appointments for the next two days. Wednesday and Thursday were going to be devoted to calling clients and focusing on the discovery requests in Giffen -v- Priem Transport Logistics et al so he could be prepared for his next meeting with Mac on Friday. He called Dorie right away to fill her in on things. His message light lit up while he was talking with Dorie and he knew it was Kurt but no longer had to care.

10

Once a civil lawsuit is filed, one to two years usually pass before it comes to trial. The time between filing and trial is used by the litigants to find out everything they can about each other's case. They engage in "discovery" which is the mandatory trading of evidence including documents, specialist reports, and testimony of witnesses through recorded depositions. Every good trial lawyer knows never to ask a question at trial he doesn't already know the answer to. Discovery enables him to accomplish that. Discovery also enables each party to evaluate the strength and weaknesses of the case. And don't kid yourself, every case has weaknesses. Ted's first task on behalf of Laurie Giffen was to create a document request to be filed along with the complaint that Mac was drafting. Talking with Charlie was very helpful. Mac already had the accident report and the report from the Bureau of Criminal Investigation. That was a good beginning. The dead trucker's name was Patrick Malone and, regardless of his leaving the planet, he would be a co-defendant in the case. The documents all related to Malone.

Ted grabbed a legal pad off the top of the stack and jotted some notes: personnel file including any disciplinary write-ups, any medical records of Malone in the possession of Priem including CDL exam results and drug and alcohol test results, any workers compensation records, any correspondence to or from a medical professional relating to Malone, any motor vehicle accident reports, any Employee Assistance Program documents, all absentee and tardy records, documentation showing hours worked for the two weeks up to and including the day of the crash, March 18, 2009, any supervisory reports relating to Malone, all training records, all records relating to educational diplomas or certificates. He thought he had a very good start, trying to anticipate what documents Priem might have. In Ted's world, the adage "knowledge is power" was particularly true. He put down the list, promising to revisit it after he got home.

He then walked down to Mike's office, closed the door, and shared with the paralegal his decision to leave Carrothers. Ted explained that he had been considering a move and the time seemed right. He also shared with Mike his goal to join, or build a practice, crank some numbers and ask Mike to join him at the earliest possible time. He assured Mike his job with Carrothers was not in jeopardy because he was the most valuable paralegal the firm had.

Mike was stunned. Ted's decision was totally unexpected and seemingly out of the blue. He really did not know what to say. They shook hands and Ted went off to draft his resignation letter. It was important that Ted officially resign before the Giffen lawsuit was filed. His resignation letter was all business, *the less said, the better* he thought. He e-mailed it to Kurt, who had already left the office for Brentwood.

The next two days were spent contacting clients and making the necessary arrangements to exit the firm. Being a partner, that process could not happen overnight - it would be unfair to the other lawyers. The ultimate consideration was that the interests of all clients had to be protected, whether or not the client was going with Ted or staying. Matters that were staying with the firm had to be reassigned and appearances in existing cases had to be filed. Ted dreaded having to go into the office over the next couple of weeks in such a lame duck state but that was the way it would have to be.

Friday could not come quick enough; he looked forward to a friendly face. He reviewed Mac's first draft of the complaint and made some minor suggestions. They agonized over what the "prayer" of the complaint (the amount they would seek in damages) should be. Given the ghastly manner of death of a father and his two young sons and the presence of alcohol, they settled on fifteen million dollars. Mac, in turn, reviewed Ted's Request for the Production of Documents and pronounced them sound. Mac's secretary put everything in final form and mailed it off to the Anders County Clerk of Court. They split the filing fee between them sixty/forty with Ted paying the larger share. They had decided that since Ted was primarily going to "carry the water" on the case, he would receive sixty percent of the fee and bear the same percentage of the costs. Giffen-v-Priem was born. After the "chick" was hatched, they left for a sandwich, a beer or two, and a long discussion about Ted's future.

Ted returned to the office early on Saturday. His plan was to work half a day and then join the family for a much-needed weekend at the cottage. He went to the office kitchen to grab a banana, make a pot of coffee, and find the Saturday edition of *The News*.

The lead story that Saturday morning was the murder of Dr. Jerry Grundy. Ted dropped his banana and burned his lip on the coffee. He had to read it twice before any of it began to sink in. Evidently, the good doctor was shot to death in one of the exam rooms within his chiropractic office the night before. The paper reported he had been shot twice and the suspected murder weapon was in the possession of the police. Two males were in custody, having been arrested at or near the scene. There were pictures of the doctor, during much better times, as well as a picture of a beat up dark green pickup truck being towed. It was clear the paper had rushed to get the story into its Saturday edition; there were no names and no statements from the police.

At that moment, Ted lost all incentive to stay at the office. He turned the lights back off, got in his car, and headed toward the lake. After the week he had just been through, topped off by news of a client's murder, he wanted, needed, to be surrounded by those who loved him.

On the trip north, his mind raced. As much as he disliked Grundy, the fact he had been shot to death was hard to fathom. But then he thought about the dead girl lying on the front seat of Grundy's car and wondered if there was truly some sort of *"natural justice"* at play. His Dad's Dad had a favorite expression: *"What goes around...."* Maybe Grundy had finally reaped seeds he himself had sown.

Thank God the in-laws had that cottage. Ted saw it as an escape, a refuge. It was a beautiful old place, not big, looking out over the lake, surrounded by tall pines so thick there was no grass, just pine needles. It was quiet, fresh, uncorrupted.....therapeutic. Everything seemingly slowed down as soon as Ted arrived. One of Ted's favorite places in the entire world was the old leather chair in front of the wood burner and he dreamed someday of being able to sit in it and stare at the fire whenever and as long as he wanted.

Ted showed the headlines to Jack, the mother-in-law and Dorie but it was understood there would be no discussion until after the kids were up in the loft for the evening. Even then, none of the four desired to foul their sanctuary by discussing this evilness from the outside.

Sunday was beautiful, restful; Ted enjoying being with the kids all day and not thinking of the immediate future. As the sun began to sink into the west end of the lake, however, it was time to return. Dorie and the kids were staying as this was the last week before the start of school. Ted thought to himself, *it was just as well; he had a lot to do.*

12

Monday was spent looking for a new spot to "land" even if it would only be temporary. Ted did not want to make any long term commitment just yet, so he thought an office-sharing arrangement with an existing firm or solo practitioner would be the way to go. Such arrangements usually included phone and receptionist and you could also bargain for secretarial support. He started by looking in the week's Bar Report, the publication of the state bar association which reported cases, pending legislation, attorney discipline, open positions, and available office space. Remarkably, two floors down in the very same building he was presently sitting in, was just such an arrangement. A solo practitioner by the name of Rosenthall had an office available and was looking to decrease his expenses. Ted knew him to say hello as they passed in the elevator but didn't know anything about his practice.

Jay Rosenthall was a tall and fit forty two year old real estate lawyer who had left a New York City mega-firm. He was a graduate of Skidmore in upstate New York and Cornell's law school. He stayed at the big firm long enough to learn the ropes, but his plan had always been to get out on his own as soon as he could. He didn't like wearing ties or suits. His hairline was receding a little faster than he liked and he wore wire-rimmed glasses. Blue jeans and shirts from Cabela's were his favorite ensemble. He earned a living counseling clients, putting together their deals and dabbling in real estate himself. He was single.

Ted called and then went down to see him.

"Hello Ted. Jay Rosenthall. Glad you came down."

"Thanks for seeing me on such short notice."

"No problem, I wasn't going anywhere. Let me show you what I have. It really isn't much but it might work." He began a guided tour of the office.

"This is Jenny, my lifeline."

"Hello, Jenny."

"Hello."

"And here is my office...then the conference room...a small kitchen over here...and this is the office we have available. It's actually a tad bigger than mine, but, as you can see, it's an inside office. Don't know what your needs are as far as seeing clients. I meet with my clients in the conference room which we designed to be a little larger than most. Fairly often, we have closings with many parties so we needed a good sized room."

Ted found the offices to be very appealing. The wall colors and fabrics were earth tone. "Understated" was the word he would later use to describe the space to Dorie.

Jay and Ted talked a little more about Ted's situation and then struck a very generous deal for Ted. It was unstated but clear, that one lawyer was helping another get on his feet and Ted would always remember that. He started moving his things the next morning.

13

It took two days to set up the new office. It was very humble, but Ted didn't care - rather, he was proud. He was officially out on his own. The first call he got was from Mac and it was not good news.

"Ted?"

"Yes, hello Mac."

"Ted, there is some bad news. Evidently Laurie Giffen has lost whatever weak grip she had on reality and they had to take her to the hospital. I'm not sure of all the details, but it doesn't sound too good. Why don't you meet me there and we will see what is going on? She's at Westmoreland."

"Mac, I'll come by and pick you up and we can go together."

When Mac entered the car, Ted asked what had happened. Mac really didn't know that much, only to say that she was found sitting in her pajamas in the middle of her bed rocking back and forth, staring at the wall. Evidently she was totally unresponsive and has remained so for the better part of two days.

When they found her room, Ted was not prepared for what he saw. Here was that small rag doll, rocking back and forth in the middle of the bed, vacantly staring. She was incredibly pale which made her red eyes look even worse, as if they were swollen. Ted wondered how much she had cried.

They introduced themselves to the doctor who indicated the trauma she had experienced had finally become too much for her to bear, however he didn't believe anything was physically wrong with her. A psychiatrist had been summoned to consult with them about a diagnosis and treatment. They really would not know too much until then.

On the way home, Mac and Ted discussed this setback and how it might affect the lawsuit. They concluded that it really did not have any impact, at least at this preliminary stage. The lawsuit on her behalf could still be pursued and, in a morbid way, may have just gained value.

The Grundy murder story did not move to the back pages until Wednesday. By then, the public had learned the two men in custody were Thomas Merrick and Larry Townes, both residents of Anders County and both with no criminal record to speak of. They were arrested at the scene and had not attempted to flee or resist. Two handguns were confiscated from the men and were being tested. Grundy had died from a fatal wound to the left side of his head. Evidently, it was a very bloody crime scene.

14

After arranging his new office, Ted spent the remainder of the week contacting clients to notify them of his move and their choice to move with him or stay with Carrothers. Ted knew the firm would mount an all-out blitz to retain the business and he could only guess what was being said about the split. He kept a running ledger of those coming with him and the billable time each had generated over the last year - not bad so far. Even if everything came, Ted knew he would have to generate more business and soon. Jenny called him to say there was a John Dietrich in the waiting room asking to see him.

"Hello, I'm Ted Chase, what can I do for you?"

"You're a hard man to find, Mr. Chase. I'm Detective Dietrich, Anders County Sheriff's Department."

"Yes, Detective."

"This is a rather unusual thing for me to do but we have some individuals in custody and they would like to talk with you about representation. Evidently they called your firm but no one there seemed to remember you. They have their first court appearance on Monday - so as not to delay things, I was asked by the Prosecutor to contact you."

"Carl?" Ted asked.

"Yes, Carl Picker."

"So you drove all the way to Crawford to track me down?"

"Yes, Picker did not want the preliminary appearance delayed for failure to get counsel, seeing as we knew who they wanted."

"You're right, this had to be a rather unusual thing for you. Who do you have in custody?"

"Their names are Merrick and Townes."

Ted struggled to appear calm after hearing the names. Somehow he managed to thank the Detective and also assure him he would contact the men immediately.

His mind was going a mile a minute pondering what had just occurred. A solo practitioner for all of a week, whose firm could not seem to "remember" him, who was labeled a "hard man to find," would be very easy to find if he took the case, the highest profile case to come that way in twenty years. He knew what a case of this magnitude could mean. He called Dorie and then he called Mac.

"Mac, Ted. How is Laurie?"

"She's unchanged. Talked with the doc this morning."

"Do they have a diagnosis yet?"

"Don't seem to. They told me to check in with them on Monday. How's the new digs?"

"Fine, all moved in. Rather cozy but I need a landscape or something so I can pretend I have a window."

"You don't have a window?"

"No, it's an inside office."

"Oh."

"Mac, have you got a minute to talk?"

"What's up?"

"The men in custody for Grundy's murder - they want to talk with me about representation."

Silence.

"Mac?"

"Ted, that is terrific. Nothing like getting out on your own and jumping in with both feet. When did you meet with them?"

"I haven't yet. I wanted to speak with you first. Mac, do you think I have a conflict? These guys may have killed a client of my firm."

"Hell no. The S.O.B. is a deceased former client of your former firm. There are no secrets or confidences of his that have to be protected. You can take the case."

Ted knew he could take Mac's advice "to the bank."

"From what I've read so far, sounds like they got these two dead to rights. Doesn't appear like it is going to be an easy case."

Mac responded, "When was the last time you had an "easy" case?"

"You have a point there."

"Easy cases are for Carrothers."

"Well, I'll go over to Anders tomorrow morning and see what's up. Initial appearance is Monday."

"Ted, call me Monday when you're done and we can talk about Laurie and these two "cold-blooded" murderers."

"Oh, thanks a lot."

15

Ted got very little sleep Friday night; he could not get his mind to slow down. The questions kept flying at him. Do these people know me? Have I done work for either of them in the past? Did someone refer them? Or perhaps they just picked my name out of the phonebook?

He was on the way to Anders County Jail by 9:00 AM Saturday morning. He was a bit anxious and nervous - feelings he hadn't experienced in a long time, at least regarding legal matters. He had Westside Steve Simmons in the CD player. Ted's way of relieving stress was to listen to Westside Steve, bard of the Crescent Tavern on Put-in-Bay. His sweet voice took Ted's mind away from whatever manner of alligator was currently lurking.

> Doesn't matter where you go
> Anywhere the cold winds blow
> There will be someone who loves you

The jailer met him in the vestibule. "Morning Counselor."

"Hi Jake, how have you been?"

"Fine thanks, and you?"

"Good, Jake. How's the boy doing?"

Jake was a bear of a man whose arms were thicker than Ted's legs. Though his close-cropped hair was white, Jake had the physique of a college football player. Ted could not remember his son's name but knew he was a Buckeye on a full scholarship.

"Doin' fine, thinks he has a shot at starting this year."

"He's just a sophomore, isn't he?"

"Yep."

"That's terrific. Hey, I hear you have some desperadoes locked up in here."

"That would be right. You gonna represent 'em?"

"I might. Is the interview room empty?"

"Yep. I'll bring 'em down. You want them both at the same time?

"Please."

The interview room was like a small public bathroom without the toilets. The faded yellow tiles on the walls were large with a good half inch of grey grout in between. Mop stains marked the bottom row of tiles. The floor was dark brown linoleum squares and there was a grey metal table in the middle. There were four green and gray chairs around it. It was small, dimly lit and it didn't smell too good.

The younger man entered the room first, dressed in an orange jail jumpsuit with loafer style tennis shoes. He was about Ted's height with short, reddish brown hair and jowly cheeks. It appeared as though he hadn't slept in a while and he needed a shave and a shower.

Following him was a taller, older man who, even in his present surroundings, seemed to carry about him an air of dignity. He had a full head of white hair, fine features and deep blue eyes. Ted thought most women would find him very attractive. He was similarly dressed.

Jake took off their handcuffs and left the room, locking the door behind him.

"Hello, my name is Ted Chase and I understand you would like to talk with me about your case."

"That's right, said the older of the two. My name's Tom Merrick and this here's Larry Townes." They shook hands and sat down.

"Listen, before we get started, there is an issue which comes up immediately. Right now, I know nothing more than what's been reported in the newspapers but there's potential conflict here between the two of you so that one lawyer could not rep..."

57

Tom Merrick cut him off mid-sentence. "We have already discussed that, Mr. Chase. Larry and I began this together and we are in it together to the end."

The phrase *"began this together"* had Ted worried already.

"Let me ask you this, why did you ask for me?"

Larry answered, "We've seen you work."

"In court?"

"Yes, when you got Grundy off," said Tom. "We were in the courtroom every day."

"You attended the trial?"

"Yes, we sat in the very back."

"Why?"

"The girl Grundy killed..... the receptionist..... she was my daughter."

Ted momentarily lost his breath. He bowed his head down, then.....very slowly........ looked up at Larry.

"You were her fiancé."

His eyes began to tear. "Yes.....I was."

How could Ted face these two men? This made no sense. Ted couldn't think straight.

"Mr. Chase? No matter the outcome of the trial, we would have felt the same. Guilty, not guilty, it didn't matter to us. We know what happened."

"We are in deep now. We need someone to believe in us, our innocence, just like you did in that trial."

"The sheriff has to know who you are and the connection to Grundy. Why hasn't this come out in the papers?"

They had no answer.

"Are you sure you want me to represent you?"

"Yes."

"Okay, look. This is enough for now (indeed, Ted thought it was too much). I will be back here tomorrow morning and we can start work on your defense. Have you been interviewed by the detectives?"

58

"They asked but we said we wanted a lawyer and then they stopped."

"Okay. Are there any other inmates here?"

"Yes."

"Have you talked about your case where you could be overheard?"

Tom said, "No. I know your concern. We were careful not to say anything."

"Look. The best way to go about it is you can talk about anything you want, but nothing about Grundy or anything connected with your case. The only person you can talk to about it, is me. Do you understand? Don't talk about it at all."

"Yes, we understand."

16

The Sunday edition of *The News* had the story back on the front page. The headline read: *"Connection between Grundy and Suspected Killers."* That was no surprise to Ted. He had wondered why it hadn't been reported earlier, however, when he began to read, the reason became clear. The article began with a long quote from Prosecutor Carl Picker and had his picture off to the side. Ted surmised Picker was slowly feeding information to the newspaper, deliberately keeping the case in the headlines. Picker was trying his case in the papers and he realized then, his own connection to Grundy would surely merit another "Picker headline."

As he was driving back to Anders to meet with his new clients, he tried to recall Saturday's discussion. He remembered Larry's words that they needed someone to believe in their innocence. These men had the strongest motive to kill known to man: revenge. They certainly had the means and opportunity to commit the crime. Yet they spoke of their innocence to their lawyer. But they had also said they were in it together and that they *"had begun it together."* If they were innocent, what had they "begun together?"

Back in the interview room with his new clients, Ted began the session with a discussion of what his role would be. He stressed that it was his duty to do everything he could, within the bounds of the law, to get them out of this jam they were in. He said it was important for them to be upfront with him and hold nothing back. He shared that some defendants hide key information from their own lawyer for fear the lawyer will just "go through the motions." He assured them both that would not be the case with him and that whatever information they shared with him was protected from disclosure by the lawyer/client relationship they now have.

Many of Ted's clients, even after this speech, still felt compelled to lie. It was the worst possible thing they could do. A criminal defense lawyer MUST be told where all the land mines are buried. Tom Merrick completely understood.

"Tom, let me start by asking you about a statement you made to me yesterday. You said that you and Larry "had begun this together." What is it that you had "begun together?"

"Mr. Chase..."

"No Tom, from here on out, it is Ted."

"Ted, when we went to Grundy's office.........when we went over there..... (Tom glanced at Larry whose head was hanging so low Ted couldn't see his face)... we were going there to kill him."

With the best poker face Ted could possibly summon, he calmly asked, "And when did you start to plan?"

"The day after Grundy's trial."

The interview took the entire morning. Ted learned that father and son-in-law-never-to-be, decided they were going to do what the law failed to do. They began by finding out the make and license number of Grundy's car which they recorded on a scrap of paper - now in the possession of the sheriff. They "checked out" the chiropractic office in the days before to determine the number of employees, hours of operation, parking arrangements and Grundy's times of coming and going. The female office manager was the only employee and she arrived a half hour before the first patient and left very soon after the last. Grundy himself usually showed up fifteen minutes before his first appointment but, most nights, stayed until at least 6:00 PM. They had an informational brochure from the office which they had made some notations on. The sheriff now possessed this as well.

On the night Grundy was murdered, they waited in Larry's old green pick up (which the sheriff impounded), in the rear lot of the building just north of the chiropractic office. From their vantage point, they could keep their eye on the two cars parked at the rear entrance. They had no view of the front

61

of the building. They watched the office manager leave and waited for Grundy to exit the building and walk to his car. They figured it would be about 6:00. They brought with them a small caliber handgun which Tom was going to use.

Six o'clock came and went yet Grundy had not come out. They waited until after 7:00. Still no Grundy. They discussed what to do and figured he must be alone inside the office doing bookwork or something. The back door was locked so they walked around to the front and were surprised to find the door unlocked. When they entered the building, the lights were all on. Nothing seemed out of place until they got to exam room four. There was blood all over the small room. Grundy was lying on the floor face up about ten feet from the door with the left side of his face blown off including his neck. His eyes were bugged out with a frozen stare of horror. They saw three holes in the wall behind where he was lying. They got blood all over their shoes (which the sheriff now had) and tracked it wherever they stepped. Larry found a handgun on the other side of the examining table and instinctively picked it up. A minute later, an Anders County deputy sheriff entered the room, weapon already drawn.

The deputy sheriff confiscated the weapon each man had, handcuffed them and walked them out to his patrol car. They offered no resistance. There, he waited for the car working the other zone to arrive and take control of the scene so he could transport the men to the sheriff's department.

Back at the department, some testing was done on their hands, followed by fingerprinting. They were placed in separate cells out of sight of each other. Two hours later, when a detective asked to speak with them, each had the good sense to ask for a lawyer.

Ted also learned that each of the men had high school educations and had spent time in the military and that Larry was an Iraqi war veteran. Both of them were lifelong residents of Anders County and had never been in trouble before. Tom was retired from Tru-Line Corp. where Larry presently worked. Larry had met Tom's daughter at a company picnic.

62

It was a case of "love at first sight," according to Larry. Their courtship began immediately and they became inseparable. She grew to depend on Larry for everything and he enjoyed that. He took her everywhere she had to go because they were so much in love and, he chuckled a bit, because she had never learned how to drive.

"Wait a minute Larry," Ted said. "Terri did not have a driver's license?"

"No, she never learned how."

When Larry deployed to Iraq, they promised each other they would marry as soon as they could upon his return.

The interview ended with a brief discussion regarding the next day's arraignment and the same admonition of the day before; not a word to anyone.

Ted's mind raced on the drive home so much so he thought it best to try *not* to think. He rolled the window all the way down and put Westside Steve on.

> I paid the devil for heaven on earth
> What did we give him and what was
> it worth

Sleep was impossible that night; his mind was on overload. He tried to place himself in the shoes of Tom Merrick, asking for the same lawyer who got his daughter's killer a "walk". He thought about what Tom had decided to do to avenge Terri's death and wondered if he could do the same had it been one of his daughters. He tossed and turned until well past two.

17

The arraignment Monday morning before His Honor Curtis Granders was for the purpose of entering a plea and requesting bond. Not Guilties were entered for each man but Ted knew bond was a long shot. Even though Ted knew neither man was a flight risk, this case was too big. True to form, Granders set a bond, but even ten percent of it was way beyond the reach of either man. They were going to have to sit until trial. Accordingly, Ted asked for a date as soon as the Court's schedule permitted. Granders set a pretrial for one week but did not address Ted's request.

After the session, Carl Picker caught up with Ted in the corridor.

"Well, Ted, it's really something, isn't it?"

"What would that be Carl?"

"I mean you got Grundy off and these two fellas come along and take him out. His acquittal ended up being a death sentence. Pretty tough to deal with I guess."

Biting his tongue, Ted responded, "Well, Carl I just try to do the best I can for each of my clients."

"Yea, but this one backfired on you a bit, didn't it?"

Ted was starting to heat up just a little.

"You know Carl, you may be right. Had you prevailed, Grundy would have done some time and *whoever* it was who did this, would not have been able to get to him. By the way, did you know that Terri Merrick did not know how to drive?"

Ted left Picker standing there, first with his mouth open and then with a scowl. Walking away, Ted thought, *the worst thing about being a lawyer is having to deal with lawyers*. He regretted immediately sharing the information with Picker about Terri but his emotions had got the better of him; he wanted to show him up and he wanted to shut him up as well.

18

When he returned to the office, there was some mail to open and some calls to return. Phil Carrothers' was the first call he returned.

"Hello Ted, how's it going three floors down?"

"Fine, Phil. What do you need?" Ted was not in the mood for any small talk.

"I just wanted to tell you that I will be representing Priem Transport in the Giffen matter."

Ted thought to himself that every civil case also has an element of luck. This was music to his ears but Ted hid his happiness. "That so? Well, I think you'll find it will be an interesting case with us two seasoned litigators going head to head." Ted couldn't resist the jab but, not surprisingly, the point was entirely lost on Phil.

"Ted, this case will never see the inside of a courtroom. It's a summary judgment case" (meaning the court would throw it out on legal grounds without a trial.)

"That so Phil? How do you see it?" Ted thought, here come the hand grenades.

"The company had no knowledge this guy Malone was drinking and on top of that, he was on some kind of frolic with the company vehicle. He was driving away from the terminal - he wasn't in the course of employment. You may have a great cause of action against him, but it ends there. As a matter of law, the company cannot be responsible. And fifteen million? Where the hell did that number come from?""

"Have you received our request for documents, Phil?"

"Yes."

"I tell you what (Ted thought it would be smart to start the hoodwinking immediately), based on what you just told me, perhaps we should get together right after you send the materials to us."

"Us?"

"Yes, McIlvaine is on the case with me."

"Sure, we need to end this thing sooner rather than later." For Phil, "fearus courtroomus" had already raised its ugly head.

So, his opponent in the case will be the litigator who has never litigated and has already shared with Ted the legal defenses he is going to assert. Nothing like showing your hand before all the cards are dealt.

Ted turned to his mail and the first piece he opened was a lawsuit captioned Kurt Carrothers Co LPA versus Theodore Chase.

Later that day, he called Mac as promised to discuss Laurie Giffen's health and her case. Laurie's status was unchanged and there was some talk of moving her to a long term facility rather than have her stay at the hospital. Ted filled Mac in on his conversation with Phil Carrothers and talked a little about the murder case.

"Mac, as long as we're doing the Giffen case together, maybe you can help me out with Townes and Merrick? I am already up to my ass in alligators and we haven't even been to a pretrial yet. Picker definitely has it in for me on this one and you know who the judge is."

"What's in it for me?"

"A date with Dorie."

"When can I start?"

"You're an asshole."

Later that night, he had a long discussion with Dorie. He really could not fathom an existence without her; she was everything to him. She was his island of calm in his profession of storms, a voice of reason in a world filled with insanity. Many times she had brought Ted back from the brink, times when he just wanted to chuck it all and go drive a beer truck.

67

19

The week went by quickly, mostly spent calling on clients, cementing relationships, and discussing reduced hourly rates due to the lack of "big firm overhead." Ted and Mac were awaiting Priem's answer to Giffen's complaint and the documents in response to their request.

Monday came quickly. It was time for the first pretrial in *"The People versus Merrick and Townes, Aggravated Murder"*.

Pretrials are informal conferences, usually in chambers, used by the Court to assist in getting the case to trial. Deadlines are set, criminal discovery (the trading of information) discussed, as well as any matter the litigants think should be brought to the Court's attention. Plea bargains routinely occupy ninety percent of the discussion. If every criminal case required a trial, the entire judicial system in this country would implode.

"Welcome gentlemen."

"Good morning, Your Honor."

"Well, we have a number of items to discuss. First of all, I note the state has a one count indictment for each defendant and there are no lesser included offenses. Is that correct, Mr. Picker?"

"Yes, Your Honor."

"So it's your intention to proceed on the count of aggravated murder and no others?"

"Yes, Your Honor."

"Of course, you realize the Court maintains the discretion to charge on "lesser-includeds" if the facts warrant?"

"Certainly, Your Honor, however, the People will waive any such instruction and proceed on the aggravated murder count only."

"Regardless of the proof?"

"Your Honor, the People have a strong case and will secure a verdict at that level."

"What you are really saying, Mr. Picker, is that you don't want to give the jury an out?"

"That's correct Your Honor."

"Mr. Chase, what have you to say about this?"

"The defendants will also waive jury charges on lesser included offenses." Picker almost fell out of his chair.

"Are you serious?" Granders asked. "Mr. Chase, these men are facing the remainder of their lives in prison without the possibility of parole! Surely, you want the jury to have as much leeway as possible to avoid that outcome."

"Your Honor, my clients did not commit this crime or any other crime. We do not wish to risk a "compromise verdict" from the jury."

"Well, haven't we all got brass balls this morning? I tell you what, we're going to have to put this on the record. Mr. Chase, I will need to inquire directly of your clients."

"I understand, Your Honor."

"How is discovery coming?"

"The defendants have not requested anything from us at this point in time, Your Honor."

"Mr. Chase?"

"Your Honor, at this time we only move for an inspection of the scene of the crime - Dr. Grundy's office. As to discovery from the prosecution, we reserve the right to request at a later date."

"No discovery? Mr. Chase, do you want to tell me what is going on here? Are you just building a case for the court of appeals by goading me into error?"

Picker was now enjoying this.

"Your Honor, the rules do not allow discovery by the People unless triggered by a request on behalf of the defendants," Ted said while keeping an eye on Picker. "We reserve the right to initiate discovery at a later date."

"Mr. Chase, what is the most popular argument made nowadays at the appellate level to try to get a conviction overturned?"

"Ineffective assistance of counsel."

"Is that your game plan here?"

"No, Your Honor. The only plan I have is to gain an acquittal for two innocent men."

"Well, so far, you are certainly going about it in a very strange way. What about plea discussions?"

"The people have no offer to make, Your Honor."

"Why does that not surprise me? So you, Mr. Picker, are risking "a walk," while Mr. Chase over here, waiving jury charges, has to win the whole enchilada. Is that it? Both of you guys have to hit home runs and nobody wants to settle for even a triple?"

Silence.

"Your Honor, there is another matter - the defense has already requested an early trial date, or, in the alternative, reduction in bail."

"So on top of everything else, you want to rush to trial? Mr. Picker, what do you have to say about this?"

"We have no objection."

"Anything else, Mr. Chase?"

"Yes, Your Honor. One last item." Handing a document to both Picker and the Judge, Ted said, "I have filed a motion to prohibit the prosecution from discussing my representation of Grundy in the manslaughter trial. That fact is neither relevant nor material to the guilt or innocence of Merrick and Townes but may serve to prejudice the jury. It is the defense's position the jury should not be allowed to know it."

Picker began to say something but the Judge cut him off mid-sentence. "I agree. Your motion will be granted. Anything else from either of you?"

Silence.

"So be it. Agnes, please get the court reporter up, we need to go on the record." Judge Granders took the bench and placed his rulings on the record, making sure to explain that both parties had agreed. He had Merrick and Townes verbally express their approval of Ted's waiver of possible jury charges. He instructed Ted to arrange the office visit with the sheriff. He then set a trial date.

Making a record had nothing to do with the defendants - it was purely Granders covering his own ass should the matter end up in the court of appeals.

Ted told his clients to "hang in" and reminded them to keep quiet. He told them he had a few matters to take care of and would be back to see them in a few days.

In the hallway, Picker, once again approached Ted.

"Ted, I'm sure you're aware the defense of "*natural justice*" is not legally recognizable in our state."

"You know what I am aware of Carl? I'm aware that juries can, and do, whatever they feel is right, oftentimes without regard to the law. OJ's jury let him walk because, rightly or wrongly, they felt it was the thing to do. How much evidence did they ignore? Carl, you can't keep Terri Merrick out of your case. You need Terri Merrick to prove motive and you know it. Isn't it ironic that you will be the one to provide the jury with exactly the reason they need to vote against you?" Ted turned his back and walked away.

.

He did not return to the office. Instead he called Jenny to let her know he would not be in until Wednesday morning. He needed a day off and he thought perhaps he and Dorie could steal a Monday evening and Tuesday up at the cottage on their own. He called Dorie.

"Hey babe, I'm on the way back from Anders. Any chance you can get Mom and Dad to stay with the kids tonight and tomorrow so we can go up to the lake by ourselves? I really need a little time to relax and go over some things without the phone ringing. I'm sure we can get back around suppertime if we have to."

"I don't see why not. I'll give Mom a call. Are you headed straight here?"

"I'll be there in about a half hour."

"Okay, I'll call Mom."

His in-laws were already at the house when Ted arrived. What a blessing they were. One of the nice things about having a getaway is that you don't have to pack anything - just get up and go. Ted enjoyed wearing his ragged jeans, faded golf shirts and worn out mocs which he left in the cottage closet year round. The pantry was kept full so grocery shopping wasn't necessary. It was a home away from home but also a home away from the rat race. Ted had used it before, on his own sometimes just to "chill out," as his son would say, and sometimes to have a quiet place to work. He planned to do a little of both this trip.

Dorie and Ted thanked the in-laws and hit the road. They both knew the kids would be happily surprised to come home from school to their grandparents. Ted thought it would be nice to stop for dinner on the way up and he suggested Hal's, one of Dorie's favorite places.

Hal's was on the main road close to the cottage. It was an old log cabin with one big dining room that had a century old back bar which ran the whole length. The floor was dark plank boards. The fireplace on the south end of the room was stone and always roaring - real wood, none of those gas log things. There was a huge moose head above the fireplace which seemingly stared at each patron all at the same time. The glow from the fireplace was reflected in the mirror of the back bar but not before being filtered through the green and amber liquor bottles on the shelves in front of it. The tables were all wood, covered with red and white checkered table cloths and there were no two chairs alike in the entire place. It was a warm, friendly, cozy place and the perfect spot to start your getaway, if even for just a day. The bonus was that the food was terrific and reasonably priced.

They both got comfortable, ordered a drink and then Dorie said, "So how goes it there *Mr. Solo Practitioner?*"

"Dorie, it goes okay. Should have left years ago. The work seems to be coming; I just did not expect to be in two "monster" cases at the same time and so soon."

"How is that Giffen lady?"

"Not good. They moved her to St. Joseph's from the hospital and no one takes that as a good sign. She just finally snapped....my God, her family was incinerated. It's tragic. No amount of money will ever make her whole. We may have to enlist the services of another expert, that is, if she doesn't improve."

"And how's Mac?"

"Oh yeah. I forgot to tell you, he's helping me with both cases now."

"He's on the Grundy murder too?"

"Yes."

"How did that come about?"

"Well....I promised him he could take you out on a date."

"He is a corrupt old codger."

"Tell me."

From that point on they talked about the kids, and what was going on in their lives, especially the older daughter who recently decided boys weren't such a bad thing after all.

It was about eleven when they finally arrived at the cottage. They immediately climbed into bed and fell asleep in each other's arms.

21

There was nothing to do on the Giffen case until Ted received the documents from Priem - that is, from Phil Carrothers. Tuesday morning, Ted spent reviewing the criminal case. He had never seen such a case. He understood why Picker was so cocky. They caught these two seemingly "in the act," both with handguns, stepping through the victim's blood. They had a motive no juror would reject and evidence of "prior calculation and design." He was especially worried about the fiancé, Larry Townes, caught with the murder weapon in his hand.

Break it down, Ted said to himself. Mac had taught him whenever you look at a case, look at the whole picture and then break it apart. Just like Mrs. Lampley in the convenience store. Her eyewitness testimony, considered on its own, could have convicted the Longer kid but when Ted broke it down, it became clear you can't see shit in those mirrors, certainly not to convict a young man beyond a reasonable doubt. Or even take Grundy, himself. The officer testifies he failed all the field sobriety tests, but when broken down, were they really fair? The individual juror realizes the unfairness of it all, and says to himself, thank God it wasn't me. I probably could not have passed those tests even sober.

Ted wondered about the short length of the examination room and the fact three shots missed. Knowing Grundy as he did, he wondered about other skeletons he may have had in the closet as well as enemies. He looked forward to inspecting the office and interviewing the office manager.

To prove their innocence, must he have Merrick and Townes admit what they were *about* to do and that someone else simply beat them to it? That is why Ted agreed to exclude jury charges on lesser included offenses. One lesser included offense to aggravated murder is "conspiracy to commit murder." He might beat murder but certainly they had conspired..... Or....could he simply appeal to the jury's collective sense of *"natural justice?"* These two defendants should get a free pass because Grundy only got what he deserved. What they did should have been done. Don't punish them, they've been through enough. Picker was absolutely right on the law; it wasn't a legally recognizable defense. However, Ted knew jurors draw upon their own values and beliefs regardless of what is or is not "legally recognizable." Picker knew it too.

He spent the morning making notes and testing theories. The afternoon he spent with Dorie doing whatever she wanted to do. The retreat seemed to come to an end too soon. Ted relished the day when he could stay as long as he wanted and only be concerned about his loved ones and no one else.

The balance of the week was spent attending to other matters to keep his new practice alive. Ted thought it remarkable how many costs were involved just to keep the doors open. There was malpractice and health insurance (the two biggies); office supplies; bar memberships; mandatory continuing legal education expense (twelve hours per year); and of course, his rent: it seemed to go on and on, and all had to be paid before he got paid. On top of all these, he had to be concerned about the lawsuit filed by Carrothers, though, not overly concerned. Ted had contacted the clients appropriately, and those who retained his services did so voluntarily. He knew the law favored him on this issue and he viewed the lawsuit as more of a nuisance and a "back at ya'" from his former firm.

On Thursday, the discovery documents from Carrothers, were delivered by messenger (all he had to do was take the elevator down three floors) and arrived in a good-sized box. Rather than start pouring over them on his own, he called Mac and arranged to meet him at the law school Friday morning.

22

"Here it is Mac. Shall we see what we've got? Why don't I start with Malone's personnel file and you can sift through the rest."

"Ted, tell me what I should be on the lookout for."

"Well, for starters, anything that could be remotely related to alcohol, prior driving infractions, disciplinary action of any type....that sort of thing."

"Okie doke."

The personnel filed revealed that Malone was a high school graduate who went to truck driving school soon after graduation. He had been with the company some fifteen years and it appeared he had a rather unremarkable career. CDL documents appeared to be in order. No EAP records. A few off-work slips from various physicians documenting bouts with the flu, that sort of thing. A few absences were documented for family funerals and out-of-town events. Looked like he also had a child support order from the court dated last year. His immediate supervisor was a man by the name of Joseph Minor.

Then Mac said, "Well...lookee here." Mac had found a workers' compensation claim from the year before for a minor hand laceration. He handed the documents to Ted. It wasn't the claim itself that was important, it was the emergency room report. Ted looked over the comp documents twice before he caught it: ETOH (alcohol) was noted during the ER visit which was supposedly for a job-related incident. *Did the company catch this?*

So last year was seemingly not a good one for Mr. Malone. Some evidence of a divorce and at least one entry for alcohol.

"Well....lookee here," said Mac again.

"Will you cut that out Mac! Now what?"

"Ted, the accident was March 18, is that right?"

"Yes."

"Attendance records demonstrate Mr. Malone took off work for a personal day the day before." In his best Irish brogue, Mac said, "Ah, me fine lad, now what d'ye think the good ole Paddy Malone was doin' the day before?"

"Mac, the coroner's report of the autopsy estimated a .18 BAC at 2:00PM the following afternoon. Wow. We'll have to talk to somebody. If he was still at .18 at 2:00, what would the number have been the evening before? Still, Mac, no real evidence the company had prior knowledge of his drinking - other than that one ER record in the comp case. Really wouldn't think that would be enough but I'm not giving up on that yet."

The remainder of the records didn't reveal anything helpful to their case. When they finished their task in the Giffen case, Ted drove over to Anders to visit with his clients if, for no other reason, to give them moral support as well as some relief from their tedium. He indicated the next event in their case would be his investigation of the murder scene and, hopefully, an interview of the office manager. He intended to have a weekend devoted one hundred percent to his family.

23

His message light was already lit when he entered the office a little after 6:00 A.M. on Monday. A secretary in the sheriff's department had left a message late Friday stating the office visit could be scheduled for Monday. She said the office manager could accommodate them and she indicated that a representative of the sheriff's department had to be present. She asked Ted to call first thing Monday morning.

At nine o'clock, Ted called and arranged to visit the office at eleven. A deputy sheriff would meet him there. When he arrived, a patrol car was waiting for him.

"Officer Klein, how the heck are you?"

"Fine, now that I am not being grilled by anyone."

"Well, I hope you didn't take it personally, just comes with the job I guess you could say."

"Yes, actually it was a learning exercise of sorts. Now I have a much better idea what to expect."

"That's the way to look at it. Every case is a learning experience for me as well, even now."

"Still, all the same, I wonder how you can do it."

"Do what?"

"Represent a scum like Grundy."

"Well, what you have to understand is that there is a difference between moral responsibility and legal guilt. Our criminal justice system is the best the world has ever seen but it is not perfect. Public policy is that every guilty man should go free *lest one innocent man be convicted.*" That's why the state's burden is so high - proof beyond a reasonable doubt. A defendant is not legally guilty until twelve people say he is however, he could still be morally responsible for his act. So I may believe he is responsible for his act morally, still my job is to get him acquitted."

"But he does not get punished."

"Not in this world."

Officer Klein entered the office first and spoke with the lone person there who Ted guessed was the office manager. He then said to Ted, "This place stinks. I am going to wait out in the car."

"I have been expecting you. Marcie Noonan."

"Ted Chase, glad to meet you." Marcie was very pleasant and appeared vaguely familiar to Ted. She was in her mid-thirties, Ted guessed.

"Do you mind if I start by looking at the exam room?"

"Go right ahead, you'll have no trouble finding it."

Room four had yellow tape across the entrance which Ted carefully moved to the side and ducked under.

It was horrific; the floor covered in blood, footprints everywhere and it was already starting to smell that putrid smell of death. Ted was not prepared for that; he covered his nose and mouth with his handkerchief. You could tell from the floor where the body laid. The wall directly behind it had three holes but they were spread out some twelve feet apart. One of them was about two feet above the baseboard while another about that same distance from the ceiling. Ted knew five bullets had been fired, these three, one in Grundy's right hip and the fatal shot to the left side of the face and neck. He took his pictures and then ducked back out the door.

"Marcie, can I speak with you?"

"Sure."

"Marcie, were you here the night the doctor was murdered?"

"Yes, I left right after the last patient arrived, musta been right about 4:30 give or take."

"You don't stay until the patient leaves?"

"No. In fact, as soon as Grundy (not Doctor Grundy, Ted noted) saw her approaching the office, he said I could go."

"They were alone in the office?"

"Yes."

"Is that unusual?"

"No. Depends on who it is."

It appeared to Ted that Marcie was a talker and that she may have something to say.

"Marcie, who was the last patient?"

"Her name was Lucille Malley."

"How do you remember that?"

"After Grundy got shot, I looked at her patient questionnaire."

"Which she filled out for the office?"

"Yes."

"Did you give her the questionnaire?"

"No, I was walking out the back door as she was coming in the front. Grundy had her do it."

"Do you remember what she looked like?"

"Not really. All I can tell you is that she was tall and had a nice shape."

Ted had an "inkling", so he took a "flyer" here.

"And that's why Grundy sent you home?"

Marcie looked Ted straight in the eyes and did not flinch, "Most likely."

"The questionnaire, do you still have it?"

"Yes, it's in the file Grundy opened in her name."

"May I get a copy of it?"

"I don't see why not." Marcie walked over to the file cabinet along the wall, and pulled several files because they were all jammed in there together. She placed them on the counter and rifled through them, looking for the one belonging to Lucille Malley. It had only the questionnaire in it. Marcie said, "The copier is in the back, I'll be right back."

When she left, Ted glanced down at the remaining files. The one right next to Malley's was marked on the side with the name Patrick Malone. Ted could not believe his eyes. He peeked inside and the very first document had a Priem

81

Transport logo at the top. Without so much as a second thought, he picked up that file and put it inside his briefcase.

Marcie returned with a photocopy of the Malley questionnaire which Ted examined.

"Don't bother trying to track her down."

"What?"

"I said you won't find her. The phone number is out of service and the address she provided is the Ramada Inn."

"You tried?"

"Yes."

"Why?"

"Well, until I read the account in the paper, I thought she would have been the last person to see Grundy alive. I wanted to talk with her."

"About Grundy?"

"Yes."

Ted put the questionnaire in the rear pocket of his briefcase.

"Marcie, can you go across the street with me and have a cup of coffee?"

"I don't see why not, nothing going on here."

On the way over, Ted gave Officer Klein the hi sign and he drove out of the lot. When they resumed their conversation, Ted asked, "Marcie, does the sheriff have a copy of Malley's questionnaire?"

"If they do, they didn't get it from me."

"They didn't ask you for it?"

"They didn't ask me for anything."

"So they don't know about Lucille Malley?"

"Don't think so. They already got the killers or at least they think they do."

"Marcie, you were sending a message to me about Grundy's treatment of ....certain........ of his patients."

"You picked up on that, huh?"

"Are you saying he may have taken liberties?"

"No, I'm saying the son of a bitch was a pervert. I knew what he was doing. The younger women with the shapes took twice as long in treatment and they were all made to completely disrobe."

"How do you...

"Look, I know. Let's leave it at that. I should have turned the cheap bastard in."

"Did anyone ever complain?"

"Oh yes. Three or four in particular."

"The women complained to you?"

"No, but the husbands and boyfriends did."

"How did you...

"Mr. Chase,...

"Call me Ted."

"Look Ted, have you ever heard the saying: "Do you want to speak with the man in charge or talk with the woman who knows what's going on?"

With a smile, "Yes."

"Well, I'm the woman who knows what's going on. Grundy didn't fool me. One of them actually wrote a threatening letter."

Ted started to get a little light-headed. "You're serious."

"Like a heart attack. I made a copy."

Ted swallowed hard, "Do you still have it?"

"You betcha."

"I don't suppose anyone else knows about this?"

"Not to my knowledge, other than whoever wrote it."

"Can I get a copy of it from you?"

"Sure, it's stashed back at the office."

"Marcie, to your knowledge, did Grundy have any other fallings out with anyone else?"

"You looking for enemies there Ted?"

"Yes."

"The only thing I could tell you is that one evening as I was about to leave, he was having a helluva row with a guy on the phone. Said some nasty things...nice language, you know?

I think it was his former partner. He still owns part of the building."

"What's his name?"

"Something Crawford, just like the city.

"Marcie, on the night Grundy was killed, did you see any unfamiliar vehicles near the office?"

"Yes, there was a green pickup truck in the lot next door. I remember the front license."

"You remember the license number!?"

"No, no, no, I just remember one of the corners was bent up."

They finished their coffee and returned to the office where Marcie gave Ted a copy of the letter she had stashed. Ted thanked her and asked her to keep their little meeting a secret, if she could. She had no problem with that.

On the way to his office, Ted decided he would not need discovery from Picker - that would trigger Ted's obligation to provide Picker with the information he just secured. Ted surmised that the sheriff's office and Picker had been incredibly sloppy in their investigation. They were so cock-sure they had the right men, they didn't see a need to consider any other possibilities. Immediately upon his arrival at the office, Ted drafted a Waiver of Discovery he would file with the court the next day. He then sat down to examine the Malone file he had just pilfered. After looking at the first two documents, he could not contain himself. He said in a loud voice, "Carrothers, you son of a bitch!"

24

At the same time, Mac was having a cup of coffee with Dr. Michael Berringer, a resident psychiatrist at St. Joseph's, and Laurie Giffen's doctor. Mac had just come from Laurie's room where her condition was unchanged: rocking incessantly, staring vacantly, unable or simply unwilling to communicate. The rocking now had a musical quality as the nuts, bolts and springs of the old metal bed were starting to loosen.

"Mr. McIlvaine..."

"Mac."

"Mac, I believe Laurie is suffering from an adjustment disorder with features of anxiety and severe depression. It started out as natural bereavement over the loss of her family, but progressed and can almost be labeled "chronic" at this time. It is her mind's reaction to the incredible stress of her loss and, in no small part, was fueled by her view of the autopsy photos."

"Doc, it's like she is catatonic."

"Yes, at least it presents that way."

"So what happens now?"

"We will try different drugs, psychotherapy and perhaps personal interactions to trigger a response - what she might react to. But sometimes, all that is needed is the passage of time."

"Is there a chance this could become permanent?"

"Yes."

"Is it a good thing to keep coming to see her?"

"Certainly. We never know what the triggers are; a face, a voice, you never know. There just may be some stimulus out there that will help Laurie come out of it."

"Doc, I am hoping against hope it won't be necessary, but if it does, would you be able to come to court to explain her condition and what her future might look like?"

"Sure."

On the way out, Mac's cell rang. It was Ted.

"Mac, any chance you can come over to the office tomorrow? I need you to look at something."

"Sure, same building, right?"

"Second floor instead of the fifth."

"I can be there about ten, that okay?"

"I'll see you then."

Ted could not wait to share with Mac the new information. He got little sleep that night.

When Mac arrived on Tuesday, Ted had the "recently acquired" Malone file opened in the conference room next to the documents Carrothers had provided in discovery.

"Nice digs. Figured out the window thing yet?"

"No." Ted wanted to chuck a derogatory remark back but gave Mac a pass this time.

"You went to see Laurie?"

"Yes, spoke with her doc. Says her present condition is a reaction to the incredible stress. He's not sure how long it will last. They are using meds and think there may be some type of stimulus that may help Laurie work herself out of it."

"Stimulus?"

"Yes. Something that might help her make a connection, a face, a voice, that sort of thing. He will come to court if we ask him to."

"Good, but it might not come to that." Mac shot a quizzical look at Ted.

"Mac, just look at this file for a minute."

"Where did you get that?"

"Grundy's office."

"Anyone know you have it?"

"No." Mac shot the same glance at Ted, put his reading glasses on and started paging through Grundy's Malone file.

After about three minutes, Mac could not contain himself: "Those bastards!"

"That's right Mac, Carrothers shit-canned most of this stuff!"

"Ted, do you understand what this means to the case?"

"I'm beginning to."

The first document, and probably the only one they really needed, was a short note from Malone's supervisor, Joe Minor, to Grundy. It read: *Jerry, Enclosed are records per your request. We believe these are isolated instances most likely due to the divorce and really do not present any problems for us. There's never been a citation. Malone is certified for doubles and we would like to keep him on the road. Please provide your report and fee bill for services rendered. Minor.* The note was on Priem Transport letterhead.

Attached to the note were three in-house write-ups for Malone for coming to work under the influence of alcohol. They occurred over the period of eleven months prior to the date Malone incinerated the Giffen family.

"Ted, do you have Charlie's phone number here?'

"It's in the other file, let me get it."

Mac called Charlie Howe from the conference room phone and placed it on speaker.

"Charlie, this is Mac, how have you been?"

"Fine, Mac. What can I do for ya?"

"Charlie, I'm here with Ted, the other lawyer on our case, and I've got you on the squawk box. Charlie, what do you know about Jerry Grundy?"

"The chiropractor?"

"Yes."

"He's dead." Ted made a face at Mac.

"Right, but do you know, did he do any CDL stuff for any of the companies?"

"Big time. A lot of companies used him."

"How so? He was just a chiro, not a real doctor."

"Well, he would sign as a doctor. No one really looked that close."

"Who used him?"

"Well, let's see, most of the big outfits in town X-Line, Trens Logistics, a lot of 'em."

"What about Priem?"

"Probably."

"Any particular reason?"

88

"Well, I don't think I have to tell you that a lot of the good drivers for these outfits are pretty good drinkers as well. It was common knowledge Grundy would say whatever needed to be said. Company wanted a guy gone - he was gone. Company wanted to protect a guy - no problem."

"As long as Grundy got paid."

"As long as Grundy got paid, that's right. Some of the drivers had a nick-name for him: Dr. Pass Go."

"Pass Go?"

"Yeah, you know, like the Monopoly game. Sometimes you draw the card that says: 'Go directly to jail. Do not pass GO. Do not collect two hundred dollars.' With Grundy, if your company wanted, you got to pass go."

"Dr. Pass Go."

"Yep, that's right."

Mac thanked Charlie once again, hung up the phone, and just stared at Ted. They discussed strategy in light of their new file acquisition, and it was decided Ted would call Phil Carrothers on Thursday. He was almost looking forward to making that call.

That evening, after dinner, Ted pondered what Carrothers had done and how it exemplified what the practice of law had become. For many lawyers like Phil Carrothers, a trial was no longer a search for the truth; rather it was a game to be won at all costs regardless of the truth. If evidence had to be "lost" in order to prevail, so be it. The end justified the means.

"Phil, Ted Chase."

"Hello, Ted."

"Look, I've had the opportunity to review all the documents, and, frankly there is not much here. (Let the hoodwinking begin.) In light of what you told me, perhaps we can speed this thing up a bit. I'll need to conduct one deposition, Malone's supervisor. If I'm going to dismiss this thing, I don't want anyone accusing me of malpractice for not going that far at least. Guy's name is Joseph Minor."

"Minor? How do you spell that?" (Now who was doing the hoodwinking?)

"Minor, with an O... M...I...N...O...R. Joseph."

Slowly..."Okay."

"Look, can we do it by agreement or do you need a notice? I figure the guy is in Anders so it's not a big deal for him to come over. Today's Thursday, I'm thinking Tuesday morning would be good."

"That's okay, I guess."

"Let's do it down here at ten. I won't send a notice. If, for some reason, that doesn't work, just call me."

"Okay."

"Oh, and Phil, since you sent me all the documents, I won't need to send Minor a subpoena to bring anything with him, will I? I mean, I already have everything."

"Right. You have everything."

"Good. See you Tuesday at ten."

The trap had been set. Ted was now looking forward to seeing Phil Carrothers.

Friday was spent at the Anders County jail. Ted wanted to report his progress to his clients. After a greeting and some preliminary small talk about the jail food, Ted got right down to business.

"What I have discovered is the sheriff and the prosecutor were so focused on you, they conducted a very sloppy investigation. They had so much evidence, they neglected to look any further. It's a bit ironic that because of that, the amount of evidence, we may have a way out of this thing. But the only way we will be able to pull it off is for you to admit what you were about to do." He looked for a reaction in their faces. Tom spoke first. "Ted, if we admit it, aren't we going to do jail time anyway?"

"Excellent question. Picker is so sure of a conviction, he asked the Court to waive instructions on lesser included offenses. What you did, your conspiracy and your attempt, are violations of the law, but because they cannot be presented to the jury, you cannot be punished for it. It is either aggravated murder or you get to walk."

Larry said, "All our eggs are in one basket."

"Yes, all the eggs are in one basket."

Ted then discussed the evidence he knew the prosecutor had: the scrap of paper with Grundy's car information, the office brochure with the scribbling on it, the bloody shoes and the footprints at the scene; the fact each one of them had a handgun and it appeared Larry's was the murder weapon and of course, the motive and the fact they were caught at the scene.

"I interviewed some people and learned Grundy had many enemies, including at least one who made a threat. Keep in mind that Picker has to prove your guilt beyond a reasonable doubt and all twelve jurors have to agree. We only need one juror on our side to "hang" the jury but our goal is to interject enough doubt into the case to get all twelve to acquit. Also, remember that jurors bring with them their own value system. There may be one or two of them who won't want to convict because the son-of-a-bitch only got what he deserved, regardless of what the evidence does or does not show."

"Jury nullification."

"That's right, Tom."

"Larry, why did you pick up the gun?"

"I don't know. I have had plenty of time to think about it and I just don't know. I'm sure I left my fingerprints on it."

"When they tested your hands, did they find anything?"

"Yes, I think so."

Tom piped up, "Residue."

"Tom, you watch CSI just like millions of other people.
Larry, let me ask you this. Did you see the holes in the wall behind Grundy's body?"

"Yes."

"What did you think when you saw them?"

"Whoever did it needs some serious range time."

"Why?"

"Because they were all over the place and the shooter could not have been more than ten feet away. That's considered point blank."

"A Desert Storm veteran with a marksman ribbon would not have left such a pattern?"

"Had it been me, I would have needed only one shot."

"Exactly."

On the drive back home, Westside Steve filled the car. Ted was concerned about the "CSI component" of his case -

the forensics, especially the fingerprint and residue evidence. His waiver of discovery was a calculated risk. Since he did not want to share Marcie's evidence with Picker, he was foreclosed from discovering what Picker had in the way of fingerprints, residue, and perhaps even DNA. He assumed the prints and even the residue, and thought he could explain them away because Larry, for whatever reason, picked up the gun. He had no clue if DNA was in the case and that frightened him. Still, it was a trade-off he was willing to make.

There are basically five reasons to conduct a deposition in a civil case and attorneys spend hour upon CLE hour learning how to do it effectively. The most important goal is to secure as much information about your opponent's case as you can. You never want to ask a question at trial you don't already know the answer to so you have to cover all the bases in your dep. The second reason is to "marry" the witness to his story. If he swears under oath in his deposition that the light was red, he had better answer the same way at trial. The third reason is to see how the deponent does under pressure. Does he cop an attitude? Does he volunteer information? How will he come across to the jury? The fourth reason is to see how opposing counsel conducts himself. Is he co-operative? Is he obstructive? Does he make frivolous objections? The final reason, in some cases, is to demonstrate to the other side how weak their case is.

For the witness being deposed, there are only two rules to follow and Ted religiously told his clients to obey them. The first rule is always, always tell the truth. Remember, six months down the road, at the trial, you will be asked the same question. You will have no problem remembering a truthful answer. The second rule is don't volunteer any information. Just answer the question asked in as few truthful words as possible. The more information you volunteer, the more questions opposing counsel will think of.

All the necessary parties and the court reporter were assembled at 10:00 AM Tuesday morning in Jay Rosenthall's large conference room. As a courtesy, coffee and some small pastries were provided. Pleasantries were exchanged and, once the court reporter got all her machinery arranged, Joseph Minor was sworn in.

Ted began, "Mr. Minor, for purposes of the record we are going to make today, can you state your full name and spell your last name please?"

"Joseph Allen Minor, M...I...N...O..R."

Ted then had a discussion with Minor on the record about how the deposition is conducted: the need for him to respond verbally; to try to avoid the Uh-huhs and Uh-uhs; to wait until Ted completed his question before he began to answer - all the normal instructions.

After securing his personal information regarding marital status, education and home address there followed a discussion about his employment history. Ted learned Minor had been with Priem some twenty years and knew Malone well.

"Mr. Minor, in the spring of 2009, what position did you hold with Priem?"

"Driver supervisor."

"And what does a 'driver supervisor' do at Priem?"

"I am responsible for scheduling the drivers, processing their time, dealing with any personal needs they may have - FMLA - that sort of thing, driver discipline; keeping CDL's current. I get involved a bit in the EAP program. I have some responsibility in workers comp should a driver report an injury.....that type of thing."

"Sounds like enough."

"They keep me pretty busy."

"How many drivers were at your location in March of this year?"

"Approximately 55."

"Out of those 55, how many were certified to drive doubles?"

"I would have to review the roster to be certain, but roughly, fifteen or so."

"Was it a goal of the company to have every driver certified for doubles?"

"Yes."

"Why?"

"Number one, it saves money - one driver moving the same amount of freight as two. Secondly, it makes scheduling a lot easier."

"Mr. Minor, are you considered the custodian of the personnel files of the drivers?"

"Well, we don't use that word, but, yeah, I maintain the files in my office."

"And where is your office located?"

"It's the first one inside the building nearest to the loading docks."

"Do you sometimes communicate with medical providers on behalf of the drivers?"

"Yes."

"How so?"

"Well, like I said....if a workers comp issue comes up or perhaps a CDL issue.... I sometimes have to communicate with physicians or their offices."

"Do you sometimes write to the physicians?

"Yes."

"And do you receive written communications from them and their offices at times?"

"Yes."

"Are these written communications to and from the physicians maintained in the personnel file of each driver?"

"Yes."

"Is there an on-site dispensary?"

"No. If there is a need for treatment, we use the local doc in the box."

"A medical center?"

"Yes."

"And in Mr. Malone's case, everything you just told me applies?"

"What do you mean?"

"I mean he was treated like the rest of the drivers and his personnel file was maintained in the same manner."

"Yes."

"How long have you known Patrick Malone?"

"Since he hired in."

Okay, let's get right down to it, thought Ted.

"Mr. Minor, to your knowledge, did Patrick Malone ever exhibit a problem with alcohol while on the job?"

"Objection, you may answer." (In a deposition, objections are made to preserve the record, however the deponent still has to answer the question.)

"No," perhaps beginning to sweat just a little.

"If he did begin to exhibit such a problem, how would it show up, if at all, in his personnel file?"

"Show a continuing objection to this line of questioning. You may answer," Carrothers said.

"Well... if there is a suspicion he is under the influence on the job, he could be sent for a test."

"At the local med center."

"Yes,"

"If he came in to work under the influence, would he be written up for that?"

"Yes."

"Would those write-ups end up within his personnel file?"

"Yes," he answered as he began sweating more.

"Mr. Minor, you mentioned CDLs and that you sometimes communicate with the doctors. For what purpose?"

"To tell them why the driver was being sent over - whether it was a regular CDL exam, a probationary one - that type of thing."

"Mr. Minor, were you aware that when Mr. Malone died on March 18, his BAC was reported by the coroner to be .18?"

"Objection."

"Yes, we learned that later."

"Were you aware that Mr. Malone took a vacation day the day before?"

"Yes."

97

"What did he do on March 17?"

"I have no idea."

"You sure?"

"Yes sir."

"Mr. Minor, handing you what has been marked as Plaintiff's exhibit one, can you review this for me? Take your time because I have some questions for you."

After several minutes passed with Minor paging through the file that was handed to him, Ted said, "For the record, have you ever seen Plaintiff's one before today?"

"Yes."

"What is it?"

"A copy of Patrick Malone's personnel file."

"Is the original of this file maintained in your office?"

"Yes."

"Is this the complete file?"

"As far as I can tell."

"Do you see any write-ups within Exhibit one documenting Malone showing up for work under the influence?"

"No."

"Where are the write-ups?"

"Objection!"

"What do you mean?"

"Mr. Minor, isn't it true Malone had been written up at least three times in 2008 and 2009 prior to March 18, for being under the influence of alcohol while on the job?"

Minor glanced at Carrothers with a look of "Now what?"

"I'll tell you what, let's do it this way...Showing you what has been marked as Plaintiff's two (Minor's letter to Grundy)...."

"Objection! Objection! How did you get that?" Carrothers was standing.

Ted calmly said, "Let the record reflect counsel is on his feet and is referring to Plaintiff's two, what appears to be a copy of a letter from Mr. Minor here to Dr. Jerry Grundy...."

Minor slumped back in his chair, looked angrily at Phil and stated to him, "You told me they did not have this!"

Ted continued, "Let the record reflect Mr. Minor's last comment was directed, not to me, but to defense counsel, Mr. Carrothers. And showing you, Mr. Minor, Plaintiff's three, four and five - write-ups of Mr. Malone for coming to work intoxicated..."

"Objection! Objection!"

"Phil, would you like to take a break and have a discussion in my office?"

"Yes!"

Ted followed Carrothers into his office and shut the door.

Phil turned on him immediately, "Where the hell did you get those documents?"

Ted was not about to answer any questions. He stepped up as quickly as he could and got in his face. Their noses were five inches apart. He balled up his fists and his neck muscles began to tighten. He let the expletives fly and he didn't care who heard him.

"None of your damn business."

"You didn't tell me......"

"Look you need to just shut up and listen. You and your friend Minor out there are in a world of hurt. I have you by the balls and you know it, and now the squeezing starts. Let me lay it out for you, 'Mr. Civil Litigator.' Here is what is going to happen tomorrow. First thing in the morning, I am filing an amended complaint asking for punitive damages from Priem in the amount of $35 million dollars. That's $50 million total and punitives aren't covered under any insurance policy I'm aware of. I know you're not too familiar with juries, but they tend to do what they think is right. Priem and that asshole sitting out there knew Malone was a ticking bomb and they put him back on the road! When the jury sees the pictures, what the hell do you think they're going to do? Malone's dead but that won't matter to them, they have a huge company with deep pockets sitting right in front of them. On top of that, how much business is Priem going to lose?

After I file the new complaint, I'm going to the prosecutor's office to swear out an affidavit of perjury against your buddy out there. He's dead. His perjury is saved in the record. And consider this. When all this comes out, when everyone realizes what Priem did, I suspect there may be an indictment or two for manslaughter. Who else in the company, besides Minor out there, is going down?

The last thing I'm doing tomorrow, and certainly the most enjoyable task of the day, will be to file a complaint with the Bar Association against you for hiding documents in discovery and suborning perjury. You just put your ticket to practice in jeopardy and you have no way out! Minor has already spilled the beans on the record and I bet he isn't even warmed up yet. Picture your country club buddies reading the Bar Report. But, you know what, Phil? You are still in control here. You have the power to make this all go away. You just get on your damn cell phone and tell Priem and their insurer you need $25 million to settle this case. Consider it a "blue light special" - today only. I will give you fifteen minutes."

Carrothers tried to say something but Ted cut him off, "Do it now, clock's ticking."

Carrothers returned in ten minutes.

"We need confidentiality." (Priem would pay as long as no one knew about it.)

"Bullshit." But then Ted thought a little. "Okay, I'll tell you what. We'll let you sweep it under the rug but it will cost you another $3 million and one other thing."

"What the hell, Ted, she's already getting $25."

"Look, if they want to hide it, they're going to have to pay. The additional $3 million is a donation to Mothers Against Drunk Driving - before the end of the year. The other thing is your firm has to dismiss with prejudice the lawsuit filed against me. That's the package and it's non-negotiable. It's all or nothing." The inclusion of his own legal matter was

100

clearly inappropriate but, at this point, Ted didn't care. He was sick of these assholes.

Carrothers didn't make a call. "We'll accept it."

"Fine. You're smarter than I thought. I'll place on the record that we have reached an 'amicable' settlement, the terms of which are confidential, and, as soon as the documents are executed, there will be a dismissal, with prejudice, of the lawsuit. I will draft the settlement documents."

They re-entered the conference room and Ted placed the stipulation on the record. Minor and Carrothers then crawled out of the office and entered the elevator. Ted could hear Minor screaming at Carrothers all the way up to the fifth floor. Ted's only regret was he would not get to see the look on Kurt's face when Phil broke the news. Minor had broken the first rule; he didn't tell the truth. What was worse; his lawyer coached him to do it.

As soon as the office cleared out, Ted called Mac. "It's over, Mac."

"How did we do?"

"Twenty-five for Laurie and three for MADD."

"Twenty-five... three? Twenty-five and three what?"

"Million."

Silence.

"Mac?"

Still silence.

"Mac?"

"Ted, I was just thinking about Laurie sitting, staring at the wall, rocking back and forth, oblivious to everything, trapped in some other world we know nothing of. Twenty-five million dollars won't mean a thing to her."

"It will buy her the best professional help possible and ensure she will always be cared for if she needs to be."

"Yes. We'll have to get probate approval, you know."

"A formality. No court would ever turn this down. I'm drafting the settlement documents, Mac. I'll have them executed by Priem and get them over to you as soon as possible. You can get approval from Probate. With this kind of money, every day that passes costs major dollars in interest."

Ted thought it remarkable that during the entire day, he gave no thought to what the Giffen case meant to him or to Mac. He was so focused on hanging Minor and Carrothers, he didn't consider fees. He was in for sixty percent of a third of twenty five million dollars.

He celebrated with Dorie that evening at an exclusive downtown restaurant. He also made a mental note to call Mike the next day to offer him a job.

29

Wednesday began with Ted drafting the comprehensive settlement agreement with the confidentiality clause that would put an end to the litigation. This took him the better part of the morning; it needed to be legally "airtight." It also had to pass muster with the Probate Court of Anders County because that Court had jurisdiction over matters dealing with Laurie Giffen. Since Mac had been appointed her guardian, the Court had to be especially diligent to avoid even the appearance of impropriety. After all, Mac, too, shared in the fruits of the litigation. When his first draft was completed, he e-mailed it to Mac for his review. Then, he picked up the phone to call Mike upstairs.

"Mike, Ted."

"Ted! What the hell happened yesterday?"

"I'm not permitted to say, other than the Giffen case was 'resolved to the satisfaction of the parties'. But that doesn't mean you can't review the file once you come to work on the second floor."

"Well, let me tell you, the shit hit the fan up here!"

"That bad, huh?"

"Worse. Everyone ran for cover. We had twenty lawyers with twenty doors shut. Haven't seen Phil since."

"Really?"

"Yeah, official word is he's taking a short vacation. So you ready for me to come over?"

"Yes, courtesy of Phil Carrothers."

"That good huh? Well, it sounds good to me. I'll give notice today but I'll need some time - to be fair to everyone up here."

"No problem. You'll be just in time to help Mac and me on the Grundy murder trial over in Anders."

"Yeah, who is going to hear it?"

"What do you mean? You know Anders is a one judge county."

"Haven't you heard? Granders has asked the Supreme Court for a temporary leave of absence effective immediately. Rumor is his wife is seriously ill."

Ted felt sorry for Granders; he wouldn't have done that unless her situation was grave. But he couldn't help thinking: every criminal case has an element of luck. Granders not on the case could be a lucky development for his clients, depending, of course, upon who his replacement would be.

"Look, Mike. As soon as you wind things up, give me a call. You'll be jumping right in with both feet."

"Will do."

Ted had to be in court in Crawford. Crawford was too small to have a full time public defender. They used volunteer attorneys willing to represent the indigent for a fraction of their usual hourly fee. Since Ted had placed his name on the list and had been approved, the appointments were starting to come. Even though yesterday's events rendered this work no longer necessary, Ted thought he just might continue.

30

Thursday's mail brought the dismissal with prejudice of Carrothers versus Chase. It also brought a reminder notice from the Anders County Court that the final pretrial in People versus Merrick and Townes was set for Monday at 2:00 in the chambers of Curtis Granders. That prompted Ted to give Mac a call.

"Mac, you've got the final pretrial down for 2:00 on Monday?"

"Yes. But I will have to meet you there. I want to stop off and see Laurie on the way. Doc encouraged visits."

"No problem. We can go together. I'll stop with you, if that's okay."

"Sure."

"Mac, Granders is not going to hear this thing."

"You know, I heard something. What did you hear?"

"He's taking a leave due to his wife's health."

"Oh, that can't be good."

"No. But it might be good for us. After I got Grundy off, I'm sure Granders took me off his Christmas card list. I was thinking about what we need to be ready for the final pretrial. I am concerned about the jury charge and thought we should have something ready. We both waived charges on lesser included offenses - it's aggravated murder or nothing."

"Ted, I'll look at it. I recall there was a case some time ago. You want some language to remind the jury it can *only* be aggravated murder. Given all the evidence the prosecutor has, we don't want the jury getting confused."

"That's right. And since Picker waived, he won't have much of an argument that a limiting instruction of sorts is not warranted."

"I'll work it up and bring it with me."

"Thanks, Mac. I'm taking off the rest of the week. I'll pick you up Monday, say noon? And, I almost forgot, Mike will be with us for the trial."

"Oh, good. I'll see you about noon."

Ted really needed a long weekend to "catch his breath" and at the same time, rest up for what lied ahead. The last couple weeks had been like no other in Ted's life. The stress of the personal and professional decisions which had to be made in that short span came down on him Thursday night; he thought his head was coming off. He took a couple of pills and went to bed at 8:30.

It was a beautiful fall weekend, probably the prettiest time of year. The colors were fantastic and bathed by the autumn sun. Ted and Dorie spent the entire Friday together, having breakfast out, doing some needed shopping, talking all the time about the kids and the future. Financially, they would be set but they promised each other their good fortune would not change them: life had been too good even without the Giffen case. They planned a family weekend at the lake and would leave as soon as the kids got off the school bus. Dorie called her parents who would meet them at the cottage.

31

On Monday, Ted and Mac arrived at St. Joseph's at a quarter to one. Lindie, the day nurse/receptionist met them and escorted them to Laurie's room.

"Lindie, any change at all?"

"No. Same thing. We have to be very careful about bedsores now. Just staring, rocking. We get her up on her feet during the day as often as we can and she does shuffle a little on her own but there's still that vacant stare and no communication. Poor thing has been through so much."

It was as reported. Laurie was sitting in the middle of the bed, legs folded like a preschooler, rocking and staring at the wall ten feet in front of her. The bed was making an almost musical sound. Ted thought to himself that the body has incredible ways to deal with both physical and mental assaults.

Mac spoke to her softly, "Laurie, it's Mac and Ted. We wanted to give you some good news. Our lawsuit is over and we did well."

Nothing.

"You will have no problems and everything will be taken care of."

Nothing.

"As soon as you get better, we'll get you a real nice place of your own."

Still nothing.

They stayed awhile, making small talk but that made Ted feel like he was at a wake rather than a hospital visit; the only thing missing was the casket. The rocking continued as they left the room.

"Lindie, will you call me if you see anything, anything at all?"

"Sure, give me your number."

32

An hour later, Ted was gazing out the singular window in the judge's chambers as he waited for the pretrial to begin. Two squirrels were gathering beech tree nuts from the courthouse lawn but were interrupted by a collared dog, free of his leash. At first, the dog did not know which one to chase but as the one escaped, the other seemingly froze and the dog darted its way. It caught the squirrel by its hindquarter and began to whip it back and forth. It was not two minutes before the squirrel lay motionless on the ground and the dog scolded by its owner.

"Gentlemen, good afternoon."

The voice was that of Richard McCarthy and it was music to Ted's ears - an element of luck.

"As you might guess, I have been assigned to take Curtis' spot in this matter. We have a lot to discuss so let's get right to it. Professor McIlvaine, it is a pleasure to have you in my court."

"Thank you, Your Honor. Pleasure to be here."

"How is the discovery progressing?"

"Done, Your Honor." No need to fill him in on that score. Ted didn't request any and Picker didn't have to provide any-they were done.

"Plea discussions?"

"There haven't been any, Your Honor. The People have a strong case and are not willing to discuss anything other than a plea to aggravated murder," Picker replied.

"That so Carl?" McCarthy asked. "Didn't OJ walk?"

"He wasn't caught with a weapon in his hand at the scene of the crime."

"Ted?"

"Your Honor, there is nothing from the People for us to consider. What can I say?"

"Okay....what are we looking at witness-wise here? Carl?"

"Your Honor, the People have the arresting officer, the coroner's investigator, the coroner for the cause of death, a ballistics expert, and a lay witness by the name of Marcie Noonan. We also intend to call Deputy Sheriff Klein who had previously arrested Dr. Grundy and discovered the dead girl, Terri Merrick."

"Mr. Chase?"

"We may call the defendants-we haven't decided on that yet. We reserve the right to call the People's witnesses in our case upon cross examination."

"Mr. Picker, I am somewhat concerned about Officer Klein and Terri Merrick."

"Your Honor, his testimony goes to the motive of the defendants in this case. We have photographic evidence to show the jury in conjunction with his testimony."

Ted jumped all over that. "Photographic? Surely, you don't intend to trot out photos of Terri with her head almost falling off?"

"Goes to motive."

"Your Honor, it goes to jury inflaming..." (Ted did not want to reveal his strategy of admitting their intent.)

"Okay, wait just a minute here. Let me see those," McCarthy said. "Carl, to your knowledge, did either of the defendants view these photos?"

"No, Your Honor. But they saw the corpse in the morgue when they had to identify her."

"Do you have photos of her at the morgue?"

"Yes."

"Let me see them." After shuffling through the photos he said, "Carl, I tend to agree with Ted here. In the morgue, it is a completely different presentation than what appears in the accident scene photos. Were the defendants present at the accident scene at any time?"

110

"No, Your Honor, not to my knowledge."

"Then I believe it would be inappropriate to show these photos to the jury as proof of motive. The defendants did not see them nor did they see for themselves the actual scene they depict."

"Ted, as to motive and the girl's death what are you thinking here?"

"Your Honor, we will agree to a stipulation to be read by the Court at the outset of the proceedings that the doctor and Terri were involved in a traffic accident and that Terri perished.....and further, that during Grundy's trial, who drove the automobile was never proven by the People and Doctor Grundy was acquitted. The People cannot ask for more as that was the outcome."

"Carl, I agree with Ted. We can't have Officer Klein or the photos. I think that would impute to the defendants knowledge they did not have. It would not be fair. What else do we have to discuss?"

What followed was a discussion of how the judge likes to conduct jury selection (almost no two judges are alike on this issue) and then Ted brought up the jury charge.

"Your Honor, as you know, charges on lesser included offenses have been waived by both parties and cannot be part of the case. The defense is concerned the jury may lose its way, so to speak, given the evidence we anticipate the People have. We have drafted a cautionary instruction regarding the absence of lesser included charges."

"Give it to me." Mac handed one to McCarthy and one to Picker. The Judge stole a glance at Mac, an acknowledgement of sorts.

"Carl, have you seen this before now?"

"No, Your Honor."

"Okay, let's do this. I am not ruling on this now. Carl, you look at it and if you have an objection, put it in writing and brief it if you want. Ted can then respond. Sounds to me

111

like we will be at this about one week. Anyone see it differently?"

In unison, "No, Your Honor.'

"Jury questionnaires will be available to you this Thursday, just check with the bailiff. We'll start with fifty and see how we go from there. The trial starts this Monday and we'll set the whole week aside. Be in chambers and ready to go at nine. I like to start on time and move these things along, so if there are any issues that come up beforehand that you can't work out, contact me. Thank you, gentlemen. "

Jokingly, Mac, who hadn't uttered a word throughout the conference, looked at McCarthy and said, "How'd I do Judge?"

"Professor, you were outstanding."

After the conference, Ted and Mac walked over to the jail to visit with Merrick and Townes.

"Tom, Larry, this is the gentleman I've told you about, James McIlvaine."

"How are you. Thanks for helping us."

"Just call me Mac. Glad to help."

Ted gave them the straight scoop. "Well, we just met with the Judge and trial starts Monday morning. We've had a bit of good luck to start. Judge Granders is not available to hear the case and we have a replacement by the name of McCarthy. I have had cases with both and I think McCarthy is a better draw for us. He thinks the trial will last about a week. We know who the prosecution is calling to testify and we have a pretty good idea what their case will be. We may have some opportunity here to make some points using their witnesses, which is always a good thing for the defense. There is one witness I will have to speak with again, Grundy's office manager. Other than her, it's just a matter of getting both of you ready. I did not tell the Court for sure that you were testifying; no use playing that card just yet. We need to get your suits here and get you cleaned up but we have all week for that. I will be back here toward the end of the week, probably Saturday, and we will discuss your testimony. I want the jury to hear from you both. Do you have any questions?"

Neither man said a word but they both realized they were in good hands.

"Okay, then. Mac and I have a lot of work to do. See you Saturday morning."

On the way back, Mac began the conversation. "Ted, how do you see this thing shaping up?"

"Well..... the way I see it, even more than most cases, the key here is establishing and maintaining credibility with the jury. The motive is clear, the evidence of their planning is overwhelming and, of course, they were seemingly caught in the act. That means, unless you see it differently, we will have to admit what they went there to do. We need the jury to believe us from start to finish. Where we have an edge is that because they were apprehended in the office, Picker did not bother to consider any other possibilities. We have at least three angry husbands and boyfriends, a disgruntled ex-business partner, and one threat letter. The last patient of the day, Lucille Malley, provided a bogus telephone number and address. Perhaps Grundy violated her before and she was getting even, who knows? Anyway, a juror could certainly see it that way and have some doubt about the guilt of our guys. I think all the jurors will be disappointed with the prosecution's investigative efforts. We're the ones who will be bringing all this to light. The beauty of it is that Picker is going to be hearing all this for the first time at the trial and it will be too late to chase any of it down. The pattern of the bullets works for us too. They're putting the murder weapon in Larry's hand and he was a certified marksman while in the military. From ten feet, there's no way he misses that badly. I mean, we have a bullet in the right hip, the fatal shot to the left neck and then, the spray all over the back wall."

"Have you given any thought to the kind of person we want on the panel?"

"Mac, I'll be reviewing my Plotkin materials this week. Right now, I'm thinking self-reliant individuals, fathers of young daughters certainly...don't know...need to look at Plotkin. Do it for every jury trial I have."

"What do you need from me?"

"Can you get the questionnaires on Thursday and then we can use Friday to review them in my office."

"Okie doke."

33

On Tuesday, Ted arranged to meet with Marcie Noonan to discuss her testimony. The prosecutor did confer with her about being a witness in the matter: they wanted her to establish the office routines; especially that Grundy was usually the last one to leave, and also the time she left the office that evening. Ted found it utterly remarkable they did not inquire further. He was not surprised to learn Marcie had only answered what was asked and had volunteered no information. He reviewed with her what was important to the defense. She seemed at ease with everything and Ted was struck by that - a real "cool cucumber." He asked if she had ever testified before but she said she had not. Ted was excited that Marcie would be called as a witness for the People, yet she had information to offer which was going to help Ted build reasonable doubt.

When he returned to the office, he jotted down some notes for the cross examinations of the coroner's investigator and the ballistic expert. He then retrieved his Plotkin materials from the shelf.

Harry Plotkin is a west coast jury consultant who Ted thought was a genius. Plotkin publishes a "Jury Tip of the Month" by e-mail, addressing each month a different facet of the jury selection process. Ted religiously printed each 'Tip' and bound them in a notebook. Before every trial, he would sit down for hours and review the notebook as a type of "mini refresher course" on the art of jury selection. It was invaluable. Ted felt he himself possessed good instincts in deciding who to accept and who to challenge but those decisions always seemed to come from his gut. Plotkin, on the other hand, could explain in detail, the mind processes and value systems at play. He explained concepts such as hindsight and confirmation bias, self-interest, nullification, and co-operation versus competition. He continually stressed that each juror brings with him a value system refined over a lifetime. The successful litigator had to determine what it was. He then had to present his case in such a way, that it would "fit" into that value system, making it easy for the juror to vote for his client. He also stressed the importance of the opening statement. Research has demonstrated that a remarkably large percentage of jurors make up their minds about the case at this preliminary stage (which is nothing more than a preview by the attorneys of what they *believe* the evidence in the case will be.) It has been shown that jurors apply their values to the conduct of the parties at the earliest possible time. If your opponent realized this and you didn't, the entire trial may become a futile exercise in trying to get the jurors to change their minds, something that does not come easily.

Ted would spend the remainder of the day and evening reviewing Plotkin. Wednesday and Thursday were spent on other files and also making arrangements to clear Ted's calendar for the coming week. The fully executed Giffen settlement agreement was received from the Carrothers law firm on Thursday. Ted noted it was "approved as to form" by a member of the Carrothers firm other than Phil. *Must still be on 'vacation,'* Ted thought to himself. He would have the document ready for Mac when he arrived on Friday so that Mac could submit it to the probate court for approval, the last step before the transfer of funds. Thursday evening, Ted had a long talk with Dorie after the kids went to bed.

"Next week is going to be a hell of a week so don't get too upset if I'm kind of 'out of it' around here."

"You mean, more than normal?" she said kiddingly.

"Very funny. Well, how about this? Why don't you start looking at flights for the week after – just for the two of us? I'll really need to unwind. There should be some good deals going down to southwest Florida. The season really doesn't start up until Thanksgiving. I'm thinking Ft. Myers

116

Beach or perhaps Naples. Maybe we could rent a gulf front condo for a week. We could sip cocktails and read paperbacks by the poolside all day, go out to eat in the evening and hang around in the condo in our birthday suits. What do you think?"

"That works for me."

"Good. I'll leave that up to you."

"So, are you ready for next week?"

"Not yet. Mac and I are going over the jury questionnaires tomorrow and I have to prep Merrick and Townes for their testimony on Saturday. Sunday, I'll have to be at the office all day, just tying everything together."

"What are they looking at?"

"Life without the possibility of parole."

"You know, Ted, they had probably weighed that out. I mean, they admitted to you what they were about to do, so I'm sure they decided it was worth the risk. Kind of ironic in a way. The end result was the same, it's just that someone beat them to it."

"That's right."

"Just think of it though. You have to wonder how many others wanted to see the guy dead."

"I'm sure there were many who did not shed a tear when they read the account of his death."

"So how many of them can you get on your jury?" she asked, chuckling just a little.

"Good question."

34

Mac arrived promptly at ten with the questionnaires. Jury questionnaires are used by most courts to secure very basic information about prospective jurors. The questionnaires are sent with the summons to jury duty and the candidates for jury service are instructed to complete them and return them as soon as possible. The questionnaires reveal name, age, address, and marital status; number of children, if any; education; employment; spouse's name and employment; prior jury service, if any; criminal convictions - that sort of thing. They provide the litigants with their first glimpse into the lives of strangers who may be asked to sit in judgment.

Ted found it interesting and rather silly that most courts did not make the questionnaires available to the litigants until the morning of trial. That just unnecessarily added to the tension, in his opinion. However, Ted also understood that by doing it that way, no one had an opportunity to pull any shenanigans prior to the trial. After all, there were certainly other Phil Carrothers out there. He was glad McCarthy made them available in this case as they could be studied at leisure, discussed, and notes made.

Mac and Ted worked past dinnertime on Friday. They developed a "ranking system" of sorts, trying to identify from the preliminary information presented, who may be a risk to the defendants and who may be sympathetic. After studying Plotkin, Ted decided he would like to have educated rather than uneducated jurors; "take-charge" types rather than followers; people who exhibit a deep sense of what is right and wrong; people who don't "blindly" accept authority simply because they are authority; and, most of all, people who would expect that the sheriff's department, and the prosecution, should have done much more to investigate this crime.

Ted thought this last item was key. He realized the People had forensic evidence that would certainly interest the "CSI juror," but Ted believed that same juror could have problems with the holes in the investigation. The prosecution has the scientific bells and whistles but they didn't do the basics. When he and Marcie Noonan trot out Grundy's sordid, history, the first thought in the minds of the jurors will be, *"How come Picker didn't tell us about this?"* More importantly, their second thought would probably be, *"How come Picker DIDN'T KNOW about this?"* Along with his belief he could score some defense points on the forensics, Ted held out hope.

Ted kept possession of the questionnaires at the end of their session so he could discuss them with Merrick and Townes the following day. The pressure was beginning to build. The fate of two innocent men was in Ted's hands.

35

Ted arrived at the Anders County jail about ten on Saturday. Both men were looking haggard; their confinement had begun to take its toll both physically and mentally. Ted was sure they were contemplating an endless future spent in even worse surroundings. Ted had to somehow get them focused on the immediate task at hand and give them hope.

"Hello Tom, Larry."

"Hello, Ted."

Best to start with encouraging news. "I have met with Marcie Noonan, the office manager, to review her testimony and she is going to be a good witness for us. The prosecutor is calling her as part of his case to establish Grundy's work habits and the fact she left him with the last patient about 4:30 or so that evening. But we will use her to prove there were a number of people who had it in for the good doctor. But the key to the whole thing will be for us to establish *your* credibility with the jury and that means we'll need to discuss what you planned. It won't be easy for either of you, but it is the absolute truth so you should not lose your way. The truth *never* changes so *do not* be afraid of it. When you admit up front your intent to commit the crime, the jury will believe you and when you tell them you never got the opportunity to carry it out, they will believe that too.

I will take each of you on direct examination. Tom will go first and carry most of the load. Tom, by the time you take the stand, the prosecutor will have offered the physical evidence we have already discussed. After we give the jury some background information about you, I will need you to verify that evidence. Then, toward the end of your testimony, we will discuss Terri and what prompted you to plan what you

120

were about to do. The jurors may not condone what you planned to do, but they will certainly understand it.

Keep in mind that when I am done, Picker will cross examine you. The key here is to tell the truth and don't cop an attitude with him. He may try to goad you or deliberately upset you. DON'T LET HIM DO IT! Give him the "Yes, sirs" and the "No sirs" and always treat him with respect no matter how he treats you. Pretend you are still in the service and are responding to a superior officer. If you do that, and don't let him rile you, the jury will hold any mistreatment he levels toward you, against him.

Larry, with you we will need to establish that a certified marksman could not have done so poorly from ten feet. We will discuss how you picked up the handgun; how your fingerprints ended up where they did and how the gunshot residue got on your hand. You have nothing to hide so just be straight with the whole thing.

On cross examination, just answer Picker's questions respectfully and truthfully. I want the jurors to identify with you and not with Picker. Do not try to anticipate where he may be going or try to "head him off at the pass." That is a mistake I have seen much too often. Remember, his goal is to make you look shifty, unsure of your testimony."

The next two hours were spent in rehearsal, first with Tom and then Larry. At the end of the session, Ted asked, "Did the family bring what you need?"

"Yes, we both have suits."

"Good. Now what questions do you have for me?"

They just stared. Ted thought they were overwhelmed and scared and they should have been.

"You have all my numbers so call me tomorrow if you need to talk. Don't worry about the time; cell, home, it doesn't matter. I need to know you are ready for Monday."

Tom said, "Ted, no matter how it comes out, Larry and I want to thank you for believing in us. We both realize how much work you have put into this on our behalf. You know, when we started down this road, we knew there was a good chance we could go down for it. We decided it had to be done, regardless."

Dorie was absolutely right.

36

On the way back from Anders, Westside Steve was crooning. It started to hit Ted as he knew it inevitably would. This was not about civil liability or money; this was about how two human beings were going to live out the remainder of their lives. Ted believed in the American jury system more than anyone but he also recognized its frailties. If OJ had been a poor black from the bad side of town, represented by a public defender two years out of school, he would have received the death penalty. Instead, a prosecutor's decision took away that risk from OJ and then the "dream team" he bought got him off entirely. It was because of this inequity that Ted did not believe in the death penalty. Our jurisprudence was simply not good enough nor fair enough to the indigent to allow for this irreversible outcome. The next worst penalty was life without the possibility of parole.

Ted knew Picker's goal had nothing to do with achieving justice or arriving at the truth. Plain and simple, his only goal was to get a conviction no matter what the cost. Ted also knew he was the only person in the entire world standing between Picker and that goal; everything was riding on Ted. There were going to be traps and landmines to be avoided at every turn.

He mentally outlined the points he would have to make in the prosecution's case - especially regarding the forensics. Then he thought of everything Marcie Noonan would have to offer and last, he contemplated how the jury would look upon two men who would admit to them in open court, under oath, that they intended to commit a murder but just did not get the chance. This case was like no other Ted had ever known or even read about. Still, he thought to himself, it's the truth and the truth is supposed to win out. However, he realized that "supposed to" was the key phrase.

He and Dorie had planned to take the kids to a movie and then dinner Saturday evening and that was just what Ted needed. It was, to Ted, the "calm before the storm;" one last normal evening before the insanity began.

37

Ted arrived at the office early on Sunday to begin his final preparation for the war. This was the way he always did it, totally alone.

A trial is like a play and the lawyer is the playwright, the producer, the director, and one of the leading actors. It is a human drama, a novel, a story that will be told for years to come. Mac had taught Ted that jurors need to hear a story - a believable one they could "buy into." So the first order of the day was for Ted to create a theme for his case. The theme had to fit the facts so that Ted could weave it throughout the presentation of the evidence. After mulling over different possibilities and practicing out loud, Ted settled on a most simple and forthright theme: "This case is about an intent to commit a crime." Those would be the first words out of his mouth and he would repeat them throughout the presentation of his case. By starting with this bombshell, Ted should gain instant credibility with the panel. Their first thought would be, *he is putting it all out there right from the start and he is not afraid of it.*

Now that he had his theme, he made an outline of his opening statement - what he expected the evidence would show. Long ago, Ted learned the importance of the opening statement, since confirmed to him by Plotkin. The statement had to be persuasive without being argumentative and, most importantly, it had to "fit" within the value systems of the jurors. If it were all these, Ted knew he would be half the way home; the jurors would be leaning his way right out of the box. Ted worked on this for the better part of the morning, pacing up and down the large conference room, talking out loud.

After taking a short break to make a fresh pot of

125

coffee, he returned to concentrate on his voir dire questions - what he would be asking the prospective jurors. Unlike a play, the trial lawyer gets to choose his audience.

Voir dire was an art. The judge would tell the jurors the goal of the voir dire was to get fair and impartial jurors but that was not Ted's goal - not even close. Ted's goal was to get jurors who would be sympathetic to the plight of his clients and he really did not mind if they were unfair to the prosecution. Ted's goal was to ask questions whose answers would reveal the values of each juror. He worked out a general outline of the areas he wished to explore.

He then reviewed his outlines of the cross examinations of the state's witnesses and also the direct examinations of Marcie Noonan, Tom Merrick and Larry Townes. He preferred to work off of outlines so that the presentation of the testimony did not appear over-rehearsed.

Ted never drafted a closing argument before the start of the trial. Instead, at the very rear of his trial notebook, he would have a few sheets labeled at the top "Points for Close." As the trial progressed, he would make notations there and then incorporate those important points into his closing argument. Ted knew criminal trials never go as planned so flexibility was the key.

He finished up about eight o'clock and he was exhausted. He called both Mac and Mike and said he was ready to go and to meet him at the courthouse at a quarter to nine the next morning.

38

The Anders County courthouse was like just about every other courthouse in rural Ohio. You never had to ask where the courthouse was when you traveled to these counties because you would always find it in the middle of the square or facing the square. Anders' was in the middle of the square surrounded by old beech trees and park benches. It was a gothic, three story structure with a tower at every corner. Wide sandstone steps from the sidewalk to the entrances gave it complete symmetry. It was constructed out of huge gray stone and the recently replaced steep roof was dark slate. The entire interior was custom marble. Ted marveled at that and wondered how much it would cost if it had to be built today. A picture of the courthouse always graced whatever promotional materials were published by the county.

He met Mac and Mike in the corridor outside Granders' chambers. Tom and Larry had not yet been brought over by the deputies. The hallways were very busy because Sunday's paper had reported the start of the trial and there were a lot of people vying for a good seat. This was a *big* deal for little Anders County; two of their own on trial for murdering a doctor to avenge the death of a loved one.

Mac asked Ted, "How do you feel?"

"Nervous now but that will pass as soon as we get going. Let's find Picker and get in chambers."

Judge McCarthy was waiting for them. "Good morning everyone."

"Good morning Your Honor."

"Gentlemen, are there any issues we need to discuss before we bring in the panel?"

"Your Honor, I just wanted to remind everyone we have a ruling there is to be no mention of my representation of

Dr. Grundy in the manslaughter case," Ted answered.

Picker was nodding his head in acknowledgement.

"And we have the issue of the jury charge."

"Yes, regarding that, there has been no opposition from the People?"

"No, Your Honor."

"Well, let's see where the evidence goes before I commit to any particular charge. You'll know before closing argument. If there is nothing else, let's bring in the panel and get this thing going."

The lawyers returned to the crowded courtroom. On the way back, Ted noticed a familiar face in the front row and he walked over. It was Danny Longer of the convenience store caper.

"Danny, what brings you here?"

"I dunno, thought I could learn something."

"What have you been up to?"

"Enrolled at State for fall quarter."

"Danny, that's terrific. Any idea what you're going to study."

"Thought maybe pre-law."

They just traded looks before the deputy escorted Tom and Larry to their seats.

Both men were clean shaven, well groomed and dressed in their Sunday best. Larry looked a little uncomfortable in his suit but that was not unusual for him. Tom, on the other hand, looked like one of the lawyers. Ted thought, *give him a briefcase and he would fool just about anyone.* The man had a sense of dignity about him and Ted envied him for it. To look like he does under this pressure was remarkable.

The Bailiff bellowed, "All rise! Hear Ye. Hear Ye. Hear Ye. The Anders County Court of Common Pleas is now in session. All those with business before the court draw near and be heard. The Honorable Richard McCarthy presiding."

"Please sit," Judge McCarthy said as he took his seat.

"The Court convenes today to hear the case of The

People versus Merrick and Townes, Aggravated Murder. Are the People prepared to go forward?"

"We are, Your Honor."

"And the Defense?"

"We are ready to proceed, Your Honor."

"All right then, Bailiff, please bring in the panel and ask the first twelve to take a seat in the box."

"All Rise!"

Everyone stood once again as the bailiff went out through the doors and returned escorting the prospective jurors into the courtroom. Like the high bench the Judge sat behind, the robes the Judge wore, this was part of the ritual - giving respect to those ordinary citizens who were picked to serve. As the prospective jurors filed in, they were somewhat taken aback by everyone standing, staring at them. Even the Judge was on his feet paying his respect to this collection of strangers. It was only then that the severity of what they were about to undertake hit most of them. They instantly became solemn.

McCarthy said, "Please be seated," and then he addressed them. "Ladies and gentlemen, welcome. Today, we begin the case of The People versus Merrick and Townes. The charge is Aggravated Murder." He then introduced everyone at both counsel tables included the defendants.

He took about five minutes to explain to them the voir dire process and that some of them would be asked to serve and others would be excused. He told them not to read anything into who is excused or to guess at the reason why. He further explained that he thought the trial would last about one week. He explained the questionnaires they had completed had already been provided to the litigants so they had some basic knowledge of each person's background. He then turned the floor over to Picker.

Picker stood behind the lectern facing the twelve jurors in the box. On his yellow pad, he had written down thirty or so questions and he began by asking juror Number Four, a young housewife by the last name of Martin, whether she had any knowledge of the matter.

Ted thought to himself, *already making a mistake*. By starting with juror Number Four, Picker unknowingly unnerved the remainder of the panel. Here they were, many in court for the first time in their lives, a judge perched above them, everyone glaring at them and not knowing if they were going to be called upon next. After the answer came, Picker jumped to Number Nine, and you could see the anxiety level rise in the entire panel. This was "Trial Practice 101" yet Picker was clueless. It was also maddening because Picker had to keep looking down at his pad to come up with the correct name of the person he was speaking with, and even with this, he sometimes got it wrong. He would then look down at the pad again, read the question, and then look up. Sometimes he would repeat the exact same question to another member of the group. You could have programmed a robot to do the same thing. Picker was completely missing his first opportunity to interact with each juror. He failed to understand that in the jury selection process what really goes on is that the jury is 'selecting' a lawyer to believe. It was simply awful. Ted had seen some second year Mock Trial students do a better job. When, mercifully, Picker was done, the floor was turned over to Ted.

Ted rose and stated, "May it please the Court, Ladies and Gentlemen of the Jury, James McIlvaine and I have the honor of representing Tom Merrick and Larry Townes in this case. The questions I ask are not meant to pry, but only to assess your ability to be fair and impartial." *Bullshit,* he thought to himself.

He looked at Juror Number One, a forty-five year old father of three by the name of Lander. In the best conversational voice he had, Ted asked, "Mr. Lander, do you have any brothers or sisters?"

"Yes, an older sister and a younger brother."

"Growing up, did you ever have a situation where you had to stick up for your little brother?"

"Yes, I did."

130

"Can you tell me about that?"

"Well, he was hitchhiking home from school one day and he was walking past the local Sunoco station where a lot of older kids hung out. They were all out of school - nineteen, twenty. One of them thought it was a good idea to go out where my brother was and start picking on him. He beat him up pretty good. My brother was only fifteen."

"What did you do?"

"Well, when I got home from football practice, I saw he was beat and I asked him what the hell, I'm sorry, I mean, what the heck happened and he told me. So I put him in my car and I drove down to the Sunoco station. There were about six of them and I knew I was about to get the snot beat out of me but I knew I had to do it. So I asked them which one of them beat up my brother. At first, they were giving me a hard time, but then they finally gave me a name and said the guy wasn't there - he had left. Actually, I don't think they liked the guy much. I'll never forget him. His name was Hall and he lived on Hall Road."

"What did you do?"

"Found his house and then he and I had it out pretty good."

"Tell me, you went into the station and saw six guys there, you said you had to do it. What did you mean by that?"

"I wanted my brother to know I would stick up for him. Also, I knew my father would have wanted it. I knew I had to do it even if I got the snot beat of me. Turned out, I did okay."

Ted was already trying his case.

Juror Number Two was a truck driver by the name of Jenks. He looked a little rough around the edges but Ted and Mac had scored him pretty high on their initial evaluation.

"Mr. Jenks, you have seen those special license plates, the red and orange ones?"

"Yes, party plates."

"I'm sorry?"

"Party plates. Judges make DWI guys put them on

131

their cars. We call 'em party plates. Drivers like to party."

"What do you think about people with party plates?"

"They should lose their licenses for a good long time."

"Tell me, do you have any military service?"

"Yes sir." He started to light up a little. "Marines. Vietnam."

"Any commendations or ribbons"

Litigators must always remember, as Ted did, that people like to tell their own story. For many of these simple Anders County folk, to have a stage such as this was unthinkable. Mr. Jenks was proud of his service to his country and very happy to share it with the world.

"Yes sir. Purple heart. Sharpshooter ribbon." Jenks felt a bit thankful to Ted for asking him the question.

Juror Number Three's name was Lisa Thompson and she was about thirty years old. (By this time, the jurors recognized Ted was going right down the line so no one worried about being called out of order. Juror Number Four, Mrs. Martin, was paying very close attention.)

"Ms. Thompson, your questionnaire indicated you had served on a jury about two years ago. What kind of case was it?"

"Car accident."

"So that was a civil case, not criminal."

"Yes."

"The burden of proof in that case was 'the greater weight of the evidence' whereas, in this case, the People's burden is 'proof beyond a reasonable doubt.' "

"That's right. I know."

"You recognize the difference?"

"Yes, I watch Law and Order." Laughter.

"You know, that brings up another issue. Mrs. Martin (the juror Picker started with), do you watch any of those law shows on TV?"

"Yes, I like The Practice."

132

"Did you see that episode where the lawyer was yelling at the judge, accusing him of not doing his job?"

"Yes."

"Would you be surprised to learn that is *not* going to happen in this case?" A snicker.

"No, I guess not."

"Well, it may happen once, and the next thing you'll see is a lawyer in handcuffs being led off to the jail." Laughter.

Even in as serious a case as this, Ted knew the value of humor and used it well. Unlike Picker, Ted was making the process interesting and even comfortable for them. He was learning about their values while, at the same time, developing a rapport and establishing his credibility. Credibility was the key. Above all else, a criminal defense lawyer had to show that he was totally convinced of his client's innocence. If the jury got even a "whiff" that the lawyer had the smallest doubt, his client was doomed.

The jury selection process would consume the first day of trial. Each side had unlimited challenges for cause and six peremptory challenges. Challenges for cause are exercised when a juror admits he cannot be impartial, knows the litigants or the lawyers, has a pressing personal matter, or perhaps a medical condition that would make it difficult for him to serve. The judge has to rule on such a challenge. Peremptories are challenges that don't need a reason. There may have been a look, a troublesome answer, a reaction to something another juror said, perhaps too much eagerness to serve, something that bothered the attorney - even if he could not articulate it. The challenges go back and forth in turn, starting with the prosecution. When they are exhausted or when both parties pass, the people in the box become the jury. Two alternates are then selected.

Because Anders was a small county and this was a "high profile" case, much of the voir dire focused on the jurors' prior knowledge of the case - what they had heard on the street or read in the papers. It was important to know they arrived with no pre-judgment. For some jurors, this would be verbally expressed but responses to questions would indicate otherwise. Ted had to be absolutely certain there were no "hidden agendas" leading a juror to respond one way in open court but, deep inside, hold a very different view. "Hidden agenda jurors" were, without a doubt, the most dangerous.

Toward the end of the day, it worked out that Ted "controlled" the last seat on the panel; Picker had used up all his peremptories and Ted had one remaining. Absent a challenge for cause, Ted decided who filled the last seat. He wasn't "thrilled" with present juror Number Twelve, a postal worker, so he took a minute to review the questionnaires he and Mac had ranked. If Ted were to challenge Number Twelve with his last peremptory, he would be stuck with his replacement. The next in line was an older gentleman with silver hair, a widower by the name of Gerald Elder. He was ranked high by Ted and Mac but there was still a danger; there may be something in his background not revealed by his questionnaire that Ted would not like. Relying upon their evaluation though, Ted took the gamble.

"Your Honor, the Defense would like to thank and excuse Juror Number Twelve, Mr. Goins."

"Alright. Thank you Mr. Goins, the bailiff will escort you back to the room. Mr. Elder, please take the empty seat. Mr. Chase, that was the last of your peremptories."

"Yes, Your Honor."

"Welcome Mr. Elder."

"Hello, Your Honor."

"Mr. Elder, you have been sitting for a good long time listening to all these questions. Is there anything you have heard thus far that would lead you to believe you could not be fair and impartial in this case?"

"No, I don't believe so, Your Honor."

"Go ahead Mr. Picker."

"Mr. Elder, your questionnaire indicates you are a widower. How long were you married?"

"Thirty eight years."

"Your wife's name?"

"Elizabeth."

"I am sorry for your loss."

"Thank you."

Ted asked Mike to get on his laptop and run the name Elizabeth Elder through the internet website of *The News*. After a few seconds, her name popped up; an obituary but also an article reporting her death in a traffic accident. She had been dead two years. She was killed by a drunk driver. Wow! Ted knew not to go there, not to tip off Picker. Picker asked a few more questions and then sat down.

"Mr. Chase, you may inquire."

"Thank you, Your Honor. Mr. Elder, I see you have never been picked for jury duty before. Is there any reason you would not want to serve on this jury which may take about a week of your time?"

"No, I consider it a civic duty. I don't need to be anywhere else. I'll be happy to serve."

Mr. Elder was accepted as the twelfth juror and, Ted thought, *maybe a leading candidate for foreman*. Two alternates were added and Merrick and Townes had a "jury of their peers."

The last official act of the day was to have the Bailiff swear in the panel. Judge McCarthy then gave them some ground rules on how they were to conduct themselves during the pendency of the case. He admonished them not to say a word to anyone, not even another panel member, about the case. This included all family members and spouses. Should anyone mention anything about the case to them, they were to immediately report that to the Court. He then dismissed them for the evening. Since he had a personal matter to tend to Tuesday morning, he indicated the presentation of evidence would start sharply at 10:00 and they were to be in the jury room no later than 9:45.

Ted and Mac had a brief discussion with their clients. Tom and Larry felt the first day went well and expressed same

135

to Ted before they were escorted out.

"Ted, I think we have a pretty nice panel," said Mac. Of the twelve we ended up with, we had ranked four 'very good' and seven 'acceptable.' We only have one of those we ranked at the very bottom. Who do you like for the foreperson?"

The foreperson was usually the most important juror to have in your corner. He or she was usually picked by the other members for a reason. The other jurors may identify some quality of leadership in that person, or recognize them as a little more educated, or maybe just a little older and seemingly wiser. The experienced trial lawyer always made an educated guess as to who that person might be and then played to them a little more than the others.

"I like Number Twelve, Mr. Elder."

"I agree. Lander is also a candidate, and that is not a bad thing either. I think it will be one of the two."

"I agree," said Ted.

"Well, you had better go home and get as much rest as you can. The fertilizer hits the ventilator tomorrow."

That's exactly what Ted did. One invaluable lesson Ted had learned was that when a day of a trial is over, it is over and there is absolutely no sense reliving it or thinking about things you could have done differently. It would only drive you insane and rob you of your objectivity for the next day.

39

It seemed to Ted his alarm went off fifteen minutes after he had gone to bed. Tuesday was another beautiful fall day and it almost felt wrong to Ted to enter the dark fortress of the courthouse only to leave when dusk arrived. It appeared even more crowded than the day before. He noticed Danny occupying the same seat he had on Monday and wondered how early he had to get there to claim it. Mac and Mike were already in chambers when he arrived as was Carl Picker.

"Good morning everyone."

"Good morning Your Honor."

"Well, Carl, Ted how long are we going to need for openings?"

Picker spoke first, "Not long Your Honor. Maybe fifteen minutes tops, for the People."

"Less than that for the Defense."

"Good. After the opening, I will read the agreed stipulation into evidence and instruct the jury they are to accept it as a fact in this case. Carl, who will you be putting on first?"

"The arresting officer followed by the coroner's investigator."

"Fine. We will see how that goes. Hopefully we will get at least one done before we have to break for lunch. Anyone have any issues to discuss?"

"No, Your Honor."

"Okay, let's get to it."

The jury was already in the box and Ted noticed that two of the jurors had either leaned over or looked back at Mr. Elder and engaged him in conversation. The Bailiff gave his "All rise!"

"Please sit. Good morning ladies and gentlemen. We will now hear opening statements from the lawyers. Since the People have the burden of going forward and the burden of proof, Mr. Picker will go first followed by Mr. Chase for the Defense. Ladies and gentlemen, what you are about to hear is not considered evidence in this case, rather it is what the lawyers believe the evidence will show. It's more like a roadmap of their case. It is given to assist you in understanding what they intend to prove. At the end of the trial, it is your duty, and your duty only, to decide whether in fact they did. Mr. Picker, you may proceed."

"May it please the Court. Ladies and gentlemen of the jury, the people's evidence in this case demonstrating the guilt of these two defendants is overwhelming."

Already a note for closing argument! By using the word "overwhelming," Picker had just written a check Ted thought he would not be able to cash. He is making the classic blunder of overstating his case right out of the box!

"The evidence will show that on the evening of August 28 of this year, Deputy Sheriff Clayton Pooley was patrolling the north side of Anders County and at about 7:15, came upon the office of Dr. Jerry Grundy. He noticed the lights on and the front door slightly ajar. Deputy Pooley recognized this as a bit unusual and he stopped to investigate. When he entered the office, in exam room four, he came upon the defendants in this case, Tom Merrick and Larry Townes with handguns drawn, standing over the body of Dr. Grundy. Dr. Grundy appeared to be shot once in the right hip and once in the left side of the neck and face. He noticed there was blood all over the floor and footprints in the blood. He had the men surrender their weapons and, at that point, he placed the two men under arrest and transported them to the sheriff's department.

Gregory Roth, the coroner's investigator, will also testify. He will give evidence that a total of five shots had been fired within exam room four, two hitting the doctor and three hitting the back wall. The slugs were collected and provided to the state's ballistic expert. The handguns

138

confiscated were also provided. A green pickup truck was found in the lot behind the building next to Dr. Grundy's office, which truck was impounded. It was later determined the truck was the property of Defendant Townes. Inside the truck was found a scrap of paper with information written on it about a certain make car and a license plate. The make and license number written on the scrap of paper matched that of Dr. Grundy's automobile which was parked behind his office on the night he was brutally murdered. There was also a brochure from Dr. Grundy's office inside the pickup truck. Through Mr. Roth, we will offer these items into evidence along with the bloody shoes taken from the defendants which, Mr. Roth will testify, match the footprints on the floor of exam room four.

The People's ballistic expert from the Bureau of Criminal Investigation is James McKay. Ballistic testing will confirm that all five bullets came from the gun that was taken from Defendant Larry Townes. Scientific testing will also confirm that there was gunshot residue on Townes' right hand, the hand which held the gun. Mr. McKay will explain gunshot residue and how it got on Townes' hand. He will also testify Townes' fingerprints were on the handgun.

Marcie Noonan, Dr. Grundy's office manager, will testify she noticed the truck in the back lot earlier that evening and that the truck had two men in it and was still there when she left. She can identify the truck for you because the front license plate had a bent up corner which she remembered very well. She will also testify that when she left the office that evening, Dr. Grundy was still there tending to the last patient.

Further, the evidence will show the wound to the left side of Dr. Grundy's neck was fatal, severing the carotid artery. Doctor James Strothers, Anders County Coroner, will testify to this fact and that the wound was caused by a bullet fired by the weapon taken from Larry Townes.

The evidence will demonstrate to you that these men had a motive to do what they did, they carefully planned it out, and carried it through and that they are, beyond a reasonable doubt, guilty of aggravated murder.

At the end of this trial, I am going to ask that you return such a verdict which you must, given the evidence in this case. Thank you."

Ted thought to himself, *never, ever tell a jury they MUST do something.* Another note for closing argument.

"Thank you Mr. Picker. Mr. Chase, you may address the jury."

"Thank you, Your Honor. May it please the Court, ladies and gentlemen of the jury. This case is about an *intent* to commit a crime. It's about two men, a father and a fiancé who planned to commit a revenge murder for the loss of a young woman by the name of Terri Merrick, Tom Merrick's daughter. (At these words, the rumble slowly started up like that of a far-away thunderstorm.) Yes, they planned it and on August 28, they went to Dr. Jerry Grundy's office to carry it out."

The jurors had looks that ranged from shock to utter non-belief at what Ted just said. The courtroom "rumbled." Out of the corner of his eye, however, Ted noticed Gerald Elders displayed no reaction whatsoever.

Judge McCarthy was banging his gavel. He kept banging and banging louder and louder. After what seemed like forever, the Judge was back in control of his courtroom. Rather than issue any admonishments or threats, he simply turned to Ted and said, "Please continue, Mr. Chase."

"Ladies and gentlemen, there was a clear intent to commit a crime, however the deed had already been done. The evidence will show that when Tom Merrick and Larry Townes entered Grundy's office, he already lay dead on the floor having bled profusely from the gunshot wound to the neck. Officer Pooley arrived and they offered no resistance and went with him willingly.

The evidence will also show that Jerry Grundy took advantage of certain female patients, the young, shapely ones, and that there were a number of people who had it in for him.

140

There was even a threat letter we will produce for you. (He looked at Picker.) The evidence will also show the last patient that evening was a lady by the name of Lucille Malley who gave Grundy a false address and phone number and has never been seen nor heard from again."

Picker was writing furiously on his pad.

"Ladies and gentlemen, there was an *intent* to commit a crime, but there was no crime committed by these two men. They are innocent."

Rumbling.

"Thank you, Mr. Chase. Now ladies and gentlemen, the parties have entered into a stipulation which I will now read to you. You are to accept this stipulation as fact in this case.

On June 26th of this year, Terri Merrick perished in a one car motor vehicle accident. The deceased in this case, Dr. Jerry Grundy, was charged with vehicular manslaughter because of her death. A trial on those charges was held in this very courtroom. At the trial, the prosecution was unable to prove that Dr. Grundy was the driver of the automobile in which Terri Merrick died, and the doctor was found Not Guilty of all charges on Thursday, August 20. The Doctor was found on the floor of his office on Friday August 28th."

"Mr. Picker, please call your first witness." McCarthy wasn't kidding when he said he liked to move these things along.

"Your Honor, the People call Deputy Sheriff Clayton Pooley."

Clayton Pooley entered from the rear of the courtroom and walked up to the inner rail. The Judge directed him to the witness chair where he was sworn. Deputy Pooley could best be described as a Marine drill sergeant in a police uniform. He was about six foot one and he was "buff." Although he was in his early forties, his body looked like it didn't have an ounce of fat on it. His features were sharp and he wore his reddish

141

brown hair in a flattop. He was impressive.

After some preliminary questions about his employment with the department, Picker asked, "Officer Pooley, were you on duty the evening of August 28th of this year?"

"Yes sir."

"That evening, did you enter the chiropractic offices of Dr. Jerry Grundy?"

"Yes sir."

"What time?"

"About 7:15."

"Why did you do that?"

"When I drove by, I noticed there were no cars parked out front but the front door was slightly open and all the lights within the office appeared to be on. It was out of the ordinary and didn't look right to me, so I stopped, called it in, and then entered through the front door."

"What did you find?"

"When I got just outside of one of the exam rooms, I heard noises so I drew my revolver and entered the room."

"What did you see inside?"

"Inside, I saw these two gentlemen (pointing), both holding handguns, looking down at the floor. Their backs were to me and I think I startled them as I entered the room."

"The two men you saw, are they in the courtroom today?"

"Yes (pointing again) they are sitting right there."

"The record should reflect the Officer is pointing to the defendants Tom Merrick and Larry Townes."

"What were they looking at on the floor?"

"Dr. Grundy who was lying in a huge pool of blood."

"Was he alive or dead?"

"Objection."

"Sustained." That was not for Pooley to determine.

Looking at Ted, Picker rephrased his question. "Could you tell if the Doctor was breathing?"

"He appeared not to be breathing."

"What did you do next?"

"I identified myself and instructed them to lay their weapons down on a counter in the room. I had them lie prone on the waiting room floor, handcuffed them, then escorted them to the car. I called into the station again and requested the other officer on patrol to come to Grundy's office to secure the scene. I waited for him in the car with these two in the back. When he arrived, I drove the two to the department."

"Officer, other than the defendants, did you see anyone else in or around the Doctor's office that evening?"

"No, no one."

"Did you have any discussion with the defendants at any time?"

"No."

"Did you read them their rights?"

"Yes."

"After you instructed them to lay their weapons down, was there any discussion at all?"

"Only my direction to them to get them into the back seat of the car."

"That evening, did you ever hear either man utter a word, either to you or to each other?"

"No, as far as I remember, neither man opened his mouth while in my custody."

"Was there any physical evidence taken from the defendants?"

"Yes. Their hands were swabbed for residue and they were both fingerprinted at the department."

"Thank you, Officer. Your witness."

Ted stood at counsel table without approaching the podium.

"Officer Pooley, You stated that Grundy was lying in a huge pool of blood, is that right?"

"Yes sir."

"You used the word "huge?""

"Yes sir."

"Can you give us an idea of the dimensions of this pool

143

of blood?"

"Well, it went out from the left side of his neck, underneath his head to the right of the body about a foot or so and even farther on the left side, maybe two feet. It went from his neck down to about his waist on both sides."

"Did you see any footprints in the room?"

"Yes."

"Was it later determined that the footprints came from the shoes of Tom Merrick and Larry Townes?" (Mac taught Ted to slowly familiarize the jury with the defendants. First they are "the defendants." Then they are Mr. Merrick and Mr. Townes. Then they are Tom Merrick and Larry Townes. And, eventually, they will be just Tom and Larry and would remain Tom and Larry throughout the remainder of the trial.)

"Yes, they had gotten some of the blood on their shoes."

"So if I understand you correctly, what the prosecution wants us to believe is they entered the room, one of them shot the doctor, then, instead of getting the heck out of there, they both just stood there and waited long enough for him to bleed out this pool from his head down to his waist, and then they walked in it?"

A snicker from the room and a stern look from the Judge toward it.

"Mr. Chase, I don't know what the prosecution wants you to believe. I just know what I saw."

"Did you get any blood on your shoes?"

"My left one."

"Officer, let me ask you this. Isn't it a more likely scenario that the blood got on their shoes because it was already on the floor *before* Tom and Larry entered the room?"

"Objection"

"No, he may answer," the Judge ruled.

"I don't know." A good answer for the defense.

"Officer, when you directed them to lay the guns on the counter, they complied without any hesitation, is that right?"

144

"Yes sir."

"But they had you outgunned, didn't they. I mean it was two to one, wasn't it?"

"Yes sir."

"You were concerned about that, weren't you?"

"You bet your….I mean, yes, I was very concerned."

"Even with this advantage over you, they followed your orders didn't they - without hesitation?"

"Yes sir."

"How many sets of handcuffs did you have on you?"

"Only one on me. The other set was in the car."

"But you had to handcuff both men?"

"Yes."

"Tell me, how did that go?"

"What do you mean?"

"I mean, who did you handcuff first?"

"Larry Townes."

"Where was your weapon when you were handcuffing Larry?"

"In my holster."

"After you handcuffed Larry, did you have to retrieve the other set of cuffs from the car?"

"Yes sir."

"Then what was Tom doing while this was going on?"

"Nothing."

"He just laid there on the floor of the waiting room, watching you handcuff Larry and waiting himself to be handcuffed?"

"Yes sir."

"That was pretty nice of him, wasn't it?"

A laugh from the room - Ted got the point across.

"Officer, neither man took any threatening action toward you, tried in any way to be evasive, or tried to flee from the scene even when presented with the opportunity, isn't that true?

"Yes, that's true."

"All they did was follow to the letter, your every

command?"

"Yes sir, they obeyed my orders."

"When was the last time that happened when you made an arrest?"

"Can't really say."

"Thank you Officer."

At that point, Judge McCarthy looked at his watch and indicated a fifteen minute recess was in order. Ted kept a close eye on the jury as they shuffled out, especially Mr. Elder.

Mac said, "I think we're off to a wonderful start. Picker was writing like a madman."

"Mac, it went okay, I guess… were you keeping an eye on the panel?"

"Yes."

"See anything?"

Mac replied, "Well some of them smiled when you discussed waiting around and walking in the blood. A few of them laughed just a bit when you asked the question about Tom here waiting to be handcuffed."

"What about Elder. Pick up anything on him?"

"No, not really. Why?"

"I don't know. When we start back up, keep your eye on him. There is something there…I'm not sure. Tom, Larry, any thoughts?"

"No, Ted, I think we're doing pretty good to start," said Tom and Larry agreed.

While everyone went out to take a fresh air break and maybe get a cup of coffee, Ted returned to counsel table and poured over his notes on Gregory Roth, who would certainly be next up. Only Danny Longer remained in his seat.

Upon resuming, McClelleland said, "Mr. Picker, your next witness, please."

"The People call Mr. Gregory Roth."

Gregory Roth was perhaps fifty years old, of average height, and quite a bit paunchy in the gut. He had thick glasses and was bald on top but the hair on the side was a bit unruly and in need of a cut. He wore a sport coat and slacks. His tie was a bit off to the side. If Pooley was Yin, Roth was Yang.

After introducing Roth to the jury, Picker reviewed his credentials. He was a certified forensic examiner who was assigned to several coroners' offices in that part of the state. It was his job to go to the scene of a crime, collect evidence, and present it to the coroner for a ruling. He was a "CSI guy," but he didn't look anything like the actors on television.

"Mr. Roth, were you called to the scene, Dr. Grundy's office, by the sheriff's office?"

"That's right."

"When did you arrive?"

"Saturday morning, August 29th at approximately 9:30."

"Had the office been secured since the evening before?"

"Yes, to my knowledge. An officer had been stationed there the entire time."

"What was the first thing you did?"

"I examined the front and rear doors."

"Why?"

"I wanted to ascertain whether there was any evidence the doors had been forced open or in any manner damaged."

"Were they?"

"No."

"Did you do any fingerprinting of the doors?"

"Yes, later, but, as you might guess, there was so much there, I could not find anything definitive as it related to Merrick or Townes. But that was to be expected."

"Then what did you do?"

"I looked over the receptionist/waiting room area."

"What were you looking for?"

"Well, just about anything that might appear out of the ordinary; a mark on a carpet, anything out of place, that sort of thing."

"Did you come across anything of significance in that area of the office?"

147

"No."

"Where did you go next?"

"To exam room four."

"Tell us what you saw."

"Well, the body was still there on the floor with the head approximately nine feet from the door, and rigor had set in. There was quite a bit of blood all over the floor surrounding the body and there were footprints in the blood. The blood came from two wounds; a gunshot wound to the right pelvic area and a massive wound to the left side of the face and neck. Most of the blood had come from the neck wound. There were three bullet holes in the wall behind where the body lay. One of the holes was about a foot and a half from the ceiling and one about the same distance from the molding at the floor. A third was way to the left of the other two about half-way up on the wall. There were two handguns laying on a small counter, a .22 caliber and a .45."

"Did you take any pictures?"

"Yes, several."

"Mr. Roth, showing you what has been marked as People's exhibits one through nineteen, can you identify these for me?"

Taking a couple of minutes to shuffle through the photos, "Yes, one through four are pictures of the front and rear entrances and the remainder were of exam room four including pictures of the corpse. These are the pictures I took."

"Did you retrieve the bullets from the wall?"

"Yes, after photographing the wall, I pried them out. They were actually lodged in the cinder block behind the drywall."

"Did you retrieve any bullets from the body of the corpse?"

"Yes, they were provided to me by Dr. Strothers when he performed the autopsy."

"What did you do with the bullets?"

"Placed them all in an evidence bag, sealed it to preserve the chain of custody, and drove them myself to the offices of BCI and handed them to James McKay."

"BCI is the Bureau of Criminal Investigation?"

"That's correct."

"Where are their offices?"

"Columbus."

"Who is James McKay?"

"A BCI Ballistics expert."

"Had you ever dealt with Mr. McKay before."

"Yes, many times."

"Did you do anything with the handguns?"

"Yes, the handguns were likewise bagged and marked and given to Mr. McKay along with the photos."

"Exhibits one though nineteen?"

"Yes."

"Did you secure any other physical evidence from the scene?"

"Yes, quite a bit."

"What?"

"Well, I secured from the sheriff's department the shoes of the defendants which I then compared to the pictures of the footprints at the scene."

"Showing you what has been marked as Exhibits twenty and twenty-one, can you tell the jury what these are?"

"Yes. Exhibit twenty is a plastic bag containing the shoes of Defendant Merrick and twenty-one contains the shoes of Defendant Townes."

"When you compared these shoes to the photos, what did you determine, if anything?"

"Well, first of all, there was blood on the shoes which matched the blood type of the deceased. Let's not forget that. Then, examining the soles of the shoes and comparing the soles with the footprints at the scene, there was a match on three out of the four shoes - both of Townes and the left shoe of Merrick."

"Did you secure any other physical evidence?"

"Yes, from the truck, a scrap of paper and a brochure."

"Showing you exhibits twenty-two and twenty-three,

149

can you identify these for the jury?"

"Yes, twenty-two is the scrap of paper and twenty-three is the brochure I took from the truck."

"Focusing on Exhibit twenty-two, can you tell the jury what the significance of this is, if at all?"

"Yes, this paper scrap has written on it 2008 CTS, red and JGDC007."

"Was that significant to you in any regard?"

"Yes. The deceased owned a 2008 Cadillac CTS, red in color, which we found parked behind his office. The license plate on the car was JGDC007."

"Were you able to determine who wrote on this scrap of paper?"

"Yes, the handwriting is similar to that of Tom Merrick."

(This last was clearly objectionable and McCarthy stole a glance at Ted, but, Ted remained seated. Because of his defense, he did not care that the writing was attributed to Tom.)

"And the brochure? Was there any writing on it?"

"The date August 28."

"Could you ascertain who wrote on the brochure?"

"No."

"Did you ascertain who the owner of the truck was?"

"Yes."

"Showing you what has been marked as People's twenty-four, can you tell the jury what this is?"

"Yes, this is a certified copy of the title to the truck which I secured from the Deputy Registrar."

"And whose truck is it?"

"Larry Townes'."

"Did you retrieve any other evidence from the truck?"

"No."

"Did you retrieve any evidence from the defendants themselves?"

"Yes, I went to the jail straight from the doctor's office. I was provided with the hand swabs and the fingerprints of each man."

"Showing you what has been marked as Exhibits twenty-five through twenty-eight, can you tell the jury what these are?"

"Yes. Twenty-five are the swabs taken from Townes and twenty-six are his fingerprints. Twenty-seven are Merrick's swabs and twenty-eight, his prints."

"Tell us about swabs."

"Hand swabs are routinely done in gunshot cases to determine if there is any residue evidence."

"What did you do with Exhibits twenty-five through twenty-eight?"

"I provided them to Mr. McKay, the ballistics expert, along with everything else I just mentioned."

"Can you give us an idea how it goes from here? The coroner has to make a ruling, is that correct?"

"Yes, the coroner is provided with my report and the report from BCI. That information, along with the autopsy findings forms the basis for the ruling."

"Thank you, Mr. Roth. Your witness."

McCarthy interrupted. "Ladies and gentlemen, I see that the lunch hour has arrived and my stomach is growling."

Laughter

"Let's stop right here and then Mr. Chase can conduct his cross examination after lunch. Please be back in the jury room at 1:25. Remember what I said at the outset. Do not discuss what you have heard thus far with anyone, especially your fellow jurors. The discussion does not begin until you retire to the jury room to deliberate at the conclusion of the evidence. See you back here at 1:25. I'd like to see Counsel in chambers."

In chambers, McCarthy pointed out that the case started well and that he did not see any problems with the schedule.

"Carl, after Ted is done with Roth, you have McKay, Dr. Strothers and Noonan, is that right?"

"Yes, Your Honor."

151

"In that order?"

"Yes, Your Honor."

"Anyone else?"

"No."

"Ted, how long do you think you will take with Roth?"

"In all honesty, Your Honor, not very long at all."

"Carl, since we're going along fairly well here, I'll let you make the call. You need to bring McKay up from Columbus, right?"

"Yes."

"Do you want to start with him this afternoon or just wait until tomorrow morning? If we start him today, it may be that we will need him tomorrow as well."

"Tomorrow would be fine, Your Honor. It would be more convenient for him."

Ted and Mac looked at each other, both realizing the mistake Picker just made. He just ensured the last thing the jury would hear that afternoon would be Ted's cross examination of Roth. Not smart. Certainly, Picker could conduct a re-direct examination of the witness, but Mac and Ted both knew efforts to rehabilitate a witness after a strong cross examination only served to emphasize his weaknesses.

"Any objections from the Defense?"

"No, Your Honor, that would be fine."

"See you back here after lunch. We'll just have Ted finish up with Roth and then we'll let them go early."

On the way out of the courtroom Mac asked, "Ted, do you have your zingers ready for Roth?"

"Zingers" were a favorite topic of Mac's. A cardinal rule of cross examination is never ask a question you don't already know the answer to. Another rule is, never, ever sit down on a bad note. If you get a "bad" answer on cross, do *not* sit down and let it fester in the minds of the jury. The only way to avoid this is to have your "zingers" ready - three or four questions you already know the answers to which

152

answers are *very good* for your case. The "zingers" are therefore reserved for the end. However, even if you have three or four, if you hit on the first one, STOP! Don't ask another question! Only if the first one fizzles, do you go on to the next one.

"I have a few."

"Good."

Ted asked Mac, "Notice anything about Elder?"

"Not that I could see. Seems like some of the other jurors defer to him a bit."

"Yeah, I caught that earlier. What about Lander?"

"No, nothing."

"Okay."

40

When trial resumed, (with Danny still in his seat,) Ted walked slowly to the podium and began, "Good afternoon Mr. Roth."

"Good afternoon."

Ted didn't beat around the bush, he went right in.

"Mr. Roth, isn't it a cardinal rule in your profession to get to the scene of a crime as soon as possible?"

"As soon as you can, yes."

"Why is that?"

"To preserve everything and view the evidence as "fresh" as possible."

"Mr. Roth, Deputy Pooley testified he came upon the scene and the body at 7:15 PM and that Grundy did not appear to be breathing. You did not see the body until over fourteen hours later, is that right?"

"That's correct."

"In fact, when you saw it, it was already stiff, isn't that correct?"

"Yes, rigor had already set in."

"Wasn't that fresh I guess?"

Laughter.

"Objection."

"I'll withdraw that last statement, Your Honor" (since the jury already heard it anyway).

"What went on within the office in that fourteen hour period?"

"I do not know."

"How many other people were in that office within that fourteen hour period?"

"I don't know."

"Was anything removed from the office in that time

period?"

"I do not know."

"Anything brought in?"

"I don't know."

Pause....let it sink in.

"Mr. Roth, the pool of blood you saw on the floor, I suppose it was starting to dry by the time you got there?"

"Yes."

"Officer Pooley described it as about three feet across and from Grundy's head to his waist. What dimension would that be?"

"Roughly two feet."

Ted walked over to the table of exhibits by the court reporter and picked up Exhibit Number seventeen, the best picture of the blood. "Mr. Roth, showing you People's seventeen, is this a picture you took of the pool of blood after the body was removed?"

"Yes, one of them."

"And by your testimony and that of Deputy Pooley, the blood would cover approximately six square feet, is that right?"

"Approximately."

"The footprints you found, were they on the edge of the blood pool?"

"Yes."

"Any idea how long it would take the heart of a dying man to pump that much blood out to the edge where the footprints were?"

"No, that would be a better question for Dr. Strothers."

"Fair enough. Mr. Roth, other than the footprints of Tom and Larry, did you find any others?"

"No."

"Are you sure?"

"Yes."

"What happened to Deputy Pooley's footprint?"

"Pardon me?"

"Deputy Pooley testified earlier this morning that he

got blood on his left shoe. Did you find his footprint anywhere?"

"No."

"I'm sorry, I didn't hear your answer."

"No, I didn't find a footprint of Officer Pooley."

A good long pause. You get the jury's attention not by speaking louder, but by being absolutely quiet.

"Did you determine the ownership of the handguns?"

"Yes and no."

"You could only trace one of the guns, isn't that so?"

"Yes, the .22 caliber belonged to Tom Merrick."

"And the .45 caliber?"

"We could not trace it. The numbers were all filed off."

"And do I understand it correctly that the .45 was determined to be the murder weapon?"

"Yes."

"Didn't you find that a little strange?"

"In what manner?"

"Well, if Tom and Larry already had in their possession an untraceable .45 to commit the crime, why on earth would they bring with them the .22 which was registered in Tom's name?"

No answer.

"Mr. Roth?"

"I have no idea."

"Isn't it possible the .45 was already there when Tom and Larry arrived?"

"Mr. Roth?"

"Anything's possible."

"Do you have any evidence to prove the .45 *wasn't* already there?"

"No."

"Let's discuss the pattern of bullets. See if I have this right. One bullet was eighteen inches from the ceiling; one was about the same distance from the floor and both of those were about five feet to the right of the body. One was all the way over on the other side of the wall, twelve feet to the left and about halfway up. One was in Grundy's right hip about three feet from the floor and one was in his left neck about five feet from the floor. That about right?"

"Yes, pretty much."

"Were there any signs of a struggle within the office?"

"No."

"And these shots were made from point blank range, less than ten feet away, is that right?"

"Yes, as far as I could tell."

Walking closer to the witness box, "Mr. Roth would you say I was about ten feet away from you at the present time?"

"Give or take."

"Mr. Picker?"

"Fine."

At that point Ted made his right hand into a gun and mimicked a person shooting absolutely wildly. Down at the floor to the right, "Pow!" To the left toward the right hip, "Pow!" Up to the ceiling toward the right, "Pow!" Toward the neck, "Pow!" Twelve feet to the left, "Pow!" His arm was flailing all over the place. Some of the jurors were smiling. Elder was not.

"Objection! Your Honor!"

"Mr. Chase, please avoid the theatrics."

"Yes, Your Honor."

"Mr. Roth, Ted said while looking directly at Jenks and not at Roth. Are you aware Larry Townes is a Desert Storm veteran with a ribbon for marksmanship?"

No answer.

"Mr. Roth?"

"No, I was unaware."

"That's what I thought. Thank you Mr. Roth."

Now let's see what Picker was going to do. Will he let that big matzo ball just hang out there or try to make some points on redirect?

"No redirect, Your Honor."

157

Gold! The jurors were leaving with the last image in their heads of Ted's wild display and knowing Townes was a certified marksman!

McCarthy then explained to the jurors they were going to stop for the day. He excused them with the same instructions but Ted wondered what the "pillow talk" would be this night among the jurors and their spouses.

As Larry and Tom were being led away, they each gave Ted the thumbs up. That gave him encouragement. He nodded back at them and then put his finger over his lips. They nodded back and left the courtroom.

Mac, Mike and Ted decided to hit Brothers' Lounge as it was only 2:45 and they could get a booth in the back and review and plan in peace and quiet. Before leaving the courtroom, Ted went over to Danny Longer.

"How am I doing so far?"

"Terrific. There's no way Townes would have missed that badly."

"You getting the blood thing?"

"Yea. I guess they just stood there until it all just stopped coming??? That didn't make much sense. If it woulda' been me, I woulda' shot the guy and got outta' there as soon as I could."

"Look, Danny, are you going to be here tomorrow?"

"Yep."

"Do me a favor. Keep your eye on the jury. Let me know if you see anything unusual - facial expressions, nervous looks, smiles, that sort of thing."

"Sure."

"Okay, see you tomorrow."

Danny Longer just received the most important assignment of his entire life. Someone had actually trusted him with a serious task. As Ted's son would say, Danny "was bustin" inside. He just became a part, albeit a small one, but a part nevertheless, of the defense of Tom Merrick and Larry Townes! He could not wait until Wednesday.

Mac and Mike already had the Great Lakes Ales on

158

the table when Ted caught up to them.

"Well, what does everyone think?"

Mike said, "So far so good. I can't believe Picker let it end that way just now."

Mac followed, "I wish I had this on video. I could show Picker to my students as an example of what *not* to do. Ted, McKay's coming with the ballistics, fingerprint and residue evidence. Do you need anything or are you set?"

"I think I'm set. The ballistics will be a big dog and pony show but we really don't care. We're conceding the .45 is what blew the hole in Grundy's neck. As for the residue and fingerprints, I have to tread very carefully there because we did no discovery. That will be a minefield to maneuver. I'll just have to be cautious. Are either of you getting any vibes from the panel?"

"Yeah, the pow, pow, pow thing got a reaction or two." They all laughed.

"Yeah, I kind of did that on the spur of the moment." More laughter.

"Well, you got your point across, I'm sure."

"Okay. You know what, I think I'm just going to go home, put my feet up and relax for a bit. I'll see you both tomorrow morning."

Ted slept well that night, he was exhausted.

41

Wednesday began with the threat of a rainstorm. It was heavily overcast and the wind had picked up quite a bit from the day before. The courthouse now took on an ominous appearance, like the dark fortress of the Wicked Witch of the West. Ted could almost hear the foreboding chant of the Witch's reluctant guards. He knew this was a big day and he had to be wary of the flying monkeys.

He watched the jury file in and once again noticed Elder conversing with another member of the panel. *There definitely was some deference working here,* he thought. He smiled as he glanced over and saw young Danny with his new yellow legal pad. McCarthy took the bench about 9:15.

"Good morning everyone. Please sit. Mr. Picker, I understand your witness is here."

"Yes, Your Honor. The People call Mr. James McKay."

Now here was an impressive witness, thought Ted, as McKay strode to the witness box to be sworn. He was tall and had a full head of blond hair that had been expensively cut. He was impeccably dressed and had quite an air of confidence about him.

Picker introduced him to the jury and reviewed his credentials.

"And how long have you been a ballistic expert for BCI?"

"Going on eleven years."

"And before that?"

"I was with Special Ops, U.S. Marine Corps., attached to Guantanamo Bay."

"Mr. McKay, were you given an opportunity to

examine evidence in this case provided to you by Gregory Roth?"

"Yes sir, five spent rounds; two handguns - a .45 and a .22; and hand swabs and fingerprints from the defendants. I was also provided with a series of photographs I understand Mr. Roth took of the scene of the crime."

Picker then had McKay verify the exhibits and establish the chain of custody by identifying Roth's name as well as his own on the plastic bags and tags as the evidence was passed one to the other.

"Mr. McKay, did you conduct any tests on the rounds?"

"Yes sir."

"For what purpose?"

"To determine whether they were fired from either of the weapons that were provided to me, the .45 or the .22."

"How do you go about that?"

"Well, first of all, the .22 was ruled out immediately as the five spent rounds were only .45 caliber. Then, regarding the .45, it is a matter of making a comparison between a recently fired bullet and the ones provided in the evidence bag."

"How do you make such a comparison?"

"Well, what you have to understand is that when a gun is fired, it leaves identifying marks on the bullets and casings. It is as unique as a human fingerprint, no two guns are alike. In fact, the marks are called ballistic fingerprints. Every time a gun is fired it leaves the exact same marks. So what we do is fire a new round into a water tank so the bullet is not damaged. Then we retrieve it and place it and the "evidence bullet" under a microscope to compare the markings to see if they are the same. It's not rocket science."

"And how did that come out in this case?"

"Well, the rounds taken from the cinder block wall were too heavily damaged but the ones taken from the corpse could be tested. By comparing the ballistic fingerprints, I could determine that the rounds found in the right hip and left side of the head, were, in fact, fired from the .45 caliber handgun, this one right here, that was provided to me," he said, lifting the evidence bag,

"People's exhibit twenty-nine?"

"That's right."

"People's exhibit twenty-nine, the .45 caliber, was the weapon that discharged the fatal shot?"

"Yes sir."

"Did you also conduct fingerprint testing of the weapons?"

"Yes sir, they were both dusted for prints."

"What did that reveal to you?"

"By comparing the fingerprints lifted from the handguns with those provided to me by Mr. Roth, I was able to determine that the prints on the .22 belonged to the Defendant, Tom Merrick. The .45, the murder weapon, had the prints of Defendant Larry Townes amon...."

Picker cut him off and Ted caught it.

"Now I understand you did some additional testing for residue, is that right?"

"Yes sir.

"Tell us a little about residue."

"Well, discharging a firearm produces combustion of the primer and powder of the cartridge. But not all of it burns. The residue of those components, the unburned portion, can be used to detect a fired cartridge. Residue can be found on the wound, or other target material and it can also be found on the clothing or hand of the person who discharged the gun."

"What method of detection is used?"

"At BCI, we use scanning electron microscopy to identify the primer residue. Boiled down, it is a super sensitive microscope."

"Now I understand certain swabs were provided to you?"

"Yes, Exhibit twenty-five is the hand swab from Defendant Townes and twenty-seven was that of Merrick."

"How is the swabbing done?"

162

"The method of collection is really quite simple. The collection tool is a chuck with a gummed surface that residue adheres to. The chuck is dragged over the surface and the residue is collected. The chuck, with the residue on the sticky surface can be directly prepared for examination in the SEM device."

"I see. Did you find any gunshot residue on the .22 caliber?"

"No. It wasn't recently fired."

"Okay, did you find any residue on Exhibit twenty-seven, the swab from Defendant Merrick?"

"No."

"What about the .45?"

"Yes, that had gunshot residue on it."

"And Exhibit twenty-five, the swab of the hand of Defendant Townes?"

"It was positive for gunshot residue that matched that on the .45"

"Thank you, Mr. McKay. Mr. Chase may have some questions for you."

"Good morning Mr. McKay."

"Good morning."

"Mr. Picker asked you about fingerprints and you stated you found Larry's prints on the .45 caliber, is that right?"

"Yes sir."

"He didn't ask you if there were any other prints on the weapon did he?"

"No sir."

"Were there any other prints on the .45 other than Larry's?"

"Yes sir, there was a partial."

Murmur from the back pews. (Bad for Picker - caught trying to hide something from the jury.)

"Was the partial a match to Tom Merrick?"

"No sir."

More murmur.

"What could you tell, if anything, about the partial?"
Ted had to be real careful here. He was on a limb in an area where he didn't already have the answers.

"It was small, most likely female."

"Did you run it through any registers or directories?"

"Yes."

"What did you come up with?"

"No matches. It probably was not enough of a sample."

"But you will admit to this jury that there was someone else who handled that weapon and we have no idea who it might be?"

"Yes, that's right."

"And you suspect from the size, it was a female?"

"Yes sir."

"Mr. McKay, is it possible that one set of fingerprints on a handgun could be obliterated by a second person picking the handgun up after the first?"

"Yes sir."

"Did one of Larry's prints overlap the partial print you found on the weapon?"

"Yes."

"Doesn't that indicate to you that the partial print was on the weapon *before* Larry touched it?"

"Possibly."

More murmur.

"Mr. McKay, being an ex-Marine, you are familiar with .45 caliber handguns are you not?"

"Yes, they are standard issue."

"They are a very powerful weapon, are they not?"

"Very. They make a large hole."

"In your opinion, would it be more difficult for a female to accurately discharge a .45 at a target compared to an ex-Army marksman?"

"Objection."

"Mr. Chase, are you asking only a hypothetical here?"

"Yes, Your Honor."

"I'll allow it. You may answer." (A very generous ruling from the bench - which criminal defendants were prone to receive.)

"Depends on who the female is, I guess."

"Fair enough. (Ted had made his point with the jury. Not smart to browbeat it.) "Mr. McKay, let's discuss the gunshot residue."

"Fine."

Ted picked up the .45 with only his right hand as though he were aiming at a target. "Mr. McKay, would you agree with me this is one way to hold and aim a .45 caliber handgun?"

"Yes."

"For the record, the stock of the weapon is tight upon and covered by the palm of my right hand with my index finger on the trigger. My middle, ring, and pinkie fingers are wrapped around the stock from right to left. My right thumb is on the left side at the top of the stock and resting on top of my middle finger. That fair to you Mr. McKay?"

"Yes."

"Mr. Picker?"

"Yes."

"Mr. McKay, if I fired the weapon like this, where would the gunshot residue likely come in contact with my hand?"

"On the outside of your hand over the top of your thumb and index finger and that part of your hand where they join together - which doctors call the snuff box."

"It would not be on the inside palm of my hand would it?"

"No."

"Why not?"

"Because the palmer surface of your hand is pressed against the stock."

"And therefore the residue cannot come in contact with it?"

"That's right."

"Let me ask you this. Is that your opinion or is that a matter of common knowledge among residue experts?"

"Both."

"If the residue *was* found on the palmer surface of the hand rather than on the outside of the thumb and index finger, is that consistent with someone picking up a weapon *after* it has been fired?"

"Yes, it could be."

"Mr. McKay, showing you People's twenty-five, please tell the jury what this is again."

"The positive residue swab from Defendant Townes"

"Does Exhibit twenty-five indicate the location of the residue?"

"It says, oh gee............" (A golden moment!)

"Oh gee what, Mr. McKay?"

He answered slowly, "It says the residue was taken from the inside of the right palm."

"Consistent with what, Mr. McKay?"

"Townes picking up the weapon after it had been discharged."

"I'm sorry I didn't get that."

McKay spoke much louder this time.

"The location of the residue is consistent with Townes picking up the gun after it had been fired."

Very long pause here, dead silence in the entire room. Silence, not noise, gets everyone's attention. Mac was smiling. His star pupil had learned well.

"That's what I thought. No further questions."

The room got loud and McCarthy had to bang his gavel.

Danny Longer was smiling along with Mac.

"Mr. Picker, any redirect?"

"No, Your Honor."

Ted immediately rose to his feet. "Your Honor, I know it is early but may we take a very short recess here before the People's next witness?" Mac smiled.

166

"Mr. Picker?"

"I have no objection if opposing counsel needs a break."

Ted thought to himself, *the only thing I need is for the jury to chew on what they just heard for a time before another witness takes the stand.*

"Very well. Ten minutes."

Ted went to the men's room even though he had no need to do so. Mac hid his face in his hands to keep the jury from seeing him laugh. Picker had no idea what was going on.

When Ted returned to counsel table, Mac looked at him with a big smile. "You dirty dog."

Ted had the look of the cat who ate the canary and said kiddingly, "What do you mean? Took the line and the sinker along with the hook didn't he?"

"The wonder of it all is that Picker is clueless," Mac replied.

42

Twenty five minutes later, McCarthy was back on the bench. (In court, there really is no such thing as a ten minute break, it always lasts longer. It's like a twenty second time out in an NBA game.)

"Mr. Picker, please call your next witness."

"The People call Dr. James Strothers."

Dr. Strothers was known to just about everyone in the courtroom. Small counties such as Anders did not retain a full time coroner because they could not afford to and, really, there was no need. Accordingly, it was always a local physician who would double as a county's coroner.

You could tell James Strothers was a physician from twenty yards. Unlike the murder victim, he appeared very distinguished. He was not tall, but he was in shape and carried himself well for a sixty-five year old. He had grey-white hair and wire-rimmed glasses. He had a well-groomed mustache. His suit was blue pinstripe and, Ted thought, *very expensive*. The lights of the courtroom were actually reflected by his shoes, they were so shiny. He carried a file in the crook of his left arm.

"Welcome, Doctor. Please be sworn and take your seat here in the box."

"Thank you, Your Honor."

"Welcome Doctor."

The Doctor nodded to Picker. At this point, Ted interrupted. "Your Honor, in the interests of saving time, the Defense will stipulate to the Doctor's qualifications, position as Coroner for Anders County, and his ability to offer the opinions he was called here today to give."

"Mr. Picker?"

"That would be fine."

"Fine. The stipulation is noted for the record."

Picker began "Doctor, as Coroner, you are charged with making rulings at times regarding the deaths of Anders County residents?"

"Yes, that is true."

"Were you called upon to make such a ruling in the death of Dr. Jerry Grundy?"

"Yes."

"Tell the jury how you go about that, please."

"Well, the evidence is gathered by the investigative sources and submitted to me for review and then I conduct an autopsy. In this case, Gregory Roth and Mr. McKay from BCI provided me with the information and evidence they had gathered."

What followed, was a half hour discussion regarding the evidence already presented in the case with the Doctor identifying what he received and establishing the chain of custody. Ted objected to none of it. Picker's discussion of the cause of death then followed.

"Doctor, what did the autopsy reveal to you?"

"Well, the victim sustained two gunshot wounds, one of which was fatal. His right pelvic bone was shattered at its junction with the long bone of the leg but that would not have killed him, though it would have been very debilitating, had he survived. The wound that killed Dr. Grundy was to the left ascending carotid artery. Basically, the .45 caliber bullet ripped the artery out of his body. May I use a medical illustration here to assist in explaining?"

"Certainly."

The doctor pulled the illustration from his file, turned toward the jury, lifted it up, and began pointing to it with his Mount Blanc.

"The carotid artery is the artery that supplies the head and neck with oxygen-rich blood. There are two such arteries in the body, the right and the left, and they follow the same course with the exception of their origin. The right comes

169

from an area known as the brachiocephalic trunk, whereas the left, the one that was destroyed here, arises from what we call the aortic arch. The left can actually be thought of as having two components, one thoracic, one cervical. You may have experienced or perhaps seen on TV that sometimes doctors measure the pulse of an individual by placing two fingers over the carotid artery as it rises through the neck - the cervical.

If the artery is "pinched shut" for any period of time, first you would faint. If it remained pinched for a longer period, you would risk brain damage as the blood supply is cut off and, ultimately, death. Obviously, if the artery is extracted from the body, death is imminent.

In this case, there is no question. Death occurred as a result of the massive destruction of the left carotid artery in the cervical area."

"Doctor, do you hold that opinion within a reasonable degree of medical certainty or probability?"

"Yes."

"Now, focusing on the evidence that was presented to you and that we just reviewed, as well as your autopsy findings, did you form an opinion as to whether or not Dr. Grundy's death was a homicide?"

"Yes, I formed an opinion."

"Once again, do you hold that opinion within a reasonable degree of medical certainty or probability?"

"Yes."

"And what is that opinion?"

"The damage to the carotid artery which led to the Doctor's death was done by a single gunshot wound which was not suicidal in origin. Another individual shot a .45 caliber bullet at the Doctor and hit him in the left side of the face and neck. It was definitely a homicide."

"Thank you. Your witness."

"Doctor, good morning."

"Good morning."

"Doctor, your role here is twofold: to determine a cause of death and to determine whether there was a homicide,

170

is that right?"

"Yes."

"Your role is not to offer an opinion on who did or did not do the deed?"

"No, that is not the role of the coroner."

"You offer no opinion on that issue."

"No, on that I am not qualified. That is for you folks to decide"

"Doctor, showing you what has been marked as People's seventeen, can you look at this for a minute? I have some questions for you."

"Yes, I have seen this before. It was provided to me by Mr. Roth."

"That is a photograph of the floor of the exam room after the body was removed."

"That's correct."

"Doctor, testimony has been given in this matter that the pool of blood you see on the floor measured approximately three feet by two feet. That look about right to you?"

"I would have no quarrel with that."

"Doctor, do you see the footprints at the outer edge of the blood?"

"Yes."

"Doctor, as you testified, the left carotid artery was ripped from Grundy's body, isn't that what you said?"

"Yes."

"Can you tell the jury how this large pool of blood came to be?"

"Well, some of it, a very small portion, would have drained from the head down, but probably over 95% of it came from what was left of the artery with the heart continuing to pump blood until Dr. Grundy succumbed."

"Doctor, in your medical opinion, considering the damage to the artery, and the amount of blood you see here on the floor, how long would it have taken for the heart to pump the blood to the area where the footprints are seen?"

"That is hard to say. The heart beats as long as the

171

brain tells it to. So the real question here is, how long did it take for the brain to stop sending that message. Given the injury to the artery and the amount of blood I see here, I would estimate seven to ten minutes. "

"Doctor, do you hold that opinion within a reasonable degree of medical certainty or probability?"

"Yes, I would say so."

"So whoever made these footprints at the outer edges of the blood pool, couldn't have done so until at least seven minutes had passed after the fatal shot?"

"Yes, that would be correct."

"Doctor, that means *if* the person who pulled the trigger...... is the *same* person who made the footprints....... that person shot the Doctor and........ instead of fleeing the scene............ remained there for another seven minutes, doesn't it?"

"It would appear that way."

"Thank you Doctor, no further questions."

"Any re-direct?" the Judge asked Picker

"Yes, Your Honor."

Oh-oh, now what?

"Doctor it's entirely possible that what Mr. Chase just described for us is exactly what happened here isn't it? I mean whoever shot the Doctor, for whatever reason, could have stayed for the period of time you mentioned, isn't that true?"

Ted and Mac sat ramrod straight up in their chairs and could not wait two seconds for the next answer; Picker had just asked a question he did not have the answer to.

"Well, it's possible....but not......"

"Thank you Doctor, nothing further."

Ted jumped up so fast his feet came off the ground. "Wait just a second here, you asked the question, let your witness answer it." Everyone in the courtroom including the jury reacted to Ted's "jump."

McCarthy was all over it. "Counsel, please approach the bench." Now the jury recognized something very important was about to happen.

All the attorneys went to the side of the bench and had a discussion outside the hearing of the jury, a sidebar conference.

McCarthy whispered, "Mr. Picker, you can either let the witness finish his response or I'm sure Mr. Chase will have some re-cross for him. Pick your poison."

"But, Your Honor, I would object…"

"Counselor, you can't object to your own question."

"Your Honor, I would like a second to confer with my witness."

"I hope that is your attempt at a joke," Ted said.

"Mr. Picker, you let the witness answer or the matter is returned to Mr. Chase."

"Yes, Your Honor, I'll finish."

When everyone returned to their seat, Picker said, "Doctor, I'm sorry to have interrupted you. What did you want to say?"

The sidebar, the first one of the trial, just emphasized what was to come next.

"What I wanted to say was the answer to your question was yes, it's possible, but not very likely. Any normal person would have wanted to get out of there immediately rather than stand around for another ten minutes and risk getting caught. It doesn't make much sense."

"Doctor, please remind the jury you are a medical doctor not a psychiatrist."

"That is true."

Nice try, Ted thought to himself.

After the Doctor was excused, McCarthy once again called the attorneys to sidebar.

"Carl, it's going on 11:30, who is left?"

"Marcie Noonan, the office manager."

"How long?"

"Not long at all, Your Honor."

"Ted?"

"We will not cross examine but will reserve the right

to call her on cross in our case."

"Ted, I'm trying to figure out the afternoon. Can you tell me who your first witness is going to be?"

"Tom Merrick." Picker smiled.

"Okay, let's do this. We'll break for lunch early and when we come back, Carl can put Noonan on and then you can call Merrick. That should take us to the end of the day. Agreed?"

"That's fine with the Defense."

"Fine," said Picker."

The attorneys returned to their respective tables.

"Ladies and gentlemen, we are going to break for lunch now. Please be back in the jury room by 12:45 and we will resume at 1:00. The same instructions apply, no discussion of the case with anyone. See you back in court at 1:00."

"All rise!"

Ted glanced and his clients who were half-smiling. Then he walked over to Danny who was holding a pad covered in scribble.

"Well, what did you see?"

"Mr. Chase, almost all the jurors had reactions to your cross examination of McKay, especially when he admitted the residue was not where it should have been."

"Almost all?"

"Yes, Number Twelve hardly reacts to anything, although he did crack a smile over the Strothers' statement at the very end. Everyone had raised eyebrows about that. I also noticed they all glanced at Picker when you used McKay to show that there was another print on the gun. They didn't look real happy about that."

"So, Danny, how do you feel about our case so far?"

"Well there seems to be enough doubt to go around, and you have not put a witness on yet."

"Okay, keep an eye and we'll talk some more later."

"Okay." Now Danny was certain his major would be pre-law.

174

"Well Mike, Mac, let's get a sandwich."

At the deli, there was little discussion about the morning session although all thought it could not have gone better. They talked about Noonan and Merrick coming up.

"I'm calling Noonan on cross as part of our case, probably last. I think she is the last witness I want the jury to hear. So after Picker does her direct and after he rests, we'll call Tom. He is ready."

"Ted, any misgivings about Tom or Larry taking the stand?"

"No. None. They are both ready. I need the jury to hear from both of them. They should have no problem explaining what they had planned to do. I think that admission will establish their credibility with the jury so the jury will believe them when they testify that the deed was already done."

They ate their sandwiches and ribbed Ted a little about the morning session. Mike said he thought Ted was going to jump on the table when Picker cut Strothers off. "Came close," said Ted.

43

The clouds were about to let loose when the defense team returned to the courtroom. Thankfully, they made it back before it started and boy did it come down - a good, old fashioned "gully washer;" the kind of rain that gives you the impression God was washing and renewing his earth.

"Mr. Picker, you may call your next witness."

"We call Marcie Noonan."

Marcie walked up, was sworn, and took her seat in the box.

"Good afternoon, Ms. Noonan."

"Good afternoon."

After establishing the customary background information, Picker asked, "Ms. Noonan, are you presently employed?"

"No, I am looking for a new job."

"And your last employment..."

"I was the office manager for Dr. Grundy up until his death."

"How long had you been so employed?"

"Approximately three years."

"Ms. Noonan, can you give us an idea of the work schedules and hours of operation of the office?"

"Yes, the office was open Monday, Tuesday, Thursday, Friday and Saturday. The last appointment was usually scheduled no later than 4:30 except that on Saturday we only worked a half day. I would usually stay until the last appointment showed but Doctor Grundy usually stayed to at least 6:00. We usually opened the office at ten in the morning."

"Was this the schedule in effect on August 28 of this year?"

"Yes."

"Do you recall that particular day?"

"Yes."

"What time did you leave the office that evening?"

"Approximately 4:30."

"How was Dr. Grundy when you left?"

"He was fine, tending to the last patient of the day."
She glanced at Ted.

"When you left for the evening at 4:30, which door did you go out?"

"We parked in the back so I went out the rear door."

"So when you left that evening, Grundy stayed behind?"

"Yes."

"And that was not unusual?"

"No, he usually stayed until 6:00."

"You said 'we' parked in the back, who is 'we'?"

"The Doctor and I."

"When you left that evening, did you notice any vehicles behind the building?"

"No, not behind the office, but behind the building next to the office, there was a green pick-up truck with two men in it."

"Had you ever seen that truck before that evening?"

"Yes, I had seen it before."

"How many times?"

"Oh gee, I don't know three or four maybe."

"Ms. Noonan, showing you what has been marked as Peoples' Exhibit thirty, do you recognize the vehicle in this photo?"

"Yes, that is the truck that was behind the other building."

"How is it that you recognize it?"

"Mostly from the license plate (pointing) right here."

"What are you pointing to?"

"The lower right corner of the plate was bent upwards - right here. That's how I remember it."

"Did you get a look at the men inside the truck?"

"No, I could see there were two but I did not get a good look at them."

"Thank you. Nothing further Your Honor."

"Mr. Chase, I understand it is your present intention not to question the witness now, but to call her in your case, is that correct?"

"Yes, Your Honor."

"Very well then. Mr. Picker, any other witnesses?"

"No, Your Honor. The People move for admission into evidence of their Exhibits one through thirty."

"Mr. Chase?"

"No objection, Your Honor."

"The exhibits are admitted without objection."

"Your Honor, the People rest."

"Ladies and gentlemen of the jury, at this time, we have a little housekeeping to do so to speak, so I am going to excuse you for ten minutes. We will get everything done and then bring you back in."

"All Rise!"

After the jury filed out, the Judge asked, "Ted, do you have a motion?"

"Yes, Your Honor."

A motion for a directed verdict of acquittal can only be made after the close of the State's case and should be done out of the presence of the jury. Ted went on the record and made his motion stating the People had failed to prove the offense beyond a reasonable doubt. Given the evidence, Ted knew he was just going through the motions. He had scored quite a few points, but it was still possible the jury had enough to convict. McCarthy summarily denied the motion as everyone expected him to. However, the record was made.

44

With the jury back, the Judge announced, "Ladies and gentlemen, the People have rested. Mr. Chase, please call your first witness."

"Your Honor, the Defense calls Mr. Tom Merrick."

Stirring.

Tom Merrick rose, and slowly, with his customary air of dignity, walked to the witness box. He took the oath, firmly and loudly saying "I do."

Ted established the background information regarding marital status, address, work history, military background.

"Tom, how many children do you have?"

"None now, but I had one, a daughter."

"Terri."

"Yes, Terri."

"She died June 26th of this year."

"No, she was murdered June 26th of this year." Ted stole a glance at the panel.

"Tom, you heard the stipulation Judge McCarthy read to the jury at the outset of the trial?"

"Yes."

"You maintain Dr. Grundy killed Terri even though he was acquitted of all charges?"

"Yes, he got off on a technicality, but he is the one who killed her."

"What technicality?"

"The prosecution could not prove who the driver of the vehicle was but we knew it was Grundy."

"How did you know?"

"Because Terri never learned how to drive a car."

More stirring.

Ted stole a quick glance at Elder who had a very stern

look on his face.

"After the Doctor was acquitted what did you do?"

Silence.

"Tom?"

Still silence.

"Tom, after Dr. Grundy was acquitted, did you do anything?"

"Yes. I'm not proud of it, but Larry and I decided we were going to punish him for what he did."

"Larry Townes?"

"Yes."

"Why was Larry part of this?"

"He and Terri were engaged to be married."

"And what exactly did you plan?"

"We were going to shoot him to death."

Was the rumble from the courtroom or the rainstorm outside? Ted couldn't tell. He heard the gavel.

"Did you plan it out?"

"Yes."

"Please tell the jury what you did."

"Well, we started by going over to his office to watch the comings and goings. We went over there four or five times in Larry's truck."

"The green pick-up with the bent license plate?"

"Yes."

"We took down the make and license number of his car and we got a brochure from his office with the office hours on it. After watching everything, we knew he stayed a little later and we knew he parked in the back. We chose August 28. We were going to wait for him in the lot next to his office and when he came out to the car, that's when we were going to do it."

"Who was going to actually pull the trigger?"

"Larry was going to drive the truck and pull up to the side of his car so that I could roll down the window and fire at him."

"You were going to be the triggerman?"

180

"Yes."

"What type of weapon?"

"My .22 caliber revolver."

"The one the People now have?"

"Yes."

"Then you would simply drive off?"

"That was the plan. We thought in the back lot there it was pretty secluded and that no one would see us, it would be safe to do it there."

"What happened?"

"Well Grundy normally came out to his car about six or so, but on the 28th, he didn't come out, so we waited a bit and went into the office about seven. The back door was locked, so we went around to the front. It was open so we walked in."

"Tom, let me ask you this, while you were still sitting in the truck in the back, did you see anyone enter or exit the office through the front door?"

"No, you could not see the front door from where we were."

"When you walked in what did you find?"

"He was lying on the floor of one of the exam rooms with a lot of blood all around him. He was dead. Larry saw the .45 off to the side and he picked it up. It was right then that the officer arrived with his gun on us. We didn't hear him come in."

"Did you give the officer a hard time at all?"

"No sir, we did everything he said."

"Tom, did you wait to be handcuffed by him?"

"Yes sir."

"Why?"

"Well he was just doing his job and it certainly looked bad at the time, but we hadn't done anything wrong. We didn't get the chance. Grundy was already dead."

"You never fired your .22?"

"No sir, neither of us fired anything."

"Thank you Tom. Your witness, Mr. Picker."

"Mr. Merrick, you admit to this jury you wanted Doctor Grundy dead?"

"Yes sir."

"Mr. Merrick, will you admit to this jury the .22 caliber handgun was never fired?"

"Yes."

"But the .45 found in Townes' hand was fired, wasn't it?"

"That's what they tell me."

"It was or it wasn't?"

"It was."

"And it was the murder weapon?"

"Yes, it was."

To Ted's surprise, Picker was doing well but he should be, after all, he had an arsenal of ammunition. No question the cross examination thus far was the high point of Picker's presentation.

"You saw no one come or go from his office when you were sitting in the back lot waiting to murder the Doctor did you?"

"No."

"And that's exactly what you were doing – you were waiting to murder the Doctor."

"Yes."

"You heard no gunshot?"

"No."

"So you saw no one, you heard no gunshots?"

"That's right."

"So we are to believe there was another person who came and went without being seen and who fired a gun, a powerful .45 caliber, not once, but five times (mimicking Ted from earlier) pow, pow, pow, pow, pow and no one heard a sound."

Very effective, Ted thought.

"We didn't hear anything."

182

"Mr. Merrick, to your knowledge, was there anyone else's footprints at the scene other than yours and Townes'?"

"No, just ours."

"Let me ask you Mr. Merrick. If you and your co-conspirator Townes over there (pointing) had gotten to him first, according to your testimony, Grundy would be dead right now anyway, wouldn't he?"

"Yes."

"Mr. Merrick, give me the name of one person you know of who wanted Dr. Grundy dead, other than you and Townes. Just one."

"I know of no one."

This last question was certainly improper, but Tom answered quickly and Ted had no time to object. The jury already heard the answer and Ted did not want to draw even more attention to it by objecting.

"Thank you, nothing further. Mr. Chase..... you can *have* your witness."

Ted looked at Mac who maintained his poker face but had tallied the points that had just been scored against the home team. Ted had violated the third cardinal rule of trial work: he had underestimated his opponent. Now, they were facing real danger here: they could not let this be the last evidence the jury would hear this day – what they would go home with. It had to be challenged. Ted had to come up with something fast to "dilute," even in some small way, the evidence the jury heard.

"Redirect, Mr. Chase?"

Mac knew Ted was in a jam so he leaned over and whispered in his ear.

"Ted, do the 'no-fear-of-the-truth' thing."

Ted rose, "Just briefly, Your Honor."

"Tom, will you agree with me that what the jury heard sounded pretty bad for you and Larry didn't it?"

"Yes, it did."

"But it was the absolute truth wasn't it?"

"Yes sir."

"So no matter how badly it sounds, you still want the jury to hear the truth, don't you?"

"Yes sir."

"You're not afraid of the truth, are you Tom?"

"No sir. I know Larry and I are innocent. Grundy was already dead."

"Thank you. Nothing further Your Honor."

"Can I say just one more thing?" Tom asked.

Ted sensed danger. He had no idea what Tom wanted to add. But, really, how could he say no to Tom in front of the jury? He was in a real spot.

"What is it, Tom?"

"No one, no one here, not Mr. Picker here or even these good folks on the jury…. could know how we felt, unless….they have lost a loved one like we lost Terri." Tom dropped his head and wiped his eye.

Ted looked at Elder. His eyes were moist and he was slowly nodding his head.

Ted took his seat.

The Judge addressed the jury, "Ladies and gentlemen, I think it best not to start another witness. I am going to let you go at this time. Please be back here tomorrow morning at 8:45 and we'll get going at 9:00. Same rules apply; no discussion of the case with anyone. See you all in the morning."

Ted had another brief discussion with Danny and then reminded Larry he would be first up in the morning.

"Mac, thanks for the life ring, man I was about to drown. Picker did better than I thought he would."

"Just trying to earn my keep there, counselor."

"Tell you what. I'm starting with Larry in the morning. Why don't you have something ready in case something similar happens? You know what his testimony is going to be."

"Will do but I may have to ask you for a raise. One date with Dorie might not be enough."

"See you in the morning. I'm going home to SLEEP with Dorie."

Mac just stood there looking at Ted who was walking away with a smirk on his face.

Ted did not sleep with Dorie that night. He hardly slept at all. Larry Townes was caught red-handed holding the murder weapon. Ted was more concerned about Larry from the very start and now Larry was going to take the stand.

45

All the eyes were once again on the panel as the Bailiff led them to their seats. Ted knew it was next to impossible to try to read their minds or their "body language." However, he still looked for clues; a slight smile, a glance. When McCarthy got everyone seated, he asked Ted to call his next witness.

"Your Honor, we call Larry Townes."

Larry walked slowly up to the stand, took the oath, and sat down.

"Larry, you heard Tom's testimony about what the two of you had planned to do and why."

Very quietly, "Yes sir."

"Do you disagree with anything Tom said?"

Again, very quietly, "No sir."

"Larry, I know this is difficult, but you will have to speak up a bit."

"Yes sir."

"Terri's death was the only reason?"

"Yes sir. It was about Terri."

"Do you have anything to add to what Tom said?"

"No, it was just like he said."

"Larry, that evening when you entered the room and saw the bullet holes in the wall, what did you think?"

"The person who put them there needs to spend some time at the range."

"Why did you think that?"

"Because they were all over the place. One by the floor, one up by the ceiling, one all the way on the other side of the room. The room is small. The shooter couldn't have been more than ten feet away."

"Ten feet.....is that considered point blank range?"

"Objection! Your Honor, this witness is not a

ballistics expert."

Fantastic! Picker took the bait!

"Your Honor, before a ruling, may I inquire regarding this witness' ability to answer?"

"Yes, please voir dire the witness on his qualifications, Mr. Chase."

"Larry were you ever in the military?"

"Yes sir."

"What branch?"

"U.S. Army."

"Did you see any action?"

"Yes sir, Desert Storm – Iraq."

"Any certifications?"

"Yes sir. I was my unit's SDM and had just about completed my sharpshooter."

"SDM?"

"Squad Designated Marksman."

"What is that?"

"In the Army, a marksman is referred to as the SDM. He has to undergo special training in the classroom and in the field. He must pass a series of exams and he has to demonstrate his ability to consistently hit targets."

"Is a marksman the same as a sniper?"

"Well sometimes the terms are used interchangeably, but they shouldn't be. A sniper is usually deployed for a specific objective. He has to learn camouflage and things like that. The marksman operates as a regular member of his unit – that's why he's called the Squad Designated Marksman – the SDM."

"Were you trained in ballistics?"

"Yes. We needed to understand flight path, rise and fall, and the MPBR of certain weapons."

"MPBR?"

"Maximum point blank range."

"Was a .45 caliber one of the weapons?"

"Yes, it is standard issue."

"Tell us what maximum point blank range is."

"It is a measure of the distance at which the round falls three inches below the line sight."

Picker had his head in his hands. Jenks, on the other hand, was smiling.

"Your Honor?"

"He may answer the question. He possesses the knowledge."

"Thank you, Your Honor." (And thank you Carl for objecting!)

"So, Larry, what is the point blank range for a .45?"

"Well over 100 yards."

"Larry, where was the .45 when you first saw it?"

"On the floor, by the examining table."

"Why did you pick it up?"

"You know, I just wasn't thinking. It was just a reaction, I guess."

"Larry, at any time, did you discharge the .45?"

"No sir, there was no need. Grundy was already dead."

"Larry, had you been the one to shoot Grundy with that .45 from ten feet, how many shots would you have had to fire?"

"One."

"Thank you. Your witness."

"Mr. Townes, I just have one question for you. You helped Tom Merrick plan the murder of Dr. Jerry Grundy and on August 28th you drove to Grundy's office to carry it out. True or false?"

"True."

"Thank you."

Actually, this last from Picker was wise. He was too smart to wade in and get clobbered. He just wanted to bring the jury back to this ugly, but true fact: Townes wanted Grundy dead.

"Thank you, Mr. Townes. You may step down. Mr. Chase, you can call your next witness."

"The defense calls Marcie Noonan as upon cross

examination."

Marcie came up and the Judge reminded her she was still under oath and invited her to take a seat.

"Ms. Noonan, as part of your employment as Office Manager, you sometimes received complaints, didn't you?"

"Yes, I did."

"What about?"

"Billing, problems with insurance, the Doctor being late for an appointment, screw ups in paperwork, things like that."

"Ever receive any complaints about inappropriate conduct by Grundy?"

"Objection!"

"Overruled. She may answer."

"Three or four.

"Did you ever witness inappropriate conduct by Grundy?"

"Objection!"

"Overruled. She may answer."

"Yes."

"Can you tell us about that?"

"Objection!"

"Mr. Picker, you're not getting the message. I believe this evidence may be relevant and I'm letting it in until I hear otherwise. I will let the record reflect your continuing objection to this line of questioning. Does that suit you?"

"Yes, Your Honor."

Judge McCarthy responded sternly, "Very well, then. Ms. Noonan, please answer the question."

"He usually made the young, shapely female patients disrobe, no matter what they were there for. Their appointments usually took twice as long as others."

McCarthy hit the gavel at least five times to get control of his courtroom.

When it finally quieted down, "And who complained about this conduct?"

"The husbands and boyfriends of the women."

"Three or four such complaints?"

"Yes."

"Anything in writing?"

"Yes, one."

Picker was about to vomit.

"Did you bring that with you today?"

"Yes."

"May I have it please?"

Marcie pulled the one threat letter from her purse.

Ted asked Picker to approach the bench and he brought the letter to the Judge. "Judge, we intend to mark this as Defense Exhibit A."

All three looked at it.

"I'll allow it if you can establish a grounds for its admission."

"Thank you Your Honor."

Picker returned to his seat, chin down.

"Ms. Noonan, as part of your employment as the Office Manager, did you process the office paperwork?"

"Yes, all of it."

"Did the paperwork include communications from patients?"

"Yes."

"What did you do with the papers when they came into the office?"

"Filed them appropriately."

"Including the communications from the patients?"

"Yes."

"Did those papers become part of the regular business records of the office?"

"Yes sir."

"Showing you Defense Exhibit A, did the office receive this through the mail?"

"Yes."

"Does it appear to you to be a communication regarding a patient of the office?"

"Yes."

"Did you show it to Dr. Grundy?"

"Yes."

"Did he tell you to file it?"

"No, he told me to destroy it."

"Obviously, you didn't."

"No."

"Did you treat this letter just like all the other communications you received?"

"Yes, I filed it." Really, she 'stashed' it.

"Is this document considered a business record of the chiropractic office of Dr. Jerry Grundy?"

"Yes."

Judge McCarthy said, "I'll allow it and note your objection Mr. Picker."

"Thank you Your Honor."

"Ms. Noonan, will you please read this letter to the jury?"

"Grundy, you fucking pervert. I know what you did to my girlfriend in your office and we're reporting you to the State Board. She came to see you because she had a knee injury. If you ever touch her again or even come near her, you're a dead man. This is not a threat. It is a promise."

"Who did the letter come from?"

"I think I know, but not for sure."

"How is that?"

"I remember a young girl and her boyfriend and I remember she had a problem with her knee. I looked at her chart."

Judge McCarthy said, "We will not have to name names here. She has confidentiality."

"Ms. Noonan, to your knowledge, did the chiropractor have any disputes with someone other than these three or four patients?"

"Yes, a Mr. Crawford."

"How do you know this?"

"I heard them in a heated argument."

"Who is Mr. Crawford?"

"A co-owner of the office building."

191

"When did you hear this argument?"

"About one week before Grundy was shot."

"Now, Ms. Noonan, I want to focus on August 28th. Did you see the truck with two men in it behind the next door building that evening?"

"Yes, about 4:30 when I left the office."

"Through the back door?"

"Yes."

"And you had seen this same vehicle, the one with the bent up license plate, before, hadn't you?"

"Yes."

"You left at 4:30, you say?"

"Yes."

"Was Grundy alone in the building when you left?"

"No, he was with the last patient of the day."

"How come you did not stay?"

"As soon as Grundy saw her, he told me I could leave."

"What did she look like?"

"She was tall and very shapely, that's all I can say. I did not get a good look at her face."

"Why not?"

"She was coming in the front and I was going out the back."

"So Grundy was alone with this woman at 4:30 on the night he was murdered?"

"Yes."

"Do you know who the woman was?"

"Well, she wrote down that her name was Lucille Malley but I don't know if that is true."

"Wrote on what?"

"On the office patient questionnaire."

"What is that?"

"It is the basic information form we have all patients complete when they come in for an appointment."

"Did you provide her with this questionnaire?"

"No. Grundy did."

"Is the patient questionnaire a regular business record of the office?"

"Yes, it is our standard practice."

"Why do you doubt the truth of it?"

"Because after Grundy was murdered, I tried to contact her."

"Why did you do that?"

"Because I thought she might have been the last person to see him alive and I wanted to ask her some questions."

"What did she tell you?"

"Nothing. I couldn't find her."

"Why not?"

"The phone number was bogus and the address she provided was the Ramada Inn."

"So Lucille Malley is a complete dead end?"

"As far as I know, yes."

"But she may have been the last person to see Grundy alive and she gave a fake phone number, a fake address, and probably a fake name."

"Looks that way, yes."

"No one has any idea who this lady is or why she was there?"

"That's right."

Rumbling. Rumbling.

"Ms. Noonan, do you have the original patient questionnaire?"

"Yes, I have it right here."

While Marcie was retrieving the form from her purse, Ted was standing in front of the defense counsel table. He turned and bent over to Mike and said, "Mike, our copy is in the rear pocket of my briefcase. Would you get that out for me?" He then turned back toward Marcie.

Mike opened Ted's worn leather briefcase and reached into the rear pocket but he retrieved two papers, not one. Mike didn't look at the documents; he simply placed them on the table right behind Ted. The paper on top was the patient questionnaire of Lucille Malley and the one below was the

Giffen retainer agreement which had been left in Ted's briefcase.

Marcie unfolded the document. "Here it is." She handed it to Ted who had the court reporter mark it as Defense Exhibit B.

Handing it right back to Marcie, "Ms. Noonan, showing you what has now been marked as Defense Exhibit B, is this the original of the Lucille Malley patient questionnaire that we have been discussing?"

Ted reached back and picked the documents off the table. He immediately recognized he had picked up more than one, but he had his copy of the questionnaire right in front of him and that was all that he cared about at the moment.

"Yes."

"Where did you find this document?"

"Grundy had opened a file for her and this was the only paper in it."

Ted looked down at his copy of the questionnaire. "In trying to contact Ms. Malley, or whatever her name may be, did you call the number 554-7907?"

"Yes."

"Results?"

"Number's disconnected."

"Did you check out the address, 5123 East Jefferson?"

"Yes."

"How did you do that?"

"Drove to it."

"And?"

"Like I said, it's the Ramada."

"Ms. Noonan, in your three years of office management for Dr. Grundy, did you ever have a similar experience?"

"No, never."

"So the first time you experienced anything like this, it just so happened to be on the evening Grundy was shot to death?"

"Seems that way."

"Ms. Noonan, were you aware there was at least one fingerprint on the murder weapon which the People's expert says is that of a woman?" This question was really to remind the jury - it had nothing to do with Marcie.

"No, I didn't know that."

"Thank you. Nothing further. Mr. Picker may have some questions for you."

Ted sat down and laid the documents on the table in front of him.

"Ms. Noonan, you and I met to discuss this case did we not?"

"Yes, twice, I think."

"In those meetings you mentioned nothing about the disgruntled patients or this Lucille Malley character or Crawford, did you?"

"No, there was no need."

"What do you mean there was no need?"

Mac and Ted sat up like lightning bolts were going through their spines! Mac whispered, "Give it to him, Marcie!"

"Remember Mr. Picker, you said you already had the men in custody who shot Grundy. You said my interview was, what was the word you used? Routine, that's it. Routine. You said you had an airtight case and just had to go through the motions. You never asked me about any of this."

Mac whispered, "Now just sit down and make it worse for yourself Carl."

"No further questions, Your Honor."

"Thank you Ms. Noonan. You're excused and I promise this time we won't bring you back."

"Thank you, Your Honor."

"Mr. Chase?"

"No further witnesses Your Honor. The Defense moves for the admission of Exhibit's A and B."

Without waiting for a peep from Picker, "So admitted."

"Your Honor, the Defense renews its motion."

195

"Ladies and gentlemen of the jury, it is now 11:30. Today we will have lunch brought in for you. The Bailiff has menus in the jury deliberation room. This is on me. Well, really, it's on Anders County. I just like to take credit for it."

Snicker

"The Bailiff will have you back in the courtroom at 1:00."

McCarthy remained on the bench after the panel filed out.

"Let the record reflect the jury is not present in the courtroom. The Defense is renewing its motion for a directed verdict of acquittal, is that correct Mr. Chase?"

"Yes, Your Honor."

"The motion will be denied. The People have presented sufficient evidence to support a conviction and we are letting the jury decide."

Ted had expected no other ruling but the record was made.

"Mac, Mike, why don't you go get a sandwich. I'm going to stay here and organize my thoughts for close."

Mike asked, "Do you want us to bring you back something?"

"No, don't feel like eating, but thanks anyway."

Danny Longer was watching from his first pew seat. He and Ted were the only two people left in the courtroom but Ted had to focus on closing argument and did not realize Danny was still there.

The first thing Ted did was organize the papers on the table. He picked up his copy of the Malley questionnaire and that is when he got a good look at the paper below it, the Giffen retainer agreement. He held the questionnaire in his right hand and the agreement was on the table in front of him. Something struck him as odd. Something wasn't right but what was it? He looked at the questionnaire. He looked at the agreement. He laid the questionnaire down on the table next to the agreement. He picked them both up very close to his face to study them, turning his head very slowly from one document to the other. Then he set them down again. He could not believe what he was seeing. His heart began to race and he felt lightheaded. How could it possibly be? Danny Longer was watching him, totally puzzled.

46

Ted realized, at least for the next hour or so, he had to focus only on making the best summation possible. He knew his case went in well and he was close. His opponent had made some blunders along the way, the last one with Marcie Noonan the most spectacular. He studied his points for close knowing a good argument would probably nail an acquittal. Picker would go first but also rebut. Ted only got to speak to the jury in-between and that was always a source of consternation.

The jury filed back in, heard the Bailiff bellow, and were told to sit by the Judge.

"Ladies and gentlemen of the jury, the presentation of the evidence is concluded in this matter leaving only three things to do. The attorneys will do their summations, I will give you instruction on the law, and then you will retire to the jury room to deliberate.

Because the People have the burden of proof in a criminal case beyond a reasonable doubt, Mr. Picker will go first, followed by Mr. Chase, and then Mr. Picker has the last word by way of rebuttal. The sequence the attorneys must follow does not mean one is more important than the other. Gentlemen, are you ready to sum up?"

In unison, "Yes, Your Honor."

"Very well, Mr. Picker, you have the floor."

"Let me begin by thanking you for your service. The jury is what makes our criminal justice system the best in the world. The Prosecution certainly recognizes it is never easy to sit in judgment of another human being, but judge you must.

The evidence of guilt in this case is overwhelming. We must start with motive. I submit to you the motive in this case, revenge, is the oldest known to man. Remember what

Merrick said. After Grundy was acquitted, they were going to "punish" him. That was the exact word he used. Isn't it a bit ironic, ladies and gentlemen, they punished a man who was exonerated, yet they come to the very same courtroom seeking exoneration for themselves.

But I must say the defense in this case was ingenious; worthy of Perry Mason, a great TV lawyer. Counsel had to figure out a way around evidence of guilt as tall as a mountain. So why not admit you intended to commit the crime, which explains the evidence, but that some unknown, unseen, unheard culprit beat you to it. And make no mistake about that, ladies and gentlemen, there were a lot of names and theories cast about, but not one single piece of concrete physical evidence linking anyone to this crime other than Merrick and Townes. You heard about the mystery woman - Malley. You heard about a man named Crawford. You heard about patients although you were provided no names. BUT.... where is the evidence one of these may have done the crime? Where is the evidence, ladies and gentlemen? I tell you where. It is right at the feet of Merrick and Townes and only Merrick and Townes.

The motive is clear and compelling - no one could quarrel with that. Townes' pickup truck with the bent license plate was seen numerous times prior to August 28. The scrap of paper recorded the make and license number of Dr. Grundy's auto. The office brochure gave them the hours of operation. The murder weapon was a .45 caliber that had Townes' fingerprints on it. The gun residue from the murder weapon was found on Townes' hand. Only the footprints of these defendants were found at the scene of the murder. And, most compelling, ladies and gentlemen, they were caught in the act! The gun was still warm and the body still bleeding. The evidence points only at these two. Don't be fooled by the smoke and mirrors of the defense. This isn't TV, and Perry Mason is not here.

Now I am sure Terri Merrick was a beautiful young person and I am equally sure Dr. Grundy had issues, but you cannot let that sway your decision. A jury just like yourselves heard all the evidence against Dr. Grundy and said "not guilty." No man has the right to substitute his decision for that of a jury. No one. Not the judge, not the prosecution and not the family of Terri Merrick.

It is the evidence that carries the day and the evidence against these men is overwhelming. There is no other explanation for this gruesome murder.

You must vote to convict. Aggravated Murder. The defendants, Merrick and Townes, purposely, and with prior calculation and design, caused the death of Dr. Jerry Grundy on August 28, 2009. The evidence allows for no other explanation."

Picker sat down.

"Mr. Chase."

"May, it please the court. Ladies and gentlemen of the jury. Mr. Picker. At the very beginning of this trial, I told you this case was about intent to commit a crime and now you know it's true. Yes, the evidence IS overwhelming just as Mr. Picker said, but it is overwhelming evidence *only* of intent - *not* of an act. As Judge McCarthy will instruct you, causation is an essential element of murder in the first degree and causation is absent in this case. The evidence, especially from Mr. Picker's own witnesses, reveals Tom and Larry performed no act which produced Grundy's death; he was already dead when they entered the office. (Ted was paraphrasing the charge the jury would hear, adopting it as his own. When the jury would hear it from the Judge, their first thought would be, yes, that is what Mr. Chase told us.)

What is the proof beyond a reasonable doubt the prosecution wants you to rely upon? Mr. Picker mentions the residue on Larry's right hand as evidence of his guilt. But remember what Mr. McKay, the state's expert, had to say on the subject. Remember the "Oh, gee" moment he had? The residue was on the *inside* of Larry's palm which is consistent with Larry picking up the weapon *after* it had been discharged.

Ted walked over to the evidence table and picked up

the .45.

"Ladies and gentlemen, the shooter would have gunshot residue here (pointing to the outside of his thumb and first finger)." Then, switching the gun to his left hand and opening his right hand and showing his palm to the jury, "Not here." He set the gun down.

Mr. Picker argues Larry's fingerprints on the .45 are proof of guilt beyond a reasonable doubt. But what did he try to hide from you? The fact there was another fingerprint on the gun - that of a woman.

Mr. Picker mentions the bloody footprints as evidence of their guilt. But recall what Coroner Strothers, another witness for the state, had to say. It isn't likely. It assumes these men shot Grundy, waited at the scene as much as ten minutes, and then walked in the blood. He testified that made no sense and he was right - it doesn't make any sense.

The bullet holes in the wall are proof beyond a reasonable doubt? On this point, we agree. They *are* proof beyond a reasonable doubt - proof that Larry was *not* the shooter. A skilled marksman trained in the use of a .45 from point blank range would not have missed so wildly, spraying bullets all over the room," he said while looking at Jenks. Returning to the evidence table, he once again picked up the .45. He turned his back to the jury and he pretended to shoot the weapon, moving his arm wildly left to right and up and down. He walked back to the table, set the gun down, and then waited about fifteen seconds before he said another word - leaving total silence in the room.

"Marcie Noonan's evidence is proof beyond a reasonable doubt? Marcie Noonan's evidence casts *nothing but doubt* on the prosecution's case. Ms. Noonan told us there were a number of people who had it in for Grundy and she told us the sorry reason why. She produced a written death threat. She told us about a woman who gave a false address, a false phone number, and probably a false name just hours before Grundy was found. Ask yourself why someone would do such a thing. What was she up to? Then recall there was a woman's fingerprint on the murder weapon, a weapon which is so powerful, it would be hard for a woman to control." (For a split second, he thought about Laurie Giffen.)

What I find quite exceptional here is that this Prosecutor has the utter gall to stand before you and ask you to disregard this evidence. He is asking you to disregard the evidence which came from *his* witness. Then he says you must, because these people she speaks of are nowhere to be found. But why? Why weren't they found? They weren't found because no one was looking for them! He never bothered to ask Ms. Noonan about them. He admitted so much when he questioned her. How did he describe his own investigation? What was the word he used? 'Routine! Just going through the motions.' That's it! But now, somehow, it is no longer routine. To Mr. Picker, it has magically transformed into proof beyond a reasonable doubt!

Also, consider the circumstances of the arrest. Tom Merrick laid patiently waiting for his turn to be handcuffed. He said the officer "was only doing his job" and he realized "how badly things looked." But, ladies and gentlemen, even then, Tom had faith in the truth.

Ladies and gentlemen of the jury, Tom Merrick and Larry Townes still have faith in the truth. They realize the jam they put themselves in because of a bad decision they made but they know they did nothing to cause the death of Jerry Grundy. Frankly, I am amazed they still believe in the criminal justice system because it had already let them down once before.

Now Mr. Picker mentions Perry Mason and says he was a great lawyer. Ladies and gentlemen, Perry Mason was a *lousy* lawyer. He never had the key to any of his cases until the very end, after days of trial. Remember? Always on the very last day of trial, the courtroom doors would open and who would walk in? Tall, good looking, silver-haired Paul Drake. He would walk up to Perry, lean over, and whisper in his ear. It was only then that Perry had the key to his case and then, surprise.....Perry would win again! I always wondered why Berger didn't lock the damn doors! (Snicker)

If Paul Drake could come through those doors he would walk up to Mr. Picker here… and whisper in his ear. And do you know what he would say? He would say (in a stage whisper) let these men go. They are innocent. They have been through enough!

Ladies and gentlemen, the criminal justice system has let these men down once before. Don't let that happen again. They are innocent. Let them go!

Thank you."

Picker rose to give what turned out to be a weak rebuttal but Ted didn't hear a word of it. He was "all in," totally exhausted, "spent." His mind was still whirling over the documents he studied at the break and he just spent his last ounce of energy trying to get through close without falling down.

The Judge decided a brief recess would be in order before he would charge the jury. It was another NBA timeout.

47

"Now, ladies and gentlemen. I will instruct you on the law. It is your duty to decide the facts and the Court's duty to provide you with the law which you will apply to those facts."

McCarthy covered all the general tenets about what is and what is not evidence, the burden of proof beyond a reasonable doubt, all the legal "boilerplate." Then he focused on the offense.

"The Defendants are charged with aggravated murder. Before you can find the Defendants guilty, you must find beyond a reasonable doubt that on or about the 28th day of August, 2009, in Anders County, Ohio, the defendants were eighteen years old or older and purposely, and with prior calculation and design, caused the death of Dr. Jerry Grundy.

Prior calculation and design means that the purpose to cause the death was reached by a definite process of reasoning in advance of the homicide, which process of reasoning must have included a mental plan involving studied consideration of the method and the means with which to cause the death. To constitute prior calculation, there must have been sufficient time and opportunity for the planning of an act of homicide, and the circumstances surrounding the homicide must show a scheme designed to carry out the calculated decision to cause the death. No definite period of time must elapse and no particular amount of consideration must be given, but acting on the spur of the moment or after momentary consideration of the purpose to cause the death is not sufficient.

Now ladies and gentlemen of the jury, there has been information (here comes Mac's limiting instruction) presented to you by way of physical evidence and by way of admission that both Tom Merrick and Larry Townes did in fact intend to commit the murder of Dr. Jerry Grundy on or about the

204

evening of August 28, 2009. I must caution you in your deliberations. The *only* charge before you is aggravated murder which I just read to you. Should you find, from your review of the evidence, intent to commit murder but a lack of causation on the part of these defendants, you must acquit. Now I will read to you the definition of causation.

Causation is an essential element of the offense of aggravated murder. Cause is an act which directly produces the death of another and without which it would not have occurred.

After you retire to the deliberation room, the first order of business is to elect a foreperson. (Ted glanced at Elder.) This person's opinion has no greater weight by virtue of being so elected. The foreperson shall help conduct the deliberations and report to the Court with the verdict. Should you have a need for anything or should you need to contact the Court, the Bailiff here will show you how to accomplish that.

"Bailiff, please escort the panel back."

"All rise!"

And the jury was gone. And now, it was out of Ted's hands. He did the best he could do. Now he just had to wait.

He approached Tom and Larry and they both put their arms around his shoulders as though they were in a huddle of sorts. They acknowledged Ted gave it everything he had for the past week. If they went down, they were prepared for that but they knew Ted gave them a good chance.

Picker graciously shook hands and complimented Ted on his presentation and Ted did the same. Mike gave the Bailiff his cell number and so did Picker. The defense team then went across the street to wait. Ted invited Danny Longer to come with them.

When they got into the back booth, the discussion began, as Ted knew it would, about whether it was good for the defendants if the jury is out for a long or short period of time. It then turned to a review of the highs and lows of the last week. Ted, however, was not thinking about the trial in any manner. He was wrestling with whether or not he should show the documents to Mac and he ultimately decided against it. He decided he would go out to St. Joseph's alone, first thing in the morning, but he really didn't even know why.

Early afternoon turned to dinnertime and dinners were ordered. The team was starting to get just a bit concerned over the time elapsing as it was generally decided the shorter the deliberations the better. Ted knew better. He knew the amount of time did not make a difference. He was thinking of Laurie Giffen.

About midway through their salads, Mike's phone rang. He looked up and said, "Time to go." Ted's heart skipped a few beats.

The emotions the criminal trial lawyer experiences during this time, sitting in Court, knowing the verdict is in and waiting to hear it...are almost incapable of description. Ted was eventually going home to his family. Where were Tom Merrick and Larry Townes going to go? Second guessing, retrying parts of the case, worry over the clients. Hoping, yet worrying, at the same time.

The courtroom was standing room only. Danny lost his first row seat so Ted had him join them at counsel table.

Judge McCarthy came out but the Bailiff was not there to yell. It didn't matter. Everyone stood. "Please sit. We have a verdict. Mr. Picker, anything before I bring the jury in?"

"No. Your Honor."

"Mr. Chase?"

"Nothing, Your Honor."

The Bailiff led the parade. "All Rise!" Even louder than normal.

Everyone was looking for the person holding the papers. It was Lander. Elder was unchanged. Ted thought he saw a small smile on Jenks' face.

"Has the jury reached a verdict?"

Lander stood, "We have Your Honor."

"In the matter of Tom Merrick, aggravated murder, what is your verdict?"

"Not guilty, Your Honor."

The courtroom erupted. The gavel started. Ted slumped just a little. Mac had his hand on Ted's shoulder. Given the evidence though, Ted was always more concerned about Larry. It seemed like forever before there was enough quiet in the room to proceed.

"In the matter of Larry Townes, aggravated murder, what is your verdict?"

"Not guilty, Your Honor." Bedlam. The Judge didn't seem to care much this time, he let it go.

Tom and Larry embraced and then the two of them embraced with Ted. The nightmare was over. They were going home. Ted felt the weight of the world off his shoulders. He also felt like he aged five years in the last five days.

McCarthy addressed the court for the last time. "This concludes the matter of The People versus Thomas Merrick and Larry Townes. Gentlemen, you are free to go."

Picker shook hands with Ted, gathered up his materials and left the courtroom as soon as he could. He was trapped by *The News* reporters in the corridor on the way out.

48

The front page of the morning *News* had no story other than Tom's and Larry's acquittal. There were three pictures including one of Picker. Picker was quoted as saying the investigation, as far as the state was concerned, was concluded. They were closing the file. They had the killers but a jury saw it otherwise. To continue to pursue it would be a waste of the taxpayers' money.

On the second page appeared a headline reporting that Priem Transport Logistics had made a three million dollar donation to Mothers Against Drunk Driving. There was a picture of Priem's CEO and the local MADD chapter president holding the check. The reporter lauded the trucking company for its generosity and "civic awareness." The article heralded the company as an example for others to follow to "give back to the community."

Ted was in his car on the way to St. Joseph's by 9:30 that morning. His mind was going non-stop and he left the CD player off. He looked at it from every conceivable angle but he couldn't figure it out. It still made no sense to him. How? He met Lindie at the desk, "Good morning."

"Good morning." She nodded toward Laurie's room. Ted could hear the musical bed even from the hallway.

When he rounded the door, there she was, unchanged, staring, rocking. But before he entered the room, Ted noticed there was a newspaper on the bed in front of her. He stared for a bit and then he returned to Lindie.

"Lindie, what's with the paper?"

"Mr. Chase, I don't know. It was the strangest thing. She shuffled out to the reception area here, this time completely on her own. It took her forever but when she noticed the paper she picked it off the coffee table right here and took it with her. I made a note for myself to tell Dr. Berringer when he got in."

Ted walked back down the hallway. Still "music." He slowly walked to the foot of the bed and got in-between the bed and the wall Laurie had been staring at for weeks. Her eyes were vacant, dead. He went around to the side of the bed so he could get as close to her as he could. He pulled the documents from his briefcase and laid them on top of the newspaper. He leaned over, his face within six inches of Laurie's. He said, "Laurie, I know. I know about Lucille Malley." No response, no change, no acknowledgement.

"But tell me, how did you know? How did you know it was Grundy who put Malone on the road?"

Silence. The bed became still. Her head tilted ever so slightly. The eyes appeared to wake. An almost imperceptible Mona Lisa smile crept across her lips. She looked directly into Ted's eyes. She raised her right hand and tenderly pulled him closer so that his ear was within inches of her mouth and he could feel the warmth of her breath. In a barely audible whisper, she slowly said, "My sister's name is Marcie."

It was Ted's turn to smile. Ted looked deep into her eyes and then he kissed her on the forehead. He left the documents on the bed.

Ted left St. Joseph's totally at peace. He and Dorie had a plane to catch.

"What the hell do you care? You bitch!" Granville Tethers didn't see the danger in what they were doing and this was his subtle way of letting his wife know her comments weren't appreciated. The two alcoholics were in the rattletrap old Buick going too fast heading from West Canaan to Crawford to pay yet another traffic fine. It was only 2:00 and they both had already had too much to drink. At least Shirley Tethers appreciated there may be some risk in appearing in Municipal Court in the condition they were in but Granville Tethers was clueless. He was still incensed about having to fork over one hundred and forty dollars to pay the goddam fine.

Stupidly, Shirley plodded on, "Granny, It's just that someone might........."

"Just shut up will you! I'm tired of your shit!"

"But Granny..."

Granny let his backhand fly and caught her just above the lip on the left side of her face. It was almost the exact same place he had caught her the night before and now inflicted a bruise on top of the one that was already there.   It was precisely at that moment the Buick entered the intersection against the light and was broad-sided from the left by the SUV.

The SUV hit so squarely into the driver side door the vehicles did not spin; the large SUV rather just plowed the beat up old sedan straight down the road. Glass was flying everywhere inside the car. The left side of Granville Tether's head was whiplashed into the door frame and Tethers lost consciousness for a few seconds. An incredibly large knot immediately appeared on his left temple and by the time the cars came to rest, Tethers was both disoriented and enraged.

Shirley was tossed inside the car but escaped without more than some strains and minor lacerations. The Buick was small and tight inside and, when the cars came to rest, the only way out now was through the passenger door. Tethers started pushing his wife out the door and then did the best he could to climb over the console to get out himself. He had little control over his body and it was clear, when he finally exited the vehicle, that he had pissed himself. He fell out the door and stumbled first to the left and then back to the right; the combination of alcohol and the blow to the head robbing him of any coordination. He fell to his knees, smacking both lips on the pavement. Then he vomited.

When he finally got to his feet, Granville Tethers could not get to the big silver SUV fast enough. "You mother," he yelled as he ran/stumbled toward the vehicle.

Young Larry Tehan Jr. was slow to extricate himself from the large car as Tethers ran toward him. The driver side door was buckled so it took some force to get it open. Larry was covered in the white dust of the air bag and his face was lacerated in several places. When he finally got erect, all six foot six, two hundred and thirty pounds, Tethers began to slow his advance. Tethers, five foot seven and one hundred and forty pounds soaking wet, immediately realized he would have to rethink a bit. He stopped about ten feet from the nineteen year old and was content to continue his verbal attack, smelling of alcohol, vomit and piss.

Shirley had tried to grab her husband but he was like a wild animal so she just stood to the right of the car and watched events unfold. She appreciated the mismatch sooner than Tethers did and thought to herself this was not going to end well. Her emotions were mixed because she sometimes dreamed of someone coming to her aid to teach her husband a lesson.

Shirley Tethers was an alcoholic abused by an alcoholic. She stayed with him because she had no one to turn to and no place to go for relief. Alcohol governed both their lives; it was truly the only thing they had left in common.

They were a pathetic couple hopelessly ensnared by their addictions.

50

It was Thanksgiving and over a year since Ted had left Carrothers. The family always spent this holiday together at the lake and the added bonus this year was Mac had joined them and was staying over until Saturday. There were eight of them altogether which made for a full house since the cottage was small. It made for a great time, everyone crowded together truly enjoying each other's company. A fire was dancing in the wood burner and the whole place filled with the aroma of roasting turkey and burning pine.

The Chase family had much to be thankful for. Ted's transition out of the firm to his own practice went without a hitch thanks to Mac's referral of the Giffen case. The Grundy murder trial ended favorably and brought with it instant notoriety which led to more business. Ted was his own boss and could shape his practice any way he desired.

Ted and Dorie decided to go for a walk around their end of the lake while Dorie's Mom put the finishing touches on the meal. They were especially interested in a rather large log home under construction about a half mile down the road.

The site for the new home was well chosen. The house sat lower than the level of the road on a slope down to the water and was situated right at the "crook' in the lake. The entire back wall of windows provided an unbelievable view of the length of the lake going to the west. The sunsets would be fantastic, thought Ted, and he was sure that had governed the site selection. The large two-tiered deck actually extended over the water and would provide the illusion one was on a boat. They walked around inside the half-built home and Ted guessed it was somewhere in the neighborhood of six thousand square feet.

Dorie's Mom was an excellent cook and the dinner, complete with her special recipe candied yams, was consumed eagerly. Ted wanted to savor every bite, every moment with his family and best friend, and every lick and dance of the fire. He loved long holiday weekends. Wednesday, he remembered, he would begin the defense of Charlie Arken in the matter of Raycher - v- Arken.

51

You always knew where the county lines were in this part of Ohio. Most of the counties were square-shaped and the roads were laid out in a grid. If someone were to tell you he was at the intersection of County Roads A and 2, you would know right where he was without even looking at a map. However, more often than not, where the counties came together, there usually was a jog in the road; one county's road never quite matched up with the other's. And that's right where the accident occurred - right at the jog in the road.

Ted was defending local farmer, Charlie Arken, who was driving his pick up pulling two grain wagons eastbound on Crawford County 2 heading toward Anders. Charlie was a hard working farmer who worked his own fields and rented several acres from other folks, usually widows of farmers or longtime friends too old to work their own fields. Sometimes it was for so much an acre, sometimes for a share of the crop - almost always corn and soy beans. Right at the jog in the road, he intended to turn left and head north on A to one of his rented plots. He actually started his turn when, out of the corner of his eye, he saw the westbound motorcycle. He stopped. He never came in contact with the bike, but the cyclist could not negotiate the "leftward" jog in the road, went straight, and ended up in the ditch. The biker's name was Bobbie Raycher, a six foot ten inch soon-to-be college freshman who was returning from his summer job at the local LaChoy food plant. He racked up his left knee pretty badly and he was the plaintiff in the case.

Ted Chase of Rosenthall and Chase Co LPA, aka Rosenthal Chase, was up against a well-known local plaintiff's lawyer by the name of Jeff Hutton. Jeff was in his early forties. He was a large man himself, but always looked like he had just gotten out of bed no matter the time of day. He needed a tailor and some lessons in personal grooming. He was thrice married and had the reputation within the county as being quite the trial lawyer. Despite the length of time he had been practicing, this was Ted's first time up against Hutton and he needed to send a message. One of the things he knew about Hutton was that he would never be described as a "workaholic" even in trial. Indeed, the first day of trial, he waltzed in wearing a rumpled corduroy jacket and carrying a completely blank legal pad.

Bobbie Raycher's allegation was the accident ruined a certain career in the NBA and Ted thought this interesting, to say the least. Bobbie had never played one minute of organized basketball at any scholastic level; however he had played a few intramural games. Ted was sure young Raycher never considered a career in the sport until he hurt his knee and hooked up with Mr. Hutton. With Raycher's history thus far, Ted was sure no jury would buy what Hutton was selling. He wondered why a lawyer would even consider such a strategy, however, it was well known that Hutton didn't let the facts get in the way of his cases. As much as Hutton was a bit of a blowhard and somewhat full of himself, Ted still liked him. He had a great sense of humor and a dry wit.

The trial did not get underway until Wednesday afternoon. It took the afternoon to seat the jury and the next order of business was a jury view of the accident scene Thursday morning. Both plaintiff and defendant had agreed that, due to the unique nature of the intersection, taking the panel out to see it would be beneficial. The judge agreed and everyone was trucked out to the scene in rented vans.

Well, sometimes the oddest things occur during a trial and this was one for the books. Ted's defense was threefold. First of all, the intersection was full of loose cinders on the outside edges which motorcyclists have to avoid at all costs. Secondly, he thought most cyclists would be leaning left into the intersection to keep up their speed and "glide" through (thus coming closer than necessary to Charlie's little caravan.)

Third, Raycher was simply going too fast. He came to rest in the ditch more than fifty feet from the center of the intersection. For most of that distance, he was airborne.

While the jury was looking at all the angles of the intersection under the watchful eye of the bailiff (no discussion was permitted), a motorcyclist approaching from the east at a pretty good rate of speed came gliding through the intersection. He leaned into it and actually went left of center to maneuver his way without slowing down. (In truth, most motorcyclists looked forward to these little jogs in the otherwise straight, flat roads.) Ted was standing right next to Jeff and they both saw the biker coming. They both started to laugh but tried to hide it from the jurors. Before the biker got to the intersection, Jeff, almost like a ventriloquist and so only Ted could hear him, said, "How much did you pay this guy coming?"

When the biker cut the corner through the intersection, and the jury saw him go left of the center line, the lawyers couldn't contain their laughter. Ted said, "I didn't have to pay her anything. Hey honey, I'll stop and get the milk on the way home." This really busted Hutton up. They both lost it. Some of the jurors laughed as well just looking at the both of them. The lawyers knew they would have to start all over: this panel was compromised. They were certain His Honor would not be happy.

Next time Ted would see Hutton, it would be no laughing matter.

52

Rosenthall, Chase was only an "infant" of a law partnership, all of six months old. Its genesis was an office sharing arrangement between real estate specialist Jay Rosenthall and Carrothers refugee Ted Chase. The arrangement worked out so well, the two lawyers entered into a partnership. They were soon joined by fellow Carrothers escapees Larry Tehan, a corporate lawyer, and Greg Rothgery, a specialist in probate and estate law. With Ted doing 100% of the litigation, both civil and criminal, a well-rounded firm had evolved in a very short time. Of counsel to the firm was Ted's good friend and former trial practice instructor, James McIlvaine - Mac, who still taught at the law school.

Kurt Carrothers Co LPA was imploding under the threat of a malpractice claim arising out of Phil Carrothers' inept handling of Giffen-v-Priem Transport. Both Priem and its insurer, Equity National, had put the firm on notice to their claim but, as yet, had not filed suit. There was ten million in malpractice coverage, however, the liability was eighteen million more. The "pillars" of the firm, its equity partners, were leaving and, like a building without pillars, the firm was imploding. The equity partners would be on the hook for any shortfall should a suit be filed and liability found. The brothers Carrothers had been neither seen nor heard from in over four weeks.

As Carrothers was shrinking, prime office space on the fifth floor was opening up and, of course, Rosenthall Chase had an immediate need. The owners of the building couldn't move fast enough to reconfigure part of the space to suit their needs and keep a good tenant. Rosenthall Chase went with six good-sized offices (two for future expansion) and two conference rooms. There was a small kitchen and six cubicles for the support staff. Out of the dust…..

Ted got the call from Equity's counsel that Friday.

"Ted, this is Frank Consul. I'm representing Equity National. They've asked me to look into possibly filing a legal malpractice action against your former firm over the Giffen debacle and I wanted to speak with you about that."

"What can I do for you?"

"Well, for starters, I have a concern regarding the agreement that was entered into between your client and Priem."

"Let me guess. You have looked at the confidentiality provisions."

"That's right and we're going to have to ask your client to waive."

"Frank, let me give you a little background. My client did not want any confidentiality clause but Priem and Equity demanded it for their protection, not ours. Now you're saying they want Laurie to waive a provision she didn't want in the first place."

"Well…."

"If you look at paragraph eight of the agreement, I think it was paragraph eight, you'll see we incorporated a liquidated damages clause into the contract in the event of a breach. If memory serves, the figure was five hundred thousand. Paragraph nine, I recall, deals with waivers and says the information can only be divulged if both parties agree. I don't have the agreement right here in front of me, but I believe my memory is correct. It wasn't that long ago."

"What you're saying is that you want to get paid."

"What I'm saying is that these terms were for the protection of your client, but since they are mutual, that is right, they'll have to pay. Assuming a half million for a breach, I would recommend to my clients the figure of three hundred thousand."

"You're not serious."

"Yes, Frank, I'm dead serious."

219

"Look Ted, I could file the suit, join your clients, and ask the trial court for a ruling."

"Yes, you could, but as soon as you file suit, you've breached the agreement, which brings the entire amount of liquidated damages into play. That would be a gutsy move on your part, betting an additional two hundred thousand dollars on a guess at what the ruling might be. On the other hand, for three hundred, you take all the guesswork out of it. You would have to invest three hundred thousand with us to take your shot at the twenty-eight million you're after. And I will tell you right now, if you have me testify as to how the whole thing came about, you have a fantastic shot at the whole amount. That, I know for sure. But, obviously, I cannot speak with you without an agreed waiver."

"Ted, you're holding us up."

"No, Frank, I'm negotiating on behalf of a client just as you are. You started from the position you wanted a waiver for nothing. I'm saying the price is three hundred thousand. Equity needs consent from us whereas we need nothing from them. We really don't care one way or the other whether you recover from Carrothers. Why don't you think about it and let me know? In the meantime, I'll confirm the numbers with my client. I'll recommend three hundred."

"Confirming" with his client meant he would, for the first time since the trial, have to speak with Marcie Noonan who had her sister, Laurie, move in with her after she was discharged from St. Joseph's. From Mac, Ted had learned that Laurie was progressing well, still under the care of Dr. Berringer and under the protective eye of her older sister Marcie. Laurie's guardianship had been transferred to her. He called her right after hanging up with Consul.

"Marcie, Ted Chase, how have you been?"

"Fine, Ted, how about you?"

"Fine. How's Laurie?"

"She's doing nicely. Coming along."

220

"Marcie, something has come up and I wanted to discuss it with you. It relates to the lawsuit and the agreement to end it."

"Oh?"

"Priem and their insurer are contemplating the filing of a malpractice action against Carrothers and they need us to waive our confidentiality. I've had some preliminary discussions with their lawyer, and I told him I would recommend accepting three hundred thousand to waive. They really need me as a witness to document their claim. It is not worth three hundred, however they are looking for a twenty-eight million dollar payday so I thought three hundred would be a good number. In the event of a breach of the agreement, we would have been entitled to five hundred."

"Ted, if three hundred is the number, we would still want you to take a fee just like before and that would mean Laurie would end up with two, right?"

"In that event, then yes."

"Didn't we have something for MADD before?"

"Yes."

"Okay, let's do this. We will go for the three. After your fee, that would be one for Laurie and one for MADD. Does that work?"

"Sure. If they won't go for three, I think we should simply tell them we won't waive. They really need us here."

"Sounds like a plan to me. Any idea when you'll know for sure?"

"I'll call them and give them a 'drop dead' date for two weeks."

"Ted, I will have to check back with you. Laurie and I may be in our new digs by then."

"Oh?"

"Yes. We're building a home up at the lake."

221

53

Rosenthall Chase was doing well. All four partners had already-established practices and were able to provide an array of services for their clients. Jay Rosenthall's expertise in real estate helped Tehan's corporate clients from time to time. Rothgery's probate practice also benefited. Of Course, Ted's expertise in litigation was beneficial to all.

Later that afternoon, Larry Tehan entered Ted's office and closed the door behind him. He had a grave look on his face which got Ted's attention right away. Before he could say anything, Ted looked at him and said, "Larry, what's wrong?"

"It's my son, Ted, I think we may have a problem."

Larry was a widower; he and his son had been "on their own" for the better part of eight years - even before Larry had joined the Carrothers law firm. Ted knew that Larry had had his hands full raising his boy with no help.

"Oh?"

"This past summer, as he was on the way to one of his ballgames, he was involved in a traffic accident. Junior swears up and down the other guy ran the light and caused the accident but, of course, the guy and his wife said otherwise. Anyway, after the collision, the guy ran over to Junior's car and was trying to start something..... until Junior got out of the car - he is six foot six and goes about two thirty. I guess the other driver was a bit of a munch. But the guy ended up in the hospital. My son swears he never laid a hand on him."

"So he has filed a lawsuit?"

"No, he died two weeks ago."

The law recognizes various degrees of criminal culpability. If Larry's son is being truthful, he has no
222

responsibility whatsoever for this fellow's death. If the accident caused the death, there could possibly be a finding of manslaughter if Junior's at fault. If Junior purposely harmed him and that's what caused his death, the "price of poker" goes up exponentially - some degree of murder could be "in play." Larry was right to be very concerned.

"Larry, what do we know about the other driver?"

"Not much. His name was Granville Tethers and he was from West Canaan. From what I know - kind of a 'ne'er-do-well.' Wife's name is Shirley. She's already got a lawyer."

"Do we know who?"

"Jeff Hutton."

"Did Hutton contact you?"

"Yes, he sent a letter advising us of his representation and asking us to refer the matter to our insurance carrier. You know, the standard stuff."

"Have you heard from the prosecutor?"

"They want to set up an interview next week but I'm not sure that's a good idea."

"Who called you?"

"Bonner."

"Larry, has your boy been in any trouble before?"

"Ted, one thing you'll have to understand is that Junior suffers from something called fetal alcohol effect."

"Your son is an alcoholic?"

"No, Ted, his mother was and she drank when she was carrying him. He doesn't have the full-blown syndrome with the facial features and all, but his conduct his whole life will be governed by it."

Ted had no knowledge of any of this.

"How does it affect his conduct?"

"For one thing, he has a very difficult time controlling his impulses."

"So he has had some trouble?"

"Yes."

That was not something Ted wanted to hear. "Larry, you'll have to get me something so I can read up on this."

"That will be no problem. After he was diagnosed, my wife got her hands on every piece of literature addressing it. I still have it all - boxes. Ted, my immediate concern is responding to Bonner."

Ted thought a bit about Junior's mother and how she must have felt when the diagnosis was made. No wonder she researched it like she did. "Well, his request puts us at risk right off the bat. If we decide to meet with him, to some degree we play out our hand right at the start. The danger is we go that route and he still decides to prosecute."

"But if we stonewall him, he'll figure we have something to hide and he'll get even more interested won't he?"

"Yes. Larry, let's do this. I need more time to get my arms around this before we make that kind of a decision. The first thing I want to do is talk with Larry Jr. and read up on this condition he has. Also, there is a traffic crash report somewhere we need to get a copy of. Why don't you ask Mike to get it for us? I will wait until Thursday or so next week and then call Bonner and advise him of my representation. I'm sure he will still want that interview and we can "push" that out to the following week. I will just tell him that I need to get up to speed. He is reasonable. He will understand. Keep in mind, if he thought he had enough to go forward already, he probably would not be concerned about getting an interview. Since the widow Tethers has already retained Hutton, my guess is he may be asserting some pressure here. His personal injury case gets a helluva lot easier if there is a finding of some level of guilt. Can Junior, that's how you call him, Junior?"

"Yes."

"Can he come in Monday to talk with me?"

"Yes."

"Larry, get me the best two or three treatments you have on this, will you?"

"I will have them here before the end of the day."

54

Over the weekend, Ted read everything Larry gave him on the subject of fetal alcohol and what an eye-opener it was. The seriousness of the condition and its prevalence within our society made Ted question why more attention had not been focused upon it. Ted learned the disease manifested itself in different manner and degree depending upon the amount of alcohol consumed by the pregnant mother and at what time during the pregnancy she drank. The most severe manifestation of the condition was Fetal Alcohol Syndrome (FAS) diagnosed, in part, by looking at the facial features of the child; small head circumference, smaller eye openings, flat midface, small chin, thin upper lip, short upturned nose, and a flat elongated philtrum (the grooves above the lip.) What could not be seen was the smaller, mis-shaped brain.

According to Larry, Junior did not suffer from the full-blown syndrome but suffered from FAE, Fetal Alcohol Effect. The facial features were not present but the damage to the brain became evident at about age three and would govern Junior's mental/emotional function throughout his entire life. Larry told Ted he will never forget how the doctor gave them the diagnosis.

Because Junior did not have the facial features of his disease, most would simply perceive him as an unruly child. They themselves would mistakenly be perceived as failed parents incapable of controlling their child. The doctor said, "The good news is you have a beautiful little boy. The bad news is that he is a beautiful little boy - his disease is not evident. People will not understand."

The doctor explained that Junior would always have difficulty translating hearing into doing, thinking into saying, reading into speaking and feelings into words. Since the brain is malformed, links are missing and learning happens in isolated clumps, seldom, if ever, connected. For example, Junior may learn how to count from one to one hundred but would be incapable of adding two plus three and coming up with the right answer. He will live his life lacking the ability to generalize and make associations, to compare and contrast, and to identify patterns. He will have problems with basic concepts such as time and money. Since the ability to process information is encumbered, he will usually act on his first impulse. The example the doctor gave was this: Consider you are waiting in a parking lot for a space to open and when it does, another car pulls in right in front of you without waiting a second. Your first reaction is to say I am going to catch up to the guy and beat the tar out of him. Your second thought is that you will simply give him a piece of your mind. Your last thought, the one you act on, is that it is just a damned parking spot so what difference does it make? If you suffered from FAS or FAE, you would act on your first thought, being unable to think it through.

Junior was very hard to raise. FAE kids mature much slower than their counterparts so school was not a good experience for Junior; the other kids thought him slow and somewhat odd and avoided him whenever possible, that is, until he went out for Little League. When he had to be disciplined or was told he could not have something he wanted, he would go into a rage and, indeed, Larry had the marks to show for it. He would also have frequent "meltdowns" when he became frustrated with a task - sometimes a very simple one. The Tehan's were advised to buy a punching bag and hang it in Junior's room and then direct him to take his frustrations out on the bag rather than them. Larry did not like that idea, so instead, bought two dozen baseballs and set up a batting cage in the backyard. Eventually, Junior learned to go out behind the garage and express his rage by throwing baseballs at a target sixty feet away. Larry had no idea Junior would grow to be six foot six and one day be capable of hurling a baseball ninety-eight

226

miles an hour. Ironically, his incredible talent was born out of his disability. Now enrolled in junior college, he was on the radar screen of several major league ball clubs. Larry was incredibly encouraged but wondered how it was going to play out, given the demons Junior's mother had bestowed upon him.

Ted learned that FAS/FAE adults almost always experience problems with finances, employment and relationships. He also learned there was no cure for the disease. The damage is permanent and the best thing you could do was make sure there was always someone there for him who understood and could help him deal with it. The last thing he learned is the disease usually goes undiagnosed; not too many mothers admit to drinking during their pregnancy. He thought back to the many criminal defendants he had represented over the years and wondered how many of them were undiagnosed.

After his crash course, Ted wondered whether the disease had ever been successfully raised as a defense to a criminal charge. He thought back to his criminal law professor's instruction on the concept of mens rea - "guilty mind." Though hard for a layman to understand, a defendant is not guilty in the absence of mens rea: if he were incapable of forming the intent, he is innocent regardless of the act. He would have his paralegal, Mike, do the research.

55

First thing Monday morning, Junior arrived at the offices of Rosenthall Chase and Ted saw he was as represented; tall, athletic and good looking. He and Ted met alone in a conference room. Young Tehan had large hands, long fingers and a firm grip.

"Your Dad says you can bring it pretty good."

"I do okay."

"Southpaw?"

"Yep."

"How high can you get it?"

"High nineties."

"What else you got?"

"Decent change-up. Slider and curveball need a lot of work. Where I'm at now, I just throw the heater past 'em."

"Who is looking at you?"

"Oakland, Detroit, Minnesota and Pittsburgh seem to show the most interest. Atlanta."

"Tryouts?"

"Yea, all of them."

"What about the Tribe?"

"Nope, haven't heard from them."

"You're kidding! Right here in their back yard and they haven't contacted you yet?"

"Nope."

"I think your Dad should contact them."

"Well the draft is next month so we'll see."

"You have to be excited."

"I was until this stuff all started."

Ted hadn't considered that aspect of the matter. Junior's chance at a baseball career may also hang in the balance here. Most people did not understand the amount of time, effort and resources a ball club had to invest to develop a pitcher. Every major league franchise had to choose wisely. Any type of delay in young Tehan's development could kill his chances.

"Junior, tell me what happened. This woman, this Shirley Tethers is saying you ran the light and then you beat the hell out of her husband."

Ted felt Junior's tension level rising confirming his recent research into his affliction. He was very interested to see his reaction.

"I did no such thing. The guy was drunk and so was she. He was the one who ran the light and caused the accident. He came running at me all covered in dirt and vomit and urine and he called me every name in the book. The guy reeked. He was a little shit and he backed off as soon as I got out of the car."

"How close did he get to you?"

"I dunno, eight, ten feet."

"Did you see any marks on him?"

"Yes sir, he had a knot on his head the size of a golf ball. Both lips were bleeding."

"Did you hit him?"

"No sir. I never laid a hand on him. I didn't have to. He never came closer than eight or ten feet."

"Junior, don't take this the wrong way, but I read up on fetal alcohol."

"Yea, and you're thinking I lost it and beat the shit out of him."

"Impulse control is an issue with fetal alcohol."

"Mr. Chase, I have had to live with it for nineteen years so please don't tell me about what you read in a book."

"Fair enough. But tell me how it was that you kept it together."

"I can't. There is no explanation. Maybe it was the effect of the crash, the airbag going off.....I don't know....I can't explain it. Maybe it was that everything happened so

229

fast. It seemed like he was on me and I was still trying to figure out what had just happened. I know I have put Dad through hell sometimes but no one can predict when the meltdowns come. When they come, I cannot stop, just ask him. No one has come up with a way to help me or any other kid out of it. My Dad told you about the batting cage?"

"Yes."

"That is just a diversion, not a solution. All I can tell you is that if this lady is saying I hit her husband, she's lying. Mr. Chase, if I had gone off on him, he would have been dead right then and there. Trust me. I don't know what I'm doing when I'm in it, but I know the results. It's not like I'm a second grader anymore."

"Where were you going at the time?"

"I had a game."

"Were you in your uniform already?"

"Yes sir."

"You say this Tethers fellow ran up to you?"

"More like he stumbled."

"Where was his wife when all this was going on?"

"She was on the other side of the car."

"How close?"

"I dunno, thirty, thirty-five feet."

"Was she involved in any way, say anything?"

"No. Not until her husband shut up."

"You believe they were both drunk?"

"Definitely. You could smell it on both of them."

"You came close enough to her to smell her?"

"Yes. After her idiot husband finished his tirade, she walked over to him and grabbed him by the elbow."

"What did he do?"

"He collapsed."

"Were there any witnesses to any of this?"

"I don't think so. I had to call 911."

"Junior, your Dad tells me you have been in some trouble before."

"Yes."

"Because of the fetal alcohol?"

"Yes. Kids at school used to pick on me because of it. They didn't understand. Every once in awhile, someone would go a little too far and I would wig out and they usually ended up on the short end of it. But they stopped picking on me in the seventh grade. I had grown quite a bit that summer and I was becoming a pretty good pitcher. My teammates were the best. The coach had my parents come in and talk with the team about it so they all understood and they became like a lifeline. They also helped my other classmates understand it better. They stood up for me. I had never had that before."

"But you still have episodes from time to time, even now?"

"Yes."

"Anything there may be some kind of record on - at college or anything with law enforcement?"

"I don't think so. Dad could probably answer that question a lot better."

"Okay. Junior, you're sure Tethers ran the light?"

"No question about it but it will probably come down to her word against mine."

"And you never touched him."

"Never."

"Okay. I'll talk with your Dad and we'll figure out what to do with Mr. Bonner. Have you talked with anyone else about this?"

"Well some of my teammates were concerned and asked me some stuff."

"How long ago was that?"

"Right after it happened."

"What did you say to them?"

"About the same as we just discussed - how the guy ran the light and then was a real jerk about it."

"Junior, other than your father and me, you can't talk with anyone about any of this from here on out. This is very important and I need to know you understand that."

"I understand."

"Good. If any of those ball clubs have any questions about any of this, you have them call me and I'll address any concerns they may have. That okay?"

"Thanks Mr. Chase. So how does all this look to you?"

"Junior, I have been doing this for longer than I care to admit but one thing I know for sure: the truth is the truth and it always comes out. Based upon what you told me, we should be just fine. We just need to get through the system. Okay?"

"Okay. Thanks."

Ted was impressed with his new client. He was beginning to appreciate the hurdles Junior had overcome and he envied him: he had a legitimate shot at Ted's dream - playing major league baseball.

Later that day, Larry Sr. and Ted sat down in Ted's office to discuss the matter.

"Ted, how does it look?"

"If everything is as Junior says, there should be no problem."

"Well, Hutton isn't wasting any time. Got this by certified mail this morning."

Larry handed Ted the complaint and Ted began his review. It requested both compensatory and punitive damages alleging Tethers' death was the result of Junior's intentional act. It was exactly what Ted expected to see, just not this soon.

"Larry, who is your insurer?"

"Equity National."

"Larry, because of the request for punitives, we are going to have to be involved in the civil suit. Equity will send a letter declining representation and there will be no coverage if this is found to be intentional."

"Okay."

"The fact Hutton filed so soon may really help us here - if Bonner seeks an indictment."

"How so?"

"Because we can start discovery in the civil case right away. We can have this Shirley Tethers in a deposition within a matter of weeks and Bonner will be powerless to stop us. We can put her under oath and ask her anything we want. You can be sure Bonner will engineer the criminal case so we don't get a preliminary hearing but we won't need one."

"What about Bonner's request for a meeting?"

"Based on this civil filing, we may want to tell him we're not interested."

"In the civil case, they'll want to depose Junior though, won't they?"

"Yes, and as long as he tells it like it is, we'll be fine."

"What is our next move?"

"Well, we answer the complaint right away and include a counterclaim because it was Tethers who caused the accident. Might as well get the civil matter underway as soon as possible so we can get that deposition before Bonner even knows about it. I'll have Mike take a stab at a first draft of the answer, counterclaim and notice of deposition."

"Thanks Ted."

"No problem Larry. You have a fine young man there. He has overcome quite a bit."

"Yes, we know."

"Hey, what is with the Tribe? How come they are not all over Junior?"

"Good question. We haven't quite figured that one out yet."

A week later, Ted got a call from Frank Consul, Equity's counsel.

"Ted, Frank Consul."

"Hello Frank."

"Ted, calling about two matters. On the Carrothers thing, Equity is offering one hundred thousand for the waiver. Let your client know and give me a call. The Tethers complaint has been referred to me for representation too. I'll guess someone from you firm will want to enter an appearance due to the punitives"

"Yes. And a counterclaim as well. Larry Tehan did nothing other than run into the side of a drunk who ran the light."

"I understand from Hutton, Bonner may be weighing in on this."

"Yes, most likely, due to this woman's allegations."

"What is your take on all this?"

"A ne'er-do-well who thinks her ship has come in. She's got Hutton. I'm sure he's filling her head with visions of a big payout. But having Hutton on the other side is good for us - he won't work the thing up."

"Well, I was concerned about the criminal side of it but if you're on this, that will be your problem, not mine - protecting his rights."

"Yes."

"Hutton told me you folks have already contacted him to get dates for a deposition of the widow."

"Yes."

"Why so soon?"

"Didn't see a need to wait. The guy is dead so there won't be much paper discovery here - don't need any medical records other than what was generated after the accident. Thought it would be good to get to this Tethers woman sooner rather than later." Ted did not want to share any other information on that score. Consul was only concerned about the personal injury suit so his question didn't surprise Ted.

Mike arranged the Tethers deposition to take place in two weeks. Normally, in a civil case of this magnitude, a death case, the defendant would not want a deposition until he has secured all the preliminary information through the exchange of paper discovery. It sometimes took months to identify and secure all the necessary medical records and other documents. Given Ted's strategy, those efforts would be contemporaneous in this case; he wanted widow Tether's testimony under oath before Bonner did anything. In the two weeks before the deposition, Mike would do what he could to secure the

234

available "public" information about the deponent that was out there - licensing, criminal records, internet information, facebook - that sort of thing. He would do the same regarding her dead husband.

Ted needed to act quickly. He called Bonner to acknowledge his request for a "sit-down", but he did that only to buy time - he was never going to let it happen. Good lawyering sometimes meant one had to engage in "diversionary tactics." There was nothing wrong with that as long you made no misrepresentations. Ted simply told Jack Bonner he needed more time to get his arms around the matter and after that, Ted would let him know about a meeting. Ted assured him Junior was going nowhere and Bonner had no real concern about that. Junior was the son of a local lawyer and he was still enrolled in junior college with a legitimate chance at the big leagues; he was not a flight risk.

As Mike went about his business on the Tethers case, Ted concentrated on other client matters and the day-to-day running of the firm. To a great extent, a law firm almost always takes on the personality of its principals and Rosenthall Chase was no exception. Every day was casual day - if you weren't going to court or had an important client meeting, casual attire was the norm. The staff was small and it was crucial to the success of the firm that they get along. Jenny took on the responsibility of office manager as she was their original employee; she had the personality for it and did a marvelous job. Unlike almost every other law firm that kept salaries as low as possible, Ted and his partners realized the benefit of establishing a reputation for just the opposite. (Lawyers never realized the resentment caused by freezing staff salaries so a partner could make two hundred seventy thousand dollars rather than two sixty.) Ted and his partners wanted only the most dedicated employees and the firm's salary and bonus structure guaranteed it. It was soon recognized in the legal community that working at Rosenthall Chase was a "plum" job. The partners also realized the importance of open communication with their employees, something that was non-existent at his former firm. The lawyers involved the staff as much as possible in every matter so that a success would be a firm, rather than an individual accomplishment and the staff could see the direct results of their labor. Failures were just as important; everyone had to realize in this business, hard work sometimes did *not* payoff.

56

After speaking once again with Marcie Noonan, Ted drafted a letter to Frank Consul rejecting Equity's offer of the hundred thousand for the waiver. Marcie and Ted discussed that Equity would probably not pony up the full three hundred but they would take nothing less than one fifty. Ted knew if Frank offered one, Ted could get at least one fifty without problem. Frankly, it did not matter; Laurie really didn't need it.

Marcie reported that Laurie was doing much better, becoming more active and even getting out a bit by herself - grocery shopping and the like. It seemed Dr. Berringer was "all in" when it came to Laurie; she could not have asked for better, according to Marcie. Marcie also said the project up at the lake seemed to be good for Laurie; she had to make some decisions about the design and also the décor - floor coverings, window treatments, that sort of thing. It kept her busy and gave her something to look forward to. Laurie still had episodes of deep depression and crying spells but Marcie reported the spells seemed to come less often. Ted was sure the financial security made her life a bit easier, however, it could never erase her ghastly memories. He promised to follow up with Marcie as soon as a figure for the waiver was agreed upon. They both knew not to go near a discussion of Grundy.

From time to time, Ted would drift to thoughts of the dead chiropractor. The matter was over and done with, ineptly investigated by the county sheriff and just as ineptly prosecuted by Carl Picker. But really, did Laurie Giffen get away with murder? In the state of mind she was in at the time, could she have been found guilty? Ted convinced himself he had looked at it from every perspective - if, for no other reason, to give himself peace of mind. Laurie had a diminished capacity defense or perhaps even full blown insanity. In every scenario that played out in Ted's mind, she was not guilty. However Ted worried this was only his internal rationalization enabling him to get past it. But what if Merrick and Townes had been found guilty? Ted knew he could clear them with the "newly discovered evidence" of Laurie's involvement. Only Ted knew the evidence was "discovered" before the murder trial concluded but he also knew no one could prove that. Did he have an obligation as an officer of the court to turn Laurie in with the information he had? Client confidences are sacrosanct in the law and attorneys have been disbarred for revealing them. However, Laurie was not Ted's client in the prosecution; she was his client in a personal injury matter against a different defendant. Ted deliberately did not research the canon of ethics on that score; he did not want to know the answer. He rationalized it further by telling himself other defendants like OJ got a "walk" they didn't deserve but Laurie certainly did, and that was okay. He also told himself if anyone were responsible for the deaths of his entire family - and in such a ghastly manner - he would have probably done the same thing.

Mac really didn't have much to offer Ted on Junior's case. He agreed with the strategy of using the civil matter to develop a defense to the criminal case, should there be one. He, like Ted, could never fully understand the dichotomy between civil and criminal cases when it came to discovery. In a civil case, there was rule upon rule governing the amount of information to be exchanged between the parties and the amount was extensive. Production of documents, depositions, expert reports all had to be exchanged so there were no surprises, no "trial by ambush". Yet it was only money or property at stake. In a criminal case, where a person's freedom and even sometimes his very existence were at stake, the mandatory exchange of information was de minimis in comparison. Hutton's premature filing, everyone on the defense side believed, was a real blessing.

The indictment was handed down a week after Ted declined Jack Bonner's offer for a meeting. Ted immediately called Bonner that same day and struck an agreement. Junior would not be picked up but would simply appear at the arraignment - the official charging of the offense. The discovery deposition of Shirley Tethers in the civil case of Tethers versus Tehan was scheduled to commence the day before Junior's arraignment. Bonner had no knowledge of the deposition.

Hutton, in his usual sartorial disaster, appeared ten minutes late for the deposition with his client. Ted had never seen worse looking corduroy. And if the jacket weren't bad enough, he had wrinkled pants to match. He had no briefcase, but did have a blank legal pad in the crook of one arm. His client was also something to behold.

Shirley Tethers, Ted knew from Mike's cursory research, was only thirty-nine years old but she looked twenty years older. Ted's first thought was, *now here is someone who has had a rough life.* Her addictions - tobacco and alcohol - were evident. Her dyed blond hair, something in-between yellow and orange, did not conceal its gray roots. Her face was best described as "craggy" and her overdone mascara failed its purpose. Her clothes smelled of cigarette smoke and her eyes were a bit bloodshot and just a little puffy. Her body type would be described by a physician as endomorphic; she was fairly tall but very heavy below the waist - like one of those inflatable clowns we had as kids, with sand in the bottom and a big red rubber nose. When you punch the nose the clown would go all the way down to the floor and then pop back up for another punch. Ted was also sure she had taken quite a few punches in her day. Her clothes were cheap and inappropriate for the event. Her jewelry was straight out of Walmart.

Not surprisingly, Hutton asked for fifteen minutes alone with his client before the deposition would begin. True to form, he had not yet counseled his client about what was about to take place. Ted directed them to one of the spare offices. Frank Consul and Ted waited, having already agreed that Ted would take the lead on the dep.

After Mrs. Tethers was sworn in by the court reporter, Ted began with the usual discussion about how a deposition is conducted and what was expected of her. He told her to answer the questions to the best of her knowledge and not to guess at the answer. He said that if she did not know the answer to a question then "I don't know" is a good answer as long as it was the truth. He told her that if she did not understand a question, she should let him know so that he could rephrase it for her.

Ted usually covered the already-known background information by making statements rather than asking questions.

"Mrs. Tethers, I understand you are thirty-nine years old and reside at Lot 37, Valley View Mobile Home Park."

"Yes."

"That is in West Canaan."

"Yes."

"How long have you lived there?"

"Going on five years."

"Maiden name?"

"Thomas."

"Employed?"

"Yes."

"Where?"

"Suds and Such Laundromat."

"And you were married to Granville Tethers about five years ago."

"That's right."

"You moved in with him at the mobile home park."

"Yes."

"First marriage?"

"Yes."

"Any relationships prior to Granville?"

"Two."

"Highest level of education you completed?"

240

"Eleventh grade."

"What school?"

"Plains."

"Plains High?"

"Yes."

"Why didn't you graduate?"

"I got pregnant."

"GED?"

"No."

"Your first relationship produced a child. Boy or a girl?"

"Girl."

"You did not marry the girl's father. Did you live with him for awhile?"

"Yes."

"How long?"

"I dunno, two, two and a half years."

"What happened?"

"He left."

"Did he help support your daughter after he left?"

"You're kidding."

"I'll take that as a no. What was his name?"

"Corey Hartnet."

"Did you take his name?"

"No."

"Seen him since he left?"

"No."

"Your second relationship - who was that with?"

"Earnest Bey."

"Did you take his name?"

"Yes."

"Children with Earnest?"

"A boy."

"Why did you take his name?"

"I thought it was going to work out and we would get married. It would be better for the children."

"How old were you when your son was born."

241

"I had just turned twenty."

"Did Earnest leave you?"

"No, I left him."

"Why?"

"Because he beat me. He was abusive."

"Did he help you with your boy?"

"No. I didn't want anything from him. I just wanted to be rid of him."

"Where are your children now?"

At this, her eyes started to tear.

"I don't know, they were adopted."

"You gave them up for adoption?"

"No. They were taken from me by Child and Family Services."

"Tell me about that."

"I got locked out of my apartment late one night during the winter and they were inside. A nosey neighbor turned me in for neglect."

"Where had you been that evening?"

"I was out with some friends."

"Drinking?"

"Yes."

"Weren't they put in temporary custody at the time?"

"Yes. I was given twenty two months to "get my act together" so I could get them back."

"That didn't happen."

"No. They were permanently taken from me." At this, she wiped her eyes and smudged her makeup.

"How old were you when that happened?"

"Twenty five."

"What do you know about the adoption?"

"Nothing, other than they went to the same family and were kept together."

"Haven't seen them since?"

"No."

"Have you been known by any other names other than Thomas, Bey or Tethers?"

242

"No."

"Any nicknames?"

"Half Moon."

"Half Moon? Tell me about that."

At this, she rolled up the sleeve on her right arm and showed Ted a tattoo of a half moon on her forearm.

Ted put it together. "Half Moon Bey?"

"Yes."

"Like the town in California."

"Yes."

"When did you get the tattoo?"

"Right after my son was born."

"Why?"

"Because he had a birthmark on his right forearm that looked like a half moon."

"I see. Then, after the tattoo, your friends started calling you Half Moon."

"Yes."

"So you were twenty five when the children were adopted and thirty four when you married Granville. Do I have that right?"

"Yes."

"Let's talk about those nine years in between. What were you doing in that time period?"

"I dunno, lived with my Mom for a while before she passed. Worked jobs here and there."

"Any other relationships?"

"No. I wasn't about to do that."

"You figured you were better off on your own."

"Yes."

"What was it like being married to Granville?"

"It had its ups and downs."

"Did he ever strike you?"

"Yes."

"How many times?"

"I dunno, a few."

"Did you ever file charges against him?"

243

"Once."

"How long ago?"

"Last year."

"Domestic abuse?"

"Yes."

"What came of it?"

"Nothing. I asked the prosecutor to drop it."

"Did Granville work?"

"Off and on."

"When was the last time he worked before he died?"

"End of last year, he was working at West End."

"The lumber company?"

"Yes."

"What did he do for them?"

"He filled orders."

"Did he quit?"

"No, he got hurt on the job and filed a workers' comp claim."

"What did he hurt?"

"His back."

"What happened to the claim?"

"The company was contesting it. It was still pending when Granny died."

"So he hadn't worked since the end of last year?"

"That's right."

"Was he receiving any assistance?"

"Yes. He got some welfare and we got food stamps."

"What is the source of your income now?"

"The laundromat and some social security from Granny, not much."

"Has your income gone up or down since Granny's death?"

"About the same."

"So you haven't lost any income due to the death of your husband."

"No, I guess not."

"But your expenses have gone down."

"What do you mean?"

"Without Granny, you have the same amount of money but less expenses. You only have the expense of one person, not two."

"Yes."

"What can you tell me about Granville's driving record?"

With this question, Ted reached into his stack of papers in front of him and pulled out a BMV printout.

"He had some violations."

"Any DUI's?"

"Yes."

"How many?"

"I dunno, two, maybe three."

"How about five?"

"I dunno, you have the paper there."

"Any license suspensions?"

"Yes."

"DUI suspensions?"

"Yes."

"Twelve point suspensions?"

"Yes, probably, I don't know."

"Did he have insurance?"

"No, he couldn't afford it."

"Because of all the citations?"

"Yes."

"What about you. Did you have a valid driver's license on the day of the accident?"

"No. It was under suspension."

"What for?"

"DUI."

"Okay, let's talk about the day of the accident. Where were you going that day?"

"Crawford."

"Why were you going to Crawford?"

"To see some friends."

"Who?"

"I dunno their names - they were friends of Granny's."

"Where did they live in Crawford?"

"I dunno."

"The accident happened at about two in the afternoon. These friends of Granny's don't have jobs?"

"Like I said, I didn't even know who we were going to see so I can't answer that question."

"So you were going to see someone - you didn't know who - and you did not know where they lived or if they worked?"

"Granny knew all that."

"And he didn't share any of that with you?"

"I guess not."

"Had you or Granny had anything to drink that day before the accident occurred?"

"No."

"You sure?"

"Yes, I'm sure."

"Was there any alcohol in the car that might have been spilled?"

"No."

"Then why is it you both smelled of alcohol right after the accident occurred?"

"Objection."

"Says who?"

"I just want to make sure of your testimony, Mrs. Tethers. You are saying, under oath, that neither you nor your husband had anything to drink the day the accident happened?"

"That's what I'm saying."

"At the hospital, did they draw any of Granville's blood?" Ted reached for another paper. He knew they had. He had the emergency room records which reported the BAC level. He asked this question deliberately to send a message that he had done his homework and that Shirley should try to stick just a bit closer to the truth. She began to fidget. In concocting her story, she failed to account for this.

246

"I dunno. You would have to ask them."

There were two things about liars: they never consider all the possibilities and they never can remember their lies. Lawyers loved them as long as they were not clients. Liars made the lawyer's job a lot easier, especially those who lied for their own gain. From the way she testified, Ted was sure she was lying about their trip to Crawford as well, however he would have to investigate that issue a little deeper. He made a note.

"Were you and your husband having any conversation in the car prior to the accident?"

"No."

"Not a word?"

"Not that I can remember."

"How fast was your car going when it entered the intersection?"

"I have no idea."

"Can you make a guesstimate?"

"No."

"Any of Granville's violations for speeding?"

"Yes."

"What color was the light when you entered the intersection?"

"Green."

How do you remember that?"

"I happened to look up right before the collision."

"Why?"

"Dunno."

"Any of Granville's violations for running a light?"

"Dunno."

"How about two?"

"Whatever, you have the paper there."

"So if the light was green for you, that means Mr. Tehan ran a red light."

"Yes."

"After the collision, what happened?"

"The young kid came running over to Granville right after he got out of the car. The kid was cursing and then took after Granny. Caught him a few times about the head before Granny even knew what hit him. I had to go over and get in between them."

"What was 'the kid' wearing?"

"A baseball uniform."

"How close did you come to him?"

"Right next to him."

"And when you got in between them, is that when the fight stopped?"

"It wasn't a fight."

"What do you mean?"

"It was a one-sided beating."

"What happened to Granny?"

"He lost consciousness and fell to the ground."

"You're certain Granny didn't run toward Mr. Tehan?"

"No, Granny never left the passenger side of our car."

"So your testimony is that Tehan ran the light and after he did that, he assaulted Granny who never made a threatening move toward him."

"That's right."

Ted did not know the answer to the next question but he wanted to see a reaction.

"Mrs. Tethers, are you aware of any security cameras located near that intersection?"

He saw a look - in poker, they would call it a "tell." She slowly said, "No. I don't." But Ted could see the fear.

Shirley thought to herself that telling her story was much harder than she ever imagined. But this was her chance, her way out, and she was not going to let the truth get in the way. The kid was the son of some rich, sonofabitch lawyer who could afford to pay. Hell, he had insurance; it wouldn't even cost him anything. It was her turn….. finally. After a life of poverty and abuse and being shit on by every man she ever met, goddamit, it was her turn! Granville was good for

248

nothing while he was alive, but she was going to be sure his death was her ticket out.

Maybe Shirley Tethers hadn't seen a newspaper that morning reporting the manslaughter indictment, or, if she had, maybe she didn't care.

"Did you see Tehan hit Granville?"

"Yes."

Where did Granville get hit?"

"The worst place was the left temple."

"Did Tehan hit him with his left or his right hand?"

"I think his right."

"Are you sure?"

"Pretty sure."

A soft knock on the door interrupted them. Jenny had opened the door just a little bit and got Ted's attention.

"Let's go off the record for a second. Mrs. Tethers would you like to use the facilities?"

"No, thank you. I'm fine."

Ted went out in the hallway, "Jenny, what is it?"

"Prosecutor Bonner is holding on line one. He wants to speak with Mr. Hutton."

"Just tell him we are in the middle of a deposition (which, Ted knew, was the exact reason he was calling - he must have got wind of it) and that Mr. Hutton will call him back." Ted was not about to let Bonner interfere. Regardless of what Bonner may have thought, he had no right to poke his nose into the civil case and Ted was not about to let him try. He wanted to get this deposition "in the can."

He returned to the room, "Okay, we're back on the record. Mrs. Tethers, how many times did Granville get hit?"

"I dunno. Several."

The deposition continued for the better part of two hours because there were many issues which had to be explored, not the least of which was what were Shirley Tether's real damages here. She already testified her income was about the same with or without Granville. The only thing

249

she seems to have lost was an abusive alcoholic who would beat her from time to time. The "companionship" she lost, she testified, was the "socializing" she did with Granville. *"Socializing,"* thought Ted, *really meant sitting in one bar or another, drinking with fellow alcoholics.* Ozzie and Harriet they were not, and not even Jeff Hutton could make them appear that way to a jury. *Widow Tethers' reaction to his last question,* Ted thought, *would tell him for certain, whether she was lying.*

"Mrs. Tethers, are you aware that Larry Tehan Jr. was indicted for voluntary manslaughter yesterday?"

And there it was......a frightened look....if just for a second...then, "No, I didn't know that. What does that mean?"

"I'm sorry Mrs. Tethers, in a deposition I am only permitted to ask the questions, not answer them. Unless Mr. Consul has some questions for you, this deposition is over. Thank you for coming in. Jeff, Jack Bonner asks that you give him a call."

Frank Consul, lawyer for Equity, was very happy with the information that had been elicited and had no questions of his own. He was especially happy because, according to this plaintiff, it was *not* the traffic accident that caused Mr. Tethers' demise, it was Junior's deliberate act *after* the accident. Consul and Equity were only concerned about negligent conduct, not deliberate.

Hutton asked of them both, "Would you like to have a brief discussion about the case before we leave?"

Clearly he wanted to get an early read on Frank and Ted about how they might be evaluating the matter. Ted looked at Shirley Tethers with the iciest stare he could muster. He wanted to send a clear message to her and her lawyer. He knew she was lying and he was not going to let her get away with it. Without even conferring with Frank, he said, "No, Mrs. Tethers has no case." Her jaw dropped and she just looked at her lawyer as if to say, "Didn't he hear any of what I just said?" Hutton knew to keep his poker face. He put his finger to his lips and nodded his head toward the door, sending her the message; just be quiet until we get out of here.

Outside the office, Shirley quickly lit up a cigarette and said, "That sonofabitch doesn't believe anything I just told him."

"Shirley, you cannot say that for sure. I am not sure what he believes or doesn't believe. Remember, we are just at the very beginning of this lawsuit and he is not going to let on whether he thinks you do or do not have a strong case. Anyway, it doesn't matter what Ted Chase believes. What matters is what we can prove to a jury."

At this last statement, a look of worry crossed her face. Hutton saw it but did not acknowledge it.

"What was he saying about surveillance cameras?"

"Many times, parking lot cameras pick up images of people or automobiles or just parts of them. Law enforcement always are on the lookout. For instance, they might get lucky and see someone on video running from a store that had just been burglarized - stuff like that. Have you seen that TV show, Caught on Tape?"

"Oh. And what about this manslaughter thing? Is that serious?"

"Very. It is a first degree felony."

"What does that mean?"

"Means if he is convicted, he could go to jail for a long time."

"How long?"

"I think the maximum on that could be ten years but don't hold me to it."

Hutton could see the wheels turning. She was weighing things out. Unlike Ted, Hutton really didn't care about his client, other than she may be his ticket to a fairly nice settlement without having to do a lot of work. Ted had certainly hit the "warts" on Hutton's case: Granville was not much of a breadwinner and the domestic abuse charge from last year certainly gutted a "grieving widow" approach to

251

things. However, the bottom line was Granville was dead and Tehan was charged. Hutton was betting the criminal case would end in a conviction, upping "the price of poker" in the civil action so settlement would be Ted's and Equity's only option. As the plaintiff in a civil case, the civil rules allowed Hutton to control which matter went forward first because he could always dismiss and re-file. There was no doubt the criminal matter would be resolved before the civil one.

"What happens next?"

"Well, the criminal case will start to heat up. There is nothing much going to happen until that gets resolved so we will certainly monitor that. If the prosecutor needs anything from us, we will have to co-operate with him."

"Testimony from me?"

"Probably."

"I thought I was done with that."

"That was only the grand jury. If the matter gets tried, you will have to testify in court."

"Whatever."

57

"No person, while under the influence of sudden passion or in a sudden fit of rage, either of which is brought on by serious provocation occasioned by the victim that is reasonably sufficient to incite the person into using deadly force, shall knowingly cause the death of another." It was a first degree felony.

Ted thought the charge interesting to say the least. Obviously, Bonner was pinning his case on Junior's alleged conduct *after* the collision occurred but it included an element of provocation on Granville's part. Not only provocation - "serious" provocation.

Shirley Tethers had just finished testifying that Granville was totally without blame in the whole affair, yet Bonner was charging a violation with an element of "serious provocation" from Granville "reasonably sufficient" to incite deadly force from Junior. Already, there was a huge "disconnect" between the civil and criminal matters! There had to be a difference in Tether's testimony before the grand jury that issued the indictment and how she just testified in the civil case. Is it possible there were already two conflicting stories saved in the record? Could she have forgotten her first set of lies already? Or…did she think it over and decide to make the testimony even "stronger" for her civil lawsuit? Ted also noted there could be no criminal culpability unless Junior had "knowingly" caused Granville's death. This is where the fetal alcohol defense entered the picture. If it got that far, an expert on fetal alcohol syndrome could be called by the defense to prove that when a fetal alcohol child is in a "rage" he is incapable of "knowingly" doing anything; his mind is devoid of all control over his body or his conduct.

Later that night, after the kids had gone to bed, Ted and Dorie were discussing Junior's cases.

"How are things shaping up?"

"Well, for starters, I don't believe a word out of this Tethers woman's mouth. You can almost see what is going on. Hutton is filling her head with dollar signs and, it appears, she will say whatever it takes. The indictment contains an element of provocation from the decedent whereas Tethers' deposition testimony does not support that in any regard. You gotta' believe Bonner would indict to the highest level possible and he only went with the manslaughter. The whole thing stinks from the getgo. I think it is a classic case of someone believing their ship has come in and they are so callous, they don't care whose life gets ruined. She won't be able to hold up under the pressure she is creating and she definitely will not be able to keep all her lies straight. We are going to have to go "balls to the walls" on this one."

With a smirk, "Like I haven't heard that before."

Ted looked at his beautiful wife and with a similar smirk said, "Oh, shut up."

"Is Mac going to help you do it?"

"Well, I have already bounced a few things off him. I'll probably ask him - nothing like having an extra set of eyes and ears on it. Many of these judges defer to Mac - some of them were even students of his - so that can't hurt."

Their discussion then focused on the kids and her parents. Evidently, in the coming weeks, the eldest daughter's class was going to have a "Career Day" and she had asked her Mom whether her Dad could come to school to give ten minutes on what it is like to be a lawyer. Ted welcomed the opportunity - it could be fun. Dorie jokingly said that she wasn't asked to come to school to talk about what it is like to raise four children.

"Very funny," Ted replied, seeing as they only had three.

Unfortunately, many lawyers are "cursed" with being a lawyer. They are incapable of acting any other way, even with their own families. That certainly was not Ted. Truth be told, his children had no concept of Ted's work because at home he was just a big kid and they loved it. He was always goofing off with them and sometimes got in trouble along with them. Many times Dorie had to start a sentence with, "Now children.....," all the time including Ted as one of them. Often, they saw him stick out his tongue behind her back or make a face - and almost as often get caught. He always acted in such a way, however, that the children never lost any respect for either one of their parents. They knew he just loved to kid around.

The next order of business was Junior's arraignment in open court. As soon as the indictment had been handed down, Ted had struck a deal with Bonner, personally guaranteeing Junior's appearance at the arraignment. This saved Junior from having to spend an evening in jail waiting for the next court session. Bonner was reasonable, certainly mindful of the fact he was prosecuting the son of a fellow county bar member. The purpose of the arraignment was to officially inform Junior of the charges and set bail. It was scheduled for the very next morning. Ted's goal was to get Junior in and out of court as quickly as possible on an "OR" bond. An "Own Recognizance" bond is reserved for those criminal defendants who the Court determines are not flight risks, those with sufficient ties within the community. All you had to do was sign a document promising you would appear. It went smoothly since Bonner had no objection to Ted's request.

The two lawyers had a brief discussion after the short hearing.
"Ted, the Grand Jury had no choice here. Based on this woman's testimony, there was more than enough to indict."
"That should not have surprised anyone."
"What do you mean?"

"I mean her game plan here is pretty transparent. She only cares about one thing and a criminal prosecution will help her get it."

"How did her deposition go yesterday?" Bonner wanted to convey his knowledge, even recognizing he had been "hoodwinked" a bit on that.

"As expected - it was a very interesting fairy tale."

"Seems like Hutton is in a bit of a hurry."

"Well, my guess is he'll let you do all the heavy lifting for the time being. Hutton and his client are using you."

"Ted, you may be right about that but given what I heard in the grand jury proceedings, I had no choice but to go forward."

"I'll tell you what you may want to do. Have her grand jury testimony transcribed and compare it to her deposition. Might save your office the embarrassment and expense of a meritless prosecution."

"I'm getting the impression you and I are not going to have any plea negotiations on this one."

"Jack, after the truth comes out in the criminal case, you are the one who is going to have the egg on his face, not Hutton. The only thing we will accept from you is a complete and final dismissal of all charges and an apology. This is a fine young man who is just getting started in life. He's overcome quite a bit, and what you and Hutton have done so far is tarnish him. This indictment will always "be on his resume" and few will remember the ultimate outcome. But I guess that is why the law recognizes causes of action for slander, libel and malicious prosecution." This last statement was meant to sound like a threat. Ted got his point across.

Unlike the Grundy murder case, Ted was giving some thought to what discovery he may gain from the prosecution and what he may have to give up in return. What he would really love to have was a transcript of the Tethers testimony before the Grand Jury but those proceedings are secret and that would not be available to him. He was sure there were probably enough discrepancies in the two versions of her testimony to gain an acquittal. For now, he would have her sworn deposition and her live trial testimony, should the matter be tried. That was more than he normally had in a criminal case. Thank you Jeff Hutton. He didn't have to worry about statements from Junior because the Sheriff's Department was never given the opportunity to take any. Junior was right; it was really going to come down to her word against his. Ted had just thrown out the question about security cameras but he made a note to speak with his paralegal to see what could be found out about that.

The following day Larry Sr. stopped by Ted's office.

"Ted, I was wondering if you might be able to stop by the house this Saturday. The Indians are going to work Junior out at the field house and one of their personnel guys wants to come by afterwards. Says he would like to discuss Junior and everything that is going on. I certainly know enough to fill him in, but I thought it would be better for him to hear it from someone other than Junior's father."

"Sure, that would be fine. What time you want me there?"

"I imagine around two would be fine."

"I will be there. Do we have an idea what they're after?"

"No, I really don't. I guess they would like to evaluate the situation as they consider their draft picks."

"Fine. I will be there right around two."

58

The Tehan home was in a very nice older section of town, with big trees and well-kept tree lawns. Houses were not inexpensive but they were not the "McMansions" the younger generation seemed, for some strange reason, to covet. Larry and his father lived in a very attractive ranch with a stone front, winding asphalt driveway and a manicured front lawn.

Ted knew that even before Larry Sr. had joined Carrothers, he had lost his wife. Though the facts were somewhat "fuzzy," it was generally known she had perished in a one car accident during the winter months. Until just recently, Ted had no idea she had had a problem and that her child would pay the price for it for his entire life. He wondered if her death was, in some way, connected to "her problem." Larry Sr. met him at the door.

"Ted, thanks for coming."

"How did the workout go?"

"Don't know. The fellow is there now and is coming over right after."

"Who is it?"

"Name's Mike Rufaulo. He's some type of assistant in player development."

"Larry, beautiful place you have here."

"Thanks Ted, Michelle really loved it here. Probably needs a bit of a woman's touch though. We have the cleaners come in three times a month just to make sure it does not get out of hand."

To Ted, the inside of the house appeared spotless. It was tastefully decorated and very neat. They sat in the living room near the large bay window right in front of the fireplace. Ted was looking at the pictures on the mantle. There were three pictures there; an older couple Ted guessed were Larry's parents, his deceased wife Michelle, and another picture of a young girl who appeared to be in her early teens.

"Larry, the information you gave me about Junior's condition was an eye-opener. I had no idea of the extent of the problem. I had heard about fetal alcohol before, but never realized the number of children who had the condition or how severe it can be. It must have been tough for you and Michelle."

"At times, especially when Larry got older and stronger. The rages were unbelievable; he had no control. The batting cage was the best idea of my entire life."

"Where did you go for help?"

"Well, believe it or not, we got a lot of support from the schools –which is very unusual. Most districts don't have the resources."

"What about support groups?"

"Hardly any. You would be surprised. You have to realize most kids who suffer from the disease are never diagnosed. Their birth parents don't come forward or admit to it."

Ted thought for a second about Larry's wife, Michelle. "You know, I wondered about that. I can give you five or six names of criminal defendants I have represented who probably had the disease."

"That would not surprise me."

"You know, maybe we can get the Firm behind this."

"What do you mean?"

"Well, we've been in existence long enough to take on some pro bono causes. Perhaps we could start a support group - fund it. I mean, your Junior was lucky, but there are others out there who don't get a chance at a real life. Obviously, you would be the person to take the lead on something like this."

"It would be a labor of love."

"Let's discuss it at the next partners' meeting. Ted looked at the pictures on the mantle.

"That Mom and Dad?"

"Yes."

"Who is the pretty young girl?"

"That's Dottie, my daughter."

"Larry, I thought Junior was an only child."

"No, Dottie was his step sister."

Ted heard the word *was* loud and clear.

"Michelle was married before?"

"No, Michelle couldn't have children. Dottie and Larry were adopted."

"Larry, I had no idea. I am sorry."

"Don't be Ted. You're representing Larry and you need to know all about him. I already shared with you the most important information about him. Dottie was about three years older than Larry when we adopted. They have the same mother but different fathers."

This was starting to sound eerily familiar to Ted.

"Who is their mother?"

"I have no idea. We were not permitted to have that information. The kids were in foster care when they came to live with us."

"Is the mother in the area?"

"Don't know."

"You never tried to contact her?"

"No. Especially not after Junior was diagnosed. We knew she was an alcoholic. We don't believe she married either man. Didn't think contact would be very beneficial for the children with that type of woman even if she were their mother, and... the children never asked."

"Where is Dottie now?"

"Dottie? I'm sorry, I thought you knew. Dottie was with my wife. They are both gone."

"Larry, please forgive me for being such an ass."

"Don't even think about it. How would you know? When I came to Carrothers, I didn't share much of anything with anyone. Didn't feel the need."

Ted returned to the first piece of advice Mac had ever given him; *don't assume anything.* Here, all along, Ted had assumed Larry was an only child and that his birthmother was Michelle and that it was Michelle who had had the problem. Now Ted's mind was racing as he was trying to remember Tethers' deposition testimony. Could it possibly be? Doesn't it fit together? He recalled her testimony about the tattoo and the birthmark. It was right about then that Larry Jr. and Mike Rufaulo came through the door. Junior had a ball jersey on but he had long sleeves underneath.

Rufaulo had done his homework and had an extensive list of questions regarding the court cases, especially the recently-filed criminal case. Ted had to be very careful in answering the questions. His goal was to convey to the Tribe's representative that everything was going to be alright - they just had to get through the system. However, since both matters were pending, he had to be careful not to divulge certain information. He prefaced his remarks so that Rufaulo understood Ted's concerns. The interview lasted the better part of forty-five minutes. Junior did not sit in.

After Rufaulo left, Junior came out of the kitchen. Ted immediately got the impression he had been within earshot the entire time.

"How'd it go?"

"Good, Junior. We answered all his questions. I think he understands we are in fine shape on these cases. Without saying it in so many words, I conveyed to him that it is this Tethers lady and her attorney who are behind this and they are just out for a payday."

Larry Sr. asked, "How did the workout go?"

"I think it went great. They had a gun on me the entire time. I couldn't hear what they were saying, but their body language looked good. About a third of the way through, they asked for the fastball. I got it up there pretty good and they started laughing after they checked out the gun."

"Did they have you throw any breaking stuff?"

"Yea."

261

"How did that go?"

"Okay. Got a few of 'em over the plate."

Junior had taken a shower and his arms were now uncovered.

"Junior, that's quite a tattoo you have on your arm there."

"Everybody says that Mr. Chase but it's not a tattoo - it's a birthmark."

Ted could see an almost perfect half moon on Junior's right forearm.

On the short drive home, Ted put Westside Steve on.

> I'm waiting on island time
> Put some rum in my tonic and lime
> With the sand and the sea when the sun goes down, well I'll be fine
> With a pretty lady and a bottle of wine
> Everybody is a friend of mine…..

Ted marveled at the extent alcohol played a part in our culture. For the great majority of us who use it in moderation, it is no problem - it is a good thing and it is not unhealthy. We sing about it, use it in social gatherings, in our ethnic customs and even in our religious ceremonies. Holidays are celebrated, newlyweds are toasted, deals are consummated, and ships are launched with alcohol. Jesus Christ Himself promoted the use of wine; its transubstantiation into the blood of Christ for consumption done every day during the celebration of the Mass. But for the Shirley Tethers of the world, it became, at first, an escape, then perhaps a crutch, and, lastly, a way of life. For her son Junior, it was an inescapable trap unfairly bestowed upon him by an unknowing mother.

Ted was now certain of what he was dealing with and it was seemingly unbelievable. What were the chances that a mother and son, separated from one another years ago, could be brought together under such circumstances? He was also

262

certain he was the only one to have made the connection. He knew it would be appropriate to share his knowledge with Larry Sr. at some time in the future, but not now; he had two roles here which he had to keep separate. He was a good friend of the family and that meant he should share the information with them and let them do with it whatever they wanted. However, he was also a lawyer defending both a criminal and a civil suit and, tactically, the information could be of great benefit in those matters but *only* when revealed at the appropriate time. He had to keep it to himself until the time was right.

59

That Monday brought Equity's check for one hundred and fifty thousand dollars payable to Laurie Giffen and a legal document outlining the disclosures to be made. Consul knew Ted and his client would accept that sum so he presented it to Ted as a "done deal." Consul was sharp. As decided, a third of this amount was going to Laurie, a third to MADD and Ted was to retain a third as his fee. The fee was based upon the prior retainer agreement entered into between Ted and his client but it would also compensate Ted for the amount of time he was going to have to spend on the matter going forward. There would be at least one deposition and, perhaps, trial testimony. But in order for that to happen, there would be time necessary to review the file and be prepped by counsel.

The disclosure agreement was for Ted to be able to testify regarding how it all came down. There was no question in Ted's mind, Equity and Priem would prevail in this litigation - it was really going to come down to how much money they would be awarded. Collection of the award, however, could be another problem - but it would be their problem and not Ted's. Ted would not admit to himself, at least not yet, that he might enjoy giving testimony in this matter against Carrothers. He had his paralegal Mike see to the execution of the document and disbursement of funds with Marcie and Laurie who now lived very comfortably out at the lake.

In the office the next day, Ted began to work up his defenses to the criminal case. The first thing he wrote down on his legal pad was: "attack the credibility of ST." He really thought this may be the only defense necessary. His second defense was a medical one: Granville died as a result of the injuries he sustained in a motor vehicle accident he, himself, had caused. His death was not due to any conduct, either negligent or deliberate, on Junior's part. Third, due to fetal alcohol syndrome, Junior was incapable of "knowingly" hurting anybody or anything; his disease robbed him of this. Lastly, Junior's actions were done in self-defense. These defenses were not consistent but lawyers were used to "pleading in the alternative." Problem was, juries did not appreciate this type of approach and Ted was well aware of that.

Ted had made arrangements to have lunch with Mac on Tuesday to "catch up" and to deliver to Mac his share of the additional monies received in the Giffen matter, their split being sixty/forty. He thought he would use the lunch to bounce some things off Mac regarding Junior's cases, especially the criminal matter. He always looked forward to being with Mac and this lunch would be especially pleasant because, frankly, Ted had neglected to fill Mac in on the negotiations with Consul. Mac was going to receive a twenty thousand dollar check seemingly "out of the blue." Ted made a mental note to remember to tell Mac he had to pick up the tab.

Mac was waiting for Ted in the first booth at Lillie's, an old fashion railcar-type diner that had the best homemade mashed potatoes and mushroom gravy in the northern hemisphere. No matter what you ordered, a meal, a sandwich, a munchie, you always ordered the mashed potatoes and gravy along with it. They were famous for it. Ted found Mac with a bowl of it, already indulging.

"What, is that an appetizer?"

"Yeah, and for my main dish I thought I would order mashed potatoes and gravy. How you doing counselor?"

"Great Mac, how about you?"

"Been good. How's your wife and my kids?"

"Everybody's good, you dufus. Here this is for you."

"What's this?"

"Your portion of the Giffen money."

"Oh, and what would that be?"

Ted then explained to Mac what had been going on in the case and what the negotiations were.

"Wow, this is great, thanks, but I'm not picking up the tab for lunch."

The two men were so close, it was somewhat scary how they thought alike. Ted just burst out laughing.

"You're an old sonofabitch."

"I know that and I don't intend to change anytime soon."

At that point, the waitress interrupted to take their orders.

"Mac, can I run some things by you on the Tehan matter?"

"Sure. What's up?"

"Well, I was putting together some ideas for the defense of the criminal case. I'm positive that will be round one, and my goal is to use that to make everything go away. I was jotting some thoughts on the defenses."

He slipped his notes to Mac across the table. Mac looked at it briefly and said, "Tell me about this Tethers woman."

"Alcoholic, neer-do-well, works in a laundromat. She's got Hutton so I'm sure she has unrealistic expectations for the civil suit and she'll do everything she can to make the criminal charge stick because of that. She's a poor liar; won't do well with a jury, in my opinion. She's about forty years old but looks sixty. And there's one other thing."

"Oh?"

"Mac, you won't believe this, but I'm almost one hundred percent sure she is young Tehan's birthmother."

"What!?"

"She told me she got a tattoo after her son was born - a half moon on her right forearm. She went by the name Bey at the time and her nickname became Half Moon Bey."

"So?"

"The reason she got the tattoo was because her son had a half moon birthmark on his right forearm."

"And Junior has the birthmark?"

"Mac, it is so well defined it too looks like a tattoo."

"Wow. If it's not true, it would be a helluva coincidence, wouldn't it?"

"That's only part of it. The ages of the children, the fetal alcohol syndrome, the timing of the adoption - it just all fits."

"Does she know?"

"No. You're the only person I have shared this with."

"What about the Tehans?"

"I thought it through and came to the conclusion it is not a good time to share it with them. There is just too much going on and I don't want to do anything which may prejudice either case. My thought is that this information could become very valuable in one or both of the cases at the appropriate time."

"But if she knew now, do you think she would continue on?"

"Mac, that's what I don't know. It is inconceivable to me that a parent could put a child in such jeopardy, even a child they lost years ago. But I just don't get the mentality of these people. Her life is in a bottle. Her husband is dead. She hasn't got shit and, most likely, never will."

"Wow. Ted, you certainly get yourself in some strange cases."

At this last statement, Ted wondered what Mac would have to say if he knew everything about the Laurie Giffen case.

"Well, that is where you come in."

"You're kidding. If you want help from me, it will cost you."

"Okay. Deal. I'll pick up the lunch tab."

"Wait a minute here. You think I am going to get involved in this mess for some friggin' mashed potatoes?"

"Of course not. You can order dessert too."

267

On the way back to the office, Ted was listening to Westside Steve. He couldn't get his mind off the luncheon conversation, especially the part about how Shirley Tethers may react once she learns the identity of her young adversary. He thought about a young, stupid girl who couldn't keep her mouth off a bottle long enough to protect the health of her unborn child and who then lost the child because she valued an evening in a bar more than the child's wellbeing. He thought about the incredible injustice; a tall, attractive young man, cursed with the inability to control his impulses but not because of anything he did - all he did was get born. He could only imagine how Larry's parents must have felt about Tethers when Larry would go off on one of his rages or when they saw the other kids in school shun him because he was so immature. How they must have cursed her even though they did not even know her. He wondered what life would have been like for young Larry had he stayed with his mother. That was, perhaps, the scariest thought of all. Ted was certain young Larry would not be enrolled in junior college with a very good chance at capturing, what was for many boys, the all-American dream, a dream he himself had once hoped to attain. Ted concluded the best thing to ever happen to Junior was that he was lost to his birthmother.

He thought about people having to take courses and secure licenses to engage in most professions, drive a car, carry a concealed weapon, sell alcohol..... and yet, there was no training or licensing required for the most important of all jobs - having and raising children. He wondered if a minimum level of proficiency should have to be demonstrated before being permitted to bring another human being into the world. Perhaps if that came about, there would be less uncared for children growing up to become irresponsible adults just like their parents. How politically incorrect is such a thought, yet, how sensible?

60

Ted was now in his favorite place in the whole world, sitting in the old, worn leather chair with his feet on the ottoman staring straight into the wood burner, watching the flames lick and dance between the pine logs. Dorie was outside on the cottage porch watching the approaching storm. They had promised each other a weekend alone at the lake while Dorie's parents watched the kids back home. Dorie said, "Ted, come on out here and take a look at this."

The sky was deep deep purple but the clouds in the distance were a bright white. There was no trace of a sun and the lake was a muddy grey, almost black, as dark as the sky. The wind had kicked up and dancing along the top of the dark water were small whitecaps. Dorie wanted Ted to see the rain approaching; a solid wall advancing in a straight line like a platoon of Continental soldiers right down the lake toward the cottage. The line of advance was marked by the raindrops hitting the water.

"Wow. Here it comes." The thought of being holed up in the small old worn wooden cottage with Dorie with nothing to do but hold each other and talk and snooze and not have a care in the world made Ted feel warm inside. The rain soon started to pelt the roof and they were forced to retreat inside to the warmth of the glowing fire and the smell of the burning pine.

Dorie was in his arms as he returned to his favorite chair. They sat for an hour it seemed, without saying anything, watching the fire's embers glow bright orange but black and they listened to the heavy rainfall hit the roof and the porch and the windows.

"Well, Dorie, what do you think? Should we just stay here for a year or two?"

"Sounds good to me but the kids may have something to say about that."

"What kids?"

"Oh, you're awful. You would miss them more than me probably. So how goes it with the Tehan boy? Is he going to be able to play baseball?"

"I hope so. Kid's got a helluva arm. Definitely has major league stuff."

"Do you think he is going to come out of all this okay? The poor kid has certainly been through enough already - losing his mother and all."

"He's going to be fine. It may not look too promising for him right now, but he's got a good lawyer."

"Yes, I know, a real humble one too."

"Let's go to bed so I can have my way with you."

"Wow, you really know how to sweet-talk a girl. It's only four o'clock there Casanova."

"So, never heard of a little afternoon delight?"

"Okay, but then you have to take me to Hal's for dinner."

"That's all it takes? You've got yourself a deal."

61

The call came into the office Wednesday morning. The caller's voice, vaguely familiar to Ted, sent an ice cold shiver through his body like a frozen knife. "Counselor, I know who killed Grundy. I'll be calling you in a few days to make financial arrangements." Click.

Lindie Danko had been working at St. Joseph's for some six years. A divorced mother of two, living in Oil City, she barely scraped by; seemed like there was always more month left over at the end of her paycheck. She watched the patients come and go, mostly members of wealthy families who had fried their brains on drugs or alcohol or both. Many of them were "discarded" children of privileged parents, others were the parents themselves. She despised them. Their addictions were labeled diseases but she truly did not believe that. They were wealthy, spoiled, weak individuals.

More than once, Danko had listened in on Laurie Giffen's sessions with Dr. Berringer but she became much more interested after she retrieved the documents from the trash that Ted had left on Laurie's bed. At first she had no idea what she was looking at, but she pieced it together just as she pieced together the papers Laurie had torn up and mistakenly believed she had discarded for good. She knew Laurie had come into quite a bit of money; she heard Ted and Mac explain to Laurie the lawsuit had ended well and Laurie would be "set for life." Those were the words that intrigued her the most and that's exactly what she wanted for herself and her family - to be set for life. Certainly there would be enough to go around for everyone - why not her too? So the horrific loss of Laurie Giffen's family now became an opportunity for Lindie Danko. She made the initial contact with Ted but she also gave herself more time to reconsider because she was scared to death. She knew it was wrong but a chance like this was not to be wasted. She convinced herself all she had to do was be careful, take it slow and think things through. She also convinced herself she was smart enough to pull it off.

Ted's mind raced. Should he immediately consult with Mac even though he had kept the information about Laurie Giffen from him? After telling Mac, it would be out of his control and Ted was truly afraid of what Mac's advice might be. Or should he go to the authorities right now? Could he somehow get their involvement without giving Laurie up? Would he have to give Laurie up? Should he? Or should he wait to see if the threat is carried out? What did the voice say? "I will be contacting you in a few days….." Why a few days? Why wasn't a demand made? And how does he determine what this person knows or thinks she knows? What if she is wrong?

Ted decided the best course was to do nothing and see if a follow-up contact is made. That would give him time to think things through. He also had his hands full with the Tehan criminal case which was set for a pretrial conference the following morning.

62

His Honor Richard McCarthy began with Prosecutor Jack Bonner. "Jack, tell me about your case."

"Your Honor, this Tehan boy caused a collision and after the accident, lost his temper and beat the tar out of this fellow Granville Tethers. Tethers sustained a fatal blow to the head and died from it weeks later. We have the eyewitness testimony of Tethers' wife who stepped in too late to save her husband."

"Ted?"

"The cause of Granville Tethers' death was his own negligence, which, given his driving record, should surprise no one. He ran a traffic light and was hit broadside by the Tehan vehicle. Tethers was driving drunk and tried to start something after the collision but stopped as soon as he realized how stupid that was. The Tehan boy is a good kid, the son of my partner, and on the verge of a career in major league baseball. Once a jury sees him and hears from him, they will not believe this Tethers woman who has already filed her personal injury suit because she cannot wait for her big payday."

"Ted, this guy was drunk?"

"Yes, Your Honor, for the sixth time."

"Six!?"

"Yes, Your Honor."

"Jack, were you aware of the driving record here?"

"Yes, Your Honor."

"Ted, the widow has already filed a lawsuit?"

"Yes, Your Honor. She has Jeff Hutton."

"Were you aware of that Jack?"

"Yes, Your Honor."

"Kind of quick, wouldn't you say?"

"Well, I would have waited a bit, I suppose."

"Sounds to me like there may be an agenda here."

"Your Honor, I have no control over that. It is what it is. I just know what we put before the grand jury; we had no trouble getting an indictment."

"Jack, everyone in this room realizes the one-sided nature of grand jury proceedings. Wasn't it a prosecutor who once said he could indict a ham sandwich? Well, it's your case, but it sounds like your opponent is going to have quite a bit of ammunition here."

Ted spoke up. "Your Honor, we haven't even scratched the surface."

"Well, Jack, Ted, I think you should each explore other ways to resolve this thing. I'll give you thirty days to complete your discovery - trial a month from now. I understand the boy is out on his own recognizance?"

"Yes, Your Honor."

"Okay, so we have no issue there. See the bailiff on the way out for a date about thirty days out. I'm thinking three days for trial," said Judge McCarthy.

"Three would be fine, Your Honor."

If you start talking deals and need some help, just call and we'll give you a date to come in. Anything else?"

"No, Your Honor."

"Okay then, we'll see you in about a month."

On the way out of chambers, Ted turned to Jack Bonner and said, "Jack, there will be no deals here. I'm not going to let Hutton or this Tethers woman ruin this young man's life. They only care about one thing and it has got nothing to do with the truth or what happened. They just want you to make it a lot easier for them. I don't need any discovery from you."

"Ted, you sound pretty sure of things."

"I know what happened and I've seen the woman testify. The boy is telling the truth. I suggest you bring Tethers in again and talk with her in earnest. My bet is, she will not be

274

able to keep track of all of her lies. You heard her grand jury testimony and you can order the transcript from the civil deposition. You can question her again. You'll have three opportunities to test her veracity. For your benefit, I suggest you do it. Perjury should have consequences."

Some, perhaps most, lawyers always talked "tough" dealing with their adversaries but Ted Chase recognized the folly in that. Just like the boy who cried wolf, no one would believe you when you needed them to and you would earn the label of a "blowhard" among your peers. It's similar to always appearing righteously indignant before the jury. When the time came during the trial to show a bit of righteous indignation, and it often does, you were incapable of it. Ted, however, firmly believed it better to "walk softly and carry a big stick." He'd had many cases with Jack Bonner and never before came across so hard or threatening. He was certain he was getting his message across. However, he was also cognizant of the pressure the indictment brought upon young Bonner. The public is now aware, and many in the community have already decided that the son of the wealthy lawyer was guilty. They wouldn't have indicted him if he weren't. Ted recognized the general consensus in our country was that lawyers were all crooks and if Junior's case were to be dismissed outright without a trial (which was what Ted was advocating), the talk within the community would be about collusion, privilege, fix and corrupt lawyers. Ted realized lawyer bashing had become a national pastime. He'd heard all the jokes. *"What is 2000 lawyers at the bottom of the ocean? A good start. How can you tell when a lawyer is lying? His lips are moving."*

Most people bashed lawyers, that is, until they needed one. Then, they wanted to find the best one they could afford. He knew a trial here, regardless of his talk with Bonner, was almost a certainty.

63

The next call came in on a Friday morning, and when it did, Ted immediately cursed himself for not speaking with the authorities sooner. Perhaps there would have been a way to investigate the call to see where it came from.

"Hello, this is Ted Chase, what can I do for you?"

"I'm calling to make arrangements."

"Are you the party who left a message before?"

"Yes." Ted sensed the nervousness in the voice which was quivering.

"What is it that you want?"

"Five hundred thousand."

"I see. And how do I know that if you were to receive that sum, I would not hear from you again?"

"You don't."

"So what exactly am I getting for that money?"

"My silence for now."

"I see. And how do I know you have the correct information?"

"Look, I know."

"What is it that you know?"

"I know your client killed Grundy."

"I have lots of clients."

"Yes, but only one who lives in a new home up at the lake."

Ted's heart skipped a beat and now it was his voice that started to crack.

"And how am I supposed to pay you this amount?"

"Just get the money Mr. Chase. You'll get instructions from me. And this is just between you and me. If I get even a sniff that the police are involved, the prosecutor will have what I have."

"What is it that you have?"

"Never mind. Just get the money. I'll let you know what to do with it." Click.

Ted started to feel like he was caught up in a grade B movie. He could not believe this was really happening. The caller obviously had the right information but who the hell could it be and how did she acquire the knowledge? What does he do next? Talk with Marcie and Laurie? Just go straight to the police? Contact someone on his own - a private investigator? He had to put an end to this but he had to protect his client. There was no course in law school that prepared him for something like this.

After thinking it over for a few days and recalling his feelings when the caller called for the second time, Ted made the call. "Detective Dietrich, this is Ted Chase. We met some time ago on the Grundy murder case."

"Certainly, won't ever forget that. Best decision those two birds made to get you."

"Thanks. Listen, I have a sensitive matter I need to discuss with you as soon as you may have some time."

"A criminal matter?"

"Yes."

"Anders County?"

"Well, that is one of the issues - it may be. I can't be sure right now."

"I don't follow you."

"Rather than talk on the phone, I'd like to come over there and sit down with you to discuss this. As soon as you have time, that is."

"Okay, how does tomorrow afternoon look for you? Say two o'clock?"

"Fine, I'll be there. Do you mind if we meet in the client interview room rather than your office?"

"No that would be fine, I guess. See you then."

"Yes, see you then. Thank you."

277

Ted was in unchartered waters; he truly was uncertain what county may have jurisdiction. It would depend upon who the person was and where the call was made. He did feel certain, however, that Detective John Dietrich was a "straight shooter" who could be trusted and would know what to do. He felt an immediate wave of calm come over him after he hung up the phone and realized he had made the right decision. He would have the better part of twenty-four hours to think through how he was going to present the matter to the detective.

John Dietrich was a bit perplexed over the call but one thing he knew for sure - Ted Chase was sharp and if he thought a matter needed to be discussed with law enforcement, there was a strong likelihood he would be right. He also took Ted's call as a bit of a compliment. Many criminal defense lawyers he had dealings with, were pompous assholes who believed confrontation was the only way to go; they were surly and often talked down to law enforcement personnel. Not surprisingly, in return, they got what they gave. Dietrich recognized Ted was respectful in his approach to them and he understood why. Ted was more skilled and certainly more sure of himself than most of his contemporaries; false bravado was unnecessary. Dietrich even told his wife once that if he ever got into a jam himself, Chase would be the one to call. He was thinking that Chase may have recognized some similar qualities and that is why Ted made the call to him rather than someone else within the department. He was actually looking forward to his meeting the next day.

64

Ted hadn't been in the client interview room in Anders County since he last met with Tom Merrick and Larry Townes and it certainly was no better. From the smell of it, Ted was willing to bet someone vomited the night before. He thought, *if these walls could talk, what stories they could tell of lives ruined - lives lost.* Most who passed through here never had a chance at a life; they were born into broken homes, poverty, or addiction, or a combination of all three. They were the children who were never loved and never learned how to love. They, like the rest of us, were made to conform to society's norms, yet, had no real way of knowing what those norms were so they were forced to pass through these walls. Mere survival was their goal and that meant stealing or selling drugs or sometimes hurting others - sometimes fatally. It was the only life they ever knew so they ended up passing through this room, where they would meet with their court-appointed lawyers, who would eventually, plead them for a two hundred and fifty dollar fee. Ted knew they seldom got justice because their lawyers considered them "throw-aways". Few defenses were ever really mounted on their behalf. There were others like Merrick and Townes who, perhaps, never belonged here, but those stories were few. Most were destined for this room the moment they were born; it was inevitable. He didn't have to wait long as Detective Dietrich came right along, entered and closed the door behind him.

"Mr. Chase."

"Please, Ted would be just fine."

"Then please call me John. What can I do for you?"

"John, I have a situation brewing and I need your guidance."

At this, Detective Dietrich felt a surge of self-pride and respect for Ted at the same time.

"Certainly."

"John, I received two calls from someone saying they have damaging information about a client and they want to be paid to keep quiet."

"I see. You have a blackmailer. Let me guess - you are concerned about client confidences."

Dietrich just confirmed that Ted had made the right decision. The fellow had a grasp of the situation in less than a minute of conversation.

"Yes, that's exactly it."

"How does this person contact you?"

"Calls my office."

"Twice?"

"Yes. First time, I really didn't know whether it was a prank or if there was anything to it at all. But they called again and made a demand for money."

"How much?"

"Half a million dollars."

"Your client's money, not yours."

"That's right."

"Only contact has been over the phone?"

"Yes."

"You don't recognize the voice?"

"The only thing I could say is it sounds vaguely familiar but I have not been able to place it. Could have been someone I have dealt with in the past but, right now, I haven't got a clue who it may be."

"Male or female caller?"

"Female."

"Really? Has she been able to prove to you her information is correct?"

"Yes."

"Is the liability to your client civil or criminal?"

Ted had to be very careful here, "Could be both."

"I see. Any pattern to the calls?"

280

"I don't understand."

"The calls come into the office. Did the calls come in at the same time of day?"

"No, not really."

"Can you remember anything distinctive about the calls?"

"No, not really. Seemed a bit nervous."

"Where did you leave off with her?"

"She told me to gather the money and then she would contact me."

"How much time did she give you?"

Ted had to think for a moment, "She didn't."

"You're kidding."

"No…I don't recall that she gave me any specific amount of time, now that I think of it. She just said she would call back."

"Sounds like we have an amateur on our hands. Have you done anything about the money?"

"No. Only thing I did was call you."

"This client of yours - does he have that kind of money?"

Ted heard the word "he" and thought it better to let that go without comment. "Yes."

"So you are waiting for another call telling you what to do with the money."

"That's right."

"But you have done nothing to get the money together."

"That's right."

"You have no way to contact this person."

"No."

"Female caller, that's interesting. Don't really hear about too many female blackmailers - it seems to be more of a male line of work. Anyone else knows about this…. your partners?"

"No."

"Did you contact the client?"

"No."

"So, as far as you can tell, this person has accurate information which could lead to significant liability for your client."

"Yes."

"You don't feel you are in any danger or jeopardy of any sort?"

Ted hadn't given that any thought up to now.

"No....can't see how."

"Don't take this the wrong way Ted, but nothing you did regarding the client could lead to any type of problem on your end - I mean a personal or professional problem for you?"

"No." Ted wished he could have answered that question with a lot more certainty.

"Okay."

"John, is there a way this can be handled without involving your entire office? The caller made it clear to me that I shouldn't involve law enforcement."

"Ted, you, more than anyone, understand you have already reported a crime. Her phone calls to you are the first steps in a plot to extort money -   an attempt, at the very least, and even that is a felony. Protocol within our office for something like this, though, does allow us to have a bit more confidentiality.... but not because of concerns for your client. Our success rate in solving this type of thing increases when we play our cards close to the vest. I'll have to report this to the Sheriff but I'll request it be kept under wraps and that I be the only one assigned to it. Given the fact it is ongoing and the deed is not yet done, the boss should have no problem with that."

"I see. Thanks. It sure would be nice if we can work through this without having to get my client involved."

"Ted, if all we're dealing with here is a guy who can't keep it in his pants and doesn't want his wife to know...."

"No, nothing like that."

"A lot more serious than that?"

282

"That's right, a lot more serious."

Upon hearing this last statement, John Dietrich wanted to push a little further but had an instinct not to, at least for now. The detective realized Ted was there because Ted valued his discretion and he did not want to jeopardize Ted's trust. Most likely, there would come a time down the road where more frank discussions about "the client" would have to be held....but not now.

"John, where do we go from here?"
"Well, obviously you'll be getting another call. My bet is it will come to your office - the caller probably has some sort of "comfort level" contacting you there. You will be getting more definitive instructions about how to get her the money, where, when... Right now, I suggest we do nothing and wait for the call to come."
"There is nothing we can do in the meantime to try to find out who this woman is?"
"No, not really."
"Can we do anything with the phones?"
"Not without getting a lot of other people involved, including a judge."
"Certainly, I should have thought that through."
"I mean we can go for phone surveillance but..."
"No. You're right, that would open up a can of worms. I don't want to go there."
"Well, the thing to do now is wait for the call. When she calls, make some notes and listen carefully to everything she has to say. Then contact me immediately. Here is my card. I'm writing my cell on the back. Day or night, doesn't matter when the call comes, you call me immediately."
"Okay,"
"Ted, I think what we will end up doing here is simple. We'll follow instructions and then try to nab her when she goes to collect. I think we're dealing with an amateur here who will be a lot more nervous than either you or me."

"I see. A lot less glamorous than on TV."

"We both know all the stuff we see on TV is bullshit."

"Yes. Hopefully she will be calling me soon. I don't like where I'm at on this right now."

"Understandable. Unfortunately, we have no control over that. When she calls you, you call me. Okay?"

"Okay. Thanks John."

On the way back to the office, Ted wracked his brain trying to figure out who this woman could possibly be. He worried about the welfare of his client but also realized the blackmailer was asserting some degree of control over him and that pissed him off. He had to dance to her tune, losing some measure of his independence, and there was nothing he could do about it. Lawyers, more than other professionals, with perhaps, the exception of doctors, don't like to take direction from anybody. But he knew that when she called, he would be forced to follow her direction to the letter. He resigned himself to the fact there was nothing further he could do but wait until she contacted him. He had all the confidence in the world in Detective Dietrich and wondered how this person thought she could possibly pull this off.

65

What happened next confused Ted and pissed him off even more. For weeks, as he prepared Junior's criminal case for trial, nothing happened. The woman was not heard from, no contact was made; Ted was left hanging. As much as he despised the power she held over him, Ted now realized this was even worse. He was preparing for his most important trial since Grundy's murder and, at the whim of this woman, he may have to drop what he was doing at a moment's notice. Even more confounding was simply not knowing where the matter stood. Did she get cold feet and abandon her plan or is she re-thinking it for some reason? Is she looking for help? Looking to involve others? Maybe she was no longer able to carry out the scheme because she is incarcerated or, perhaps, even dead? The matter was on his mind every waking hour and Ted hated the distraction. When Ted was preparing for trial, regardless of whether criminal or civil and no matter who for, he always gave it his undivided attention. This threat robbed him of his concentration when he was supposed to be focusing on Junior Tehan, not only a young man he truly admired, but also the son of a good friend and law partner. And what about Laurie Giffen? Did the blackmailer just decide, *"oh, the hell with it"* and now intended to divulge whatever information she had, even without being compensated, rendering Ted powerless to protect his former client? Then another possibility crossed his mind: *if the blackmailer is caught, won't she give Laurie up anyway? Why wouldn't she? Could her information about Laurie be used as a bargaining chip in her own prosecution? What prosecutor wouldn't be willing to "deal" to put a murderer behind bars, especially one who seemingly got away with her crime?* Ted *knew* he would certainly "go there" if *he* were representing such a woman. The more he thought about it, the more he recognized the situation to be a "no win," and the more distracted he became.

Finally, the trial date was here. In two days, young Larry Tehan, a lifelong sufferer of fetal alcohol syndrome, would be on trial for his freedom. It was a Saturday morning and, as was his custom, Ted was all alone in his office with his case spread out over the large conference room table.

Ted had all his ducks in a row, having met with Mac, who would co-counsel the case with him, and Mike, his paralegal, the week before. Ted's witness list included Junior, of course, his father, two of Junior's teammates and his baseball coach (who had witnessed Junior's rages), and Dr. Stanton Adler, a nationally recognized expert on fetal alcohol. The trial team had spent weeks putting the case together, "coaching" the witnesses, preparing the documentary evidence including Junior's medical records, and strategizing. However, Ted was the only member of the team who knew it was his ambition to never call a witness. His plan was to attack, attack, attack the credibility of the state's witnesses, especially Shirley Tethers, and then seek a directed verdict of acquittal from Judge McCarthy. He not only needed to win the goddam case, he had to win it in such a convincing fashion there would be no lingering public doubt about Junior's innocence. Getting McCarthy to "throw the case out" after the prosecution rested was the only way he could accomplish that. He was reviewing Plotkin when the call came in.

"Counselor, listen carefully. You have the money?"

Ted immediately got the feeling he was being watched. While it was true the caller always contacted him at the office, it was unusual for him to be there on a Saturday unless he had something special going on. Perhaps this woman was aware Junior's trial began Monday or….she had been watching.

"Yes."

"You put the money in that big black briefcase of yours - the one like the airline pilots use. You know the one I am talking about?"

"Yes." She was familiar with a briefcase he owned!?
"You leave that briefcase behind the dumpster up at Hal's. Put it in between the dumpster and the row of hedges behind it. You know where I'm talking about?"

"Yes."

"You have it there by midnight Monday."

"This Monday?"

"Yes."

"Look, I'm in the middle of some...."

"Never mind. I know what you're in the middle of. You have it there this Monday evening by twelve. You understand?"

"Yes." Ted was boiling up inside.

"If it's not there or you try to pull anything with the police, the deal is off. Your "girlfriend" gets screwed. You got it?"

"Yes, it will be there."

"Fine."

Click.

Ted put the receiver down and immediately picked it back up to call John Dietrich.

"John, she just called."

"Did you pick up on anything?"

"No. I still don't know who she is."

"What's the deal?"

"She wants the money by midnight on Monday behind the dumpster at Hal's."

"Hal's, on the way to the lake?"

"Yes."

"How does she want the money?"

"You mean denominations?"

"Yes."

"She didn't say. She just asked if I had it and I told her yes. She wants it in a certain briefcase I have. She seemed to be familiar with it."

"She knew of a particular briefcase you have?"

"Yes. It is a large black one - the one we usually take to court."

"Is it the kind that has clasps on the top with combinations?"

"Yes."

"Good. We're not going to wait that long. I'll send my son by to pick up the case today. You going to be at the office much longer?"

"I'll be here until about six."

"Is there a way for my son to get that from you but be out of sight?"

"Just have him pull around back."

"Okay. He'll be there in a half hour."

"John, how is all this going to work?"

"Well, I will contact the owner of Hal's today and give him a heads-up. When I get the case, I'll load it with paper heavy enough to feel like the money. She made a mistake asking for that particular briefcase."

"How so?"

"Because we can lock it. If I don't miss my bet, she won't think to check the contents before she grabs it and, if she does, we'll have it locked. So I think she'll shoot by, throw it in her car and take off. I'll arrange with the restaurant to park in back among the help. I'm pretty sure there is a view of the dumpster from there. When she goes to leave, the crime is complete and I'll be right behind her. It's not rocket science, Ted."

"So what do I do?"

"Just give the briefcase to my son and then forget about the whole thing. I'll take care of everything. I'll report back to you Tuesday morning."

"Okay. You're the boss."

An immediate calm came over Ted. He knew the matter was in good hands; he had done the right thing getting the detective involved. He was also incredibly relieved he would not have a role in the exchange or anything that

288

occurred thereafter.   And.... finally, the nightmare was going to come to an end. He gave the case to John's son a half hour later and then he returned to Plotkin and the approaching storm.

66

It took almost a day and a half to seat a "jury of Junior's peers," a rather strange concept in our jurisprudence when you consider these "peers" really had nothing in common with young Larry Tehan. However, overall, the defense team was happy with the panel.

Judge McCarthy informed the lawyers that after putting the jurors through a day and a half of the selection process, the Court would devote Tuesday afternoon to the lawyers' opening remarks and let the State begin its case Wednesday morning. This was music to Ted's ears as it meant he would be the last person the jury would hear on Tuesday. Every trial has an element of luck. Ted was not surprised when Bonner notified the Court his first witness Wednesday morning would be Shirley Tethers. This was also music. Ted firmly believed what jury consultant Harry Plotkin "preached;" a very large percentage of jurors don't wait to hear a witness or view a piece of evidence, rather, they hear the opening remarks of counsel and determine which view of the world more closely resembles their own. Nine times out of ten, they adopt that view right then, before the evidence is presented.

Establishing his credibility with the panel from the "getgo" was also of paramount importance. If the jury got even the smallest "whiff" Ted did not totally believe in his client's innocence, Junior would be doomed.

At the same time the prosecution and defense team were exiting chambers, John Dietrich was pulling into the lot at the Sheriff's Department following Monday night's activities. He was completely and utterly exhausted. He had been up for forty hours straight but he knew Ted wanted to hear from him as soon as possible, and - he did not look forward to making his report. He went directly to the courthouse and found Ted and the other members of the defense team in one of the small counsel rooms adjacent to McCarthy's courtroom.

"John, you look exhausted." Ted entered the hallway closing the door behind him and the two men walked toward the huge window at the very end of the hall.

"I'm fine, just tired. It's been a long night."

"And?"

"It did not end well."

"What happened?"

"She's dead."

Ted's knees almost buckled. He stopped.

"Dead!? John, Jesus Christ, what happened?"

"Ted, she came and grabbed the case just as we thought and started toward Anders. But she made me as I followed her and she panicked. She took off. I thought for a moment I would let her go - I already had the plate but who knows - that may have been a dead end. So I kept up with her. I could see in the car she was going nuts. She just kept going faster and faster. She got to the Birney Road and she lost it there. You know that large curve near Esson's fruit stand? She went off the right side and hit those trees. The car was crumpled ......it caught on fire. Ted, I tried, but I couldn't even get near it. By the time help got there, the car was totally engulfed - it was an inferno."

Ted bowed his head down to conceal his face from the detective and slowly said...."Who was it?"

"Name's Linda Danko. Ring any bells?"

"Danko? No."

"Nickname was Lindie - she was an RN at St. Joseph's."

Ted felt a sharp pain in his left chest. He sat down on the marble bench in front of the window and put his face in his hands.... and he thought of the documents he had left on Laurie's bed. He kept his poker face and looking down at the floor he slowly said, "My God. Husband, any kids?"

"Kids, no husband."

Ted thought: *She died in a fiery crash on the Birney Road. My God......oh my God. She was incinerated on the Birney Road.*

67

The public's fascination with all things legal never ceased to amaze Ted. On Wednesday morning the courtroom was packed with Jeff Hutton "hiding" in the corner. Once again, Ted found himself "center stage" in Anders County. His opening statement the day before had gone well, setting up his attack on the State's witnesses, especially their first witness, Shirley Tethers. His first goal this day was to stay focused on the task at hand and not dwell on Monday evening's events or Linda Danko's fate.

The contrast was stark. Young Tehan's tall, athletic frame was draped in clothing from Brooks Brothers - "business casual" as instructed by Ted. Tethers' bottom-heavy figure, on the other hand, reminded Ted of the Sunday morning ads from the local discount chain. No matter how hard she tried, she looked cheap. Ted thought it really wouldn't matter what she wore, Tethers' lifestyle had left indelible marks. Her orange-yellow hair was in steep contrast to the overdone mascara on her face and her puffy, bloodshot red eyes. Young Tehan smelled of Drakkar Noir. Shirley smelled of cheap booze and cigarettes. Ted once again pondered Junior's attempt to overcome the effects of his fetal alcohol syndrome in comparison with Shirley Tethers' seemingly voluntary descent into the depths of alcoholism. Both of them suffered from diseases, there was no doubt, however Ted could only think, *if one had been avoided, the other would have never occurred.*

"Good morning everyone. Today we'll begin the presentation of evidence. Since the State has the burden of proof, they will present their case first. The order of presentation has no significance other than someone must necessarily go first. Mr. Bonner you may call your first witness."

"Thank you Your Honor. The State calls Shirley Tethers."

Bonner led her carefully through her testimony. Much like her deposition, Tethers tried to come across as the grieving widow. She testified on the day of the accident, she and Granville were on their way to see friends when Tehan ran the light and hit their car. She testified Tehan was incensed, got out of his car and charged Granny. She stated the defendant was at least a foot taller than her husband and probably eighty pounds heavier. She said Junior was using profanity and it was clear to her that he was out to hurt Granville. She indicated her husband got hit about five or six times about the head and neck in the course of minutes. One blow caught Granny on the left side of his forehead and a large knot appeared almost immediately. After the altercation, Granny was disoriented and lacked all co-ordination. He was transported to the emergency department of Westmoreland, was admitted, and eventually succumbed to his injuries. At the close of her testimony, Bonner asked, "Mrs. Tethers, the individual who ran into your car and attacked your husband, is he in the courtroom today?"

"Yes."

"Would you please point him out for the jury?"

"That's him, sitting right there next to Mr. Chase."

"Let the record reflect the witness has pointed out Larry Tehan Jr. No further questions Your Honor."

"Mr. Chase."

"Thank you Your Honor." Ted was going for broke. He wanted to end this *now*. He didn't want the matter to proceed further than the State's "star" witness. If he could crush her right then and there, there would be no doubt in anyone's mind about Junior's innocence for years to come.

"Mrs. Tethers, Mr. Bonner forgot to ask you how much money you've sued Junior for."

"Objection, Your Honor."

"Goes to self-interest Your Honor."

"I'll allow it."

"You want to know how much money Mr. Chase?"

"Yes, how much money are you seeking in your lawsuit? You do remember your lawsuit, don't you?"

"Yes."

Picking up a copy of the complaint, "Says here you want two point five million. That sound about right?"

"Yes, you have the paper there."

"Now tell the jury how many times your husband assaulted you in the month before the accident."

"Objection."

"Sustained."

Ted knew it would be sustained and he didn't care. It was the question that mattered, not the answer. He needed to communicate to the jury what the agenda was here. Now they wondered about the answer they were not permitted to hear.

"How many charges of domestic abuse did you file against your husband?"

"Objection! Your Honor…"

"Sustained."

Same effect.

"Mrs. Tethers, isn't it a fact your husband was intoxicated the day of the accident and it was he who ran the light and caused the accident?"

"He had been drinking."

"You saw the blood alcohol report from Westmoreland, didn't you?"

"Yes."

"And he was legally drunk, wasn't he?"

"He had been drinking but it was the boy who ran the light, not Granny."

"Okay, let's go with your version of the facts. After the collision, Junior got out of the car and he and Granville were within striking distance of one another, is that right?"

"Yes."

"Where were you when this was going on?"

"What do you mean, I was right there next to them."

"How close were you to Junior."

"Not more than three feet."

"What was Junior wearing that day?"

"A baseball uniform."

"Short sleeves, long sleeves?"

"Short sleeves."

"You testified your husband got hit in the left side of his forehead, is that right?"

"Yes."

"By Junior's right hand?"

"Yes."

"Mrs. Tethers, are you aware Junior is left handed?"

"No."

"I'm sorry, I didn't hear your answer."

"I said no!"

"You are sure you saw Junior hit your husband in the head with his right hand?"

"Yes, that's what I said!" Shirley was starting to get mad.

"You were right there, you saw Junior extend his right arm with no sleeve and hit Granville in the head?" Ted had to get her irretrievably "married" to her testimony and repeating the question to upset her was the tactic.

"Yes, what is it about that you don't understand Mr. Chase?" Now she was starting to lose it.

"Did Junior have any distinctive marks on his right arm?"

"What do you mean?"

"Your testimony is you saw his bare right arm as he reached out and hit your husband and I want to know if you saw any distinctive marks on his right arm."

"No. Nothing."

"You sure?"

"Yes, I'm sure!"

"Your Honor, may counsel approach the witness?"

"Yes."

"Junior, come with me."

Ted and Junior approached the witness stand. Shirley Tethers fidgeted because she did not know what was coming and had no idea what to expect. When they were right in front of her, Ted looked to Junior and quietly said, "Junior, roll up your right sleeve." Junior had no idea why but he followed Ted's direction. Ted reached for Junior's right arm and guided him slowly to the front of the witness stand.

"Mrs. Tethers, what do you see?"

She looked down at his right arm and its perfect half moon birthmark. She glanced at Ted with a look of such horror, both men were startled. She lost her breath. She could not speak. Her eyes, beginning to water, fixed upon Junior's right arm and then up to his face. Her overdone mascara began to run. She reached out and touched the birthmark just as she did the minute Junior had come into the world. She wanted to touch his face. The tears were flowing now. She wiped her face and the mascara mess made her appear almost ghoulish.

Ted's insides were churning. His eyes began to tear as well. For a split second he thought of his children. He could not imagine the emotion roiling up inside her but he had to force himself. He had a hard time getting it out. He asked once more, "Mrs. Tethers, what do you see?"

She dropped her head in her arms and began crying so hard, her body heaved. Bonner was calling on the judge for a recess. The jury was straining to see what was happening and Junior appeared almost frightened.

"Again........ Mrs. Tethers, what do you see?"

Finally, she looked up and said, "I want this to stop.....please stop. Granny ran the light....he ran the light. This boy didn't do anything....there was no fight. Granny never got hit. This boy didn't do anything....."

The courtroom erupted. The judge was banging his gavel. She tried to stand but she could not move her legs. Ted reached to steady her and Bonner came up to escort her from the stand. She only looked at the floor.....she never looked up. The jury was fixed on her as she slowly made her way back. The judge continued to bang the gavel.

A half hour later on the courthouse steps, Larry Sr. patted Ted on the back. "Ted, fantastic job. That cross examination was marvelous."

Ted watched Shirley Tethers, still crying, half-running up the street away from the courthouse, her right hand covering her face to hide the mess, her left arm flailing in the air as she went. It was only 11:30 and, as she arrived at the bar on the corner, she stopped, glanced back at the courthouse, stood for an instant at the door.......and then she went in. There would be no payday, no way out for Half Moon Bey. She retreated to the demons who always comforted her, this time totally alone in the world.

Ted turned to Larry and said, "No, Larry. It really wasn't. Let's go get a cup of coffee."

About the Author

Michael J. Reidy is a graduate of St. Ignatius High School, the University of Akron, and Case Western Reserve School of Law. He is a proud member of Ross, Brittain and Schonberg CO., L.P.A., a boutique labor, employment and workers' compensation defense firm in Cleveland, Ohio where he tries cases on behalf of employers.

Mike wrote Intent to Commit in an effort to increase public awareness of the medical/legal impact of alcoholism and the incredibly unfair and debilitating condition suffered by children of alcoholic mothers – fetal alcohol syndrome.

Mike is married to Michele and they have three children including one who is adopted.

Visit Mike's website at www.michaelreidy.net

CPSIA information can be obtained at www.ICGtesting.com
Printed in the USA
BVOW072309080112

279867BV00001B/5/P